Praise for *Photo Finished* by Christin Brecher

"A cozy with a keen eye. With the click of a shutter, we're off to solve a whodunit that is clever with twists and turns galore. Brecher has a winner with this new series that will delight cozy mystery readers!"
—**Abby Collette, author of *A Killer Sundae***

"From F-stops to the F-train, Liv's expert eye makes her the ultimate cozy detective in Christin Brecher's *Photo Finished*. Photographer Liv Spyers and her trusty camera lens charms readers (and the NYC elite) without ever losing focus on the investigation. Expert composition and timing culminates in a portrait of a complex mystery!"
—**Olivia Blacke, author of the Brooklyn Murder Mysteries**

"Brecher pens a twisty-turny, witty and wonderful, mysterious romp through New York City that was a pure delight to read. Liv Spyers is the sassy and warmhearted amateur sleuth we'd all like to be, and it's a pleasure to join her as she follows the clues through her sharp-eyed photographer's lens. Highly recommend this mystery, which is sure to please."
—***New York Times* bestselling author Jenn McKinlay**

"Distinctive characters complement a well-paced plot that takes several unexpected twists and turns. Brecher has upped her game with this superior cozy."
—*Publishers Weekly*

MUGSHOTS OF MANHATTAN

A SNAPSHOT OF NYC MYSTERY

CHRISTIN BRECHER

Kensington Publishing Corp.
www.kensingtonbooks.com

KENSINGTON BOOKS are published by

Kensington Publishing Corp.
119 West 40th Street
New York, NY 10018

All Kensington titles, imprints, and distributed lines are available at special quantity discounts for bulk purchases for sales promotion, premiums, fund-raising, educational, or institutional use. Special book excerpts or customized printings can also be created to fit specific needs. For details, write or phone the office of the Kensington Special Sales Manager: Attn. Special Sales Department. Kensington Publishing Corp., 119 West 40th Street, New York, NY 10018. Phone: 1-800-221-2647.

The Kensington and Teapot logo is a trademark of Kensington Publishing Corp.

ISBN: 978-1-4967-3883-7
First Kensington Trade Edition: September 2023

ISBN: 978-1-4967-3884-4 (ebook)

10 9 8 7 6 5 4 3 2 1

Printed in the United States of America

To Mark, Jen and Cate

CHAPTER 1

Click
"Over here! Over here!"
Flash
"Felix, what was it like working with Bisa on her first film?"
Snap
"Ben Goldfarb! Any comments on future movies for Bisa?"
Zoom
"Dev! Dev! Hey, Dev! How do you feel about your girl-friend crossing over from music to film? Dev!!"

As a photographer for Regina Montague Studios, New York City's premier events photography company, I don't do papa-razzi. At least, that is, not like the dozens of celebrity photographers who were screaming questions and taking photos around me. Admittedly, I stood close by them, with my camera hanging from my neck, and a full day of shooting A-list stars ahead of me. I was walking a fine line.

Balanced on a pair of strappy heels, I stepped through the slit of a store tags-just-removed, pale gray silk dress and onto a red carpet to start work at the highly anticipated, three-day extravaganza hosted by Grammy-winning, superstar, diva-extra-ordinaire . . . Bisa. My elegant outfit for an eleven o'clock brunch reflected my first *how do I nail this job?* conundrum.

My invitation–or the invitation I'd received in a packet of detailed materials for the most exciting job I'd ever landed–said *Dress Casual.* I breathed a sigh of relief that I'd gone *Casual Festive* instead. One *how-do-celebrities-celebrate?* decision down, with loads more to go, and I was looking forward to every nuanced challenge ahead. In that same spirit, my entrance was timed well behind those ahead of me, and way before the next limousine arrived.

The *flashes* and *clicks* and *snaps* and *zooms* spontaneously died in the welcome to my arrival on the red carpet. Not unexpected, given the excitement around Oscar-winning Felix Montgomery and the rest. It would've been fun to be mistaken for a guest, but I found the silver lining in my obscurity. I indulged in a full-blown grimace over the burning, quarter-sized blister on my left foot.

Granny had been right about the shoes.

"You'll be sorry," she'd said last night, shaking her thick, black, eighty-year-old hair. She wore her *I'm not saying anything, but all I'm saying is . . .* expression.

"They're perfect," I answered, reaching into an Old Threads: New Life shopping bag for the mate of the nonreturnable vintage shoe I'd just put on.

We were in my small studio, Liv Spyers Photography, which is in the two-steps-down, sidewalk storefront of my grandparents' West Village brownstone. I also live there. My lifelong best friend, Maria Ricci, was in my bedroom, looking for earrings for me, while Granny arrived from upstairs to offer food and moral support.

I'm a twenty-eight-year-old, and it might sound too cozy to live below my grandparents, but the setup works well for us. About two years ago, my grandparents decided to move their business, Carrera Locksmiths, to the first floor of their "original charm" townhouse to bring in some rent and we all believed we'd hit the jackpot. Amidst the neighborhood's polished homes and chic stores of my new neighborhood, I threw my hat into the ring to make it in New York. And my aged grandparents were able to call me anytime to help at the store, change a lightbulb, and take out the trash.

As a woman of Italian descent on my mother's side, from a family that loves its heritage, I belted out Old Blue Eyes' "New York, New York" when Maria and I drove a U-Haul over the bridge from our hometown in New Jersey almost two years ago. By the end of my first week, I'd turned my grandparents' old key store, which hadn't been updated since they'd bought the building back when the Village's real estate was unimaginably affordable, into my business's headquarters. Their former stockroom became my private residence, consisting of a single bed, two jam-packed closets of clothes, and a bathroom you pretty much need to climb over the bed to reach. It also has a window with iron bars across it, so I can safely see daylight when I wake up.

Truth: Things hadn't been looking all too good for me at first. Then, I met the queen of event photography, Regina Montague, a few months ago and scored a bona fide, career boosting job as a junior photographer for her. The gig spiraled into all sorts of trouble, but when you give me a chance, I don't give up easy. I pulled it together and earned Regina's respect. While keeping my studio active to build my private portrait business, I'd been covering the summer's wedding season as one of Regina's stable of photographers. Work is work, and I never take my career breaks for granted.

Maria popped her head around the divider between my one-room workspace and my bedroom door. She eyed my shoes approvingly.

"Don't worry, Granny. They're Manolos," she said, as if the brand is known for its comfort. She held a pair of dangly earrings from my dresser toward me, navigating tissue paper and shopping bags that littered my floor. "I still can't believe you're working for Bisa."

"Maria, *carina*, you've said that six times since I walked in five minutes ago. Eat while it's still hot," said Granny. She stood at the small red Formica counter of my Pullman kitchen, along the length of one wall of my studio, over a steaming platter of chicken parmesan she'd brought from upstairs. The inviting aroma was torture given that I was doing a fashion show of my purchases and could not risk dripping cheese onto the gold dress I was wearing, but which we'd all decided was a no-go.

"They were talking about Bisa on NY1 this morning," Granny said, handing Maria a plate of heaven. "Pat Kiernan reported that these little mini-concerts she's going to do on Thursday were sold out less than three minutes after they went on sale this morning. Pat has aged so nicely, don't you think? He went so gray, but he has such nice white teeth. He said Bisa arrived today to a mega mansion she's built at the tip of Roosevelt Island, where they filmed the movie. They showed pictures of the house. It's stupendous."

"Yeah, she tried to begin building while they were filming the movie but construction was too loud, so she hired like hundreds of people afterward to make sure it was finished on time," Maria said as she settled into my desk chair to enjoy her small feast. "She's named the place *Todo Amor.* That means *All Love* in Spanish, Granny. Perfect, don't you think?"

"Like the name of her movie, *All About Love,*" Granny said, nodding approvingly.

"And Bisa's donating her new building to the City as a music school after this weekend," Maria said, fist pumping in appreciation of her idol.

"Livia, do you know all of these details?" Granny continued. She knew I would never go into my gig blindly, but, like most New Yorkers, it was hard to resist talking about the days ahead. "She's having two days of parties with, they're saying, all of Hollywood invited. Traffic is going to be terrible. And, she's performing in three pop-up concerts on Thursday afternoon, which is apparently the new Saturday? What does that even mean? I've also never heard of a pop-up concert, but what do I know? And then Friday is the premiere of *All About Love* at Radio City Music Hall. The movie looks sweet, which impressed me because she's so va-va-voom. We'll see if she can act, but I tell you, Bisa can sing."

"This is delicious, Granny," Maria said, dabbing tomato sauce from her chin. "If they had pop-up concerts for chicken parm you'd be the next Bisa."

"I should be so lucky."

I got a kick out of the fact that Granny was a newly minted Bisa fan considering she only requested Alexa play hits from the old Rat Pack. Dean, Sammy, Frank. Now she was following the pop singer's epic takeover of New York City. In fact, I'd heard her listening to Bisa's song "Eyes on the I" while she was cooking upstairs earlier. And singing to it, too.

I had no doubt even Granny's adulation was part of Bisa's plan. After all, the superstar had top billing in her first sure-to-be blockbuster movie, opposite none other than Felix Montgomery. Plus, she had written and performed three songs for the film ahead of her upcoming Diamond Blue Tour. Hence, the inspiration behind the three pop-up concerts. She was going to drop one single at Liberty Island, the South Bronx, and at the scene of her first screen kiss on Roosevelt Island. New Yorkers are a passionate group of people and don't share their space with just anyone, yet somehow this town was about to be no more than Bisa's stage for three days. And no one could get enough of it. Bisa Mania had swept the City.

Even Roosevelt Island, which has never been a Manhattanite's idea of sophistication or glamour, was now a hot topic of conversation. The small sliver of land nestled between Queens and Manhattan in the East River was on fire. The *New York Times* reported real estate, developed on the ruins of prisons and hospitals, rose four percent in the months after Bisa announced she would headquarter herself there for the premiere and concert celebrations. That's where things stood in New York.

"Can you at least score me a ticket to one of her shows?" Maria said.

"I wish, but I can't get you a ticket to anything," I said. I rose from the guest chair across from my small desk to test my new strappy sandals. "At least not yet. Maybe once Bisa and I are besties she'll do me a favor."

"Really?" Maria beamed at me like I was Santa. At that moment, I honestly thought she'd be fine if I dumped her as a bestie for Bisa, assuming I got her the tickets.

"Seriously, you are breaking my heart, Maria. I would crash any party, endure any sample sale, and fall on my face out of an Uber at three in the morning with you, but I was kidding. Bisa isn't going to speak one word to me. Tomorrow morning, I'm taking photos at a small breakfast before the all-night kick-off party, the *Diamond Corazón*. The concerts follow the next afternoon so I don't think I'll have time to become besties with Bisa tomorrow."

"*Diamond Corazón* means *Diamond Heart*," Maria said to Granny, as self-appointed translator after four years of high school Spanish.

"Wednesday and Thursday, from start to, my finger will be glued to my shutter button," I said. "That's it."

"Fine, but I will be on your stoop, waiting for details when you return home," my dear friend said.

"You can wait in our living room. It's safer. And take a photo of Mateo DeLuca. Tell him I say hi," my granny said with a twinkle in her eye for her favorite young Italian star. She'd gone straight to the theater to see him in *Lady Duff's*

Crossings, unable to wait for it to stream on Netflix. "Poppy won't mind. We're all allowed a celebrity crush, right?"

"Except I won't be chitchatting with anyone," I said. "My job is to photograph Bisa and other celebrities at the parties and backstage at the concerts. My instructions are for stylish images rather than the usual step-and-repeat media shots. Regina says Bisa wants to own the story of these next few days rather than have the paparazzi take over. And then, she's going to sell them to whichever media outlet will pay her the most with extra royalties to us when they sell. It's a big job."

"If it's such a big job, why did they hire only one photographer?" Maria said.

I shrugged. I'd wondered the same thing, but hadn't gotten much of an answer from Regina when I'd asked. In her defense, she'd been laid up on painkillers after falling off her bike while lighting a cigarette and pedaling up Sixth Avenue last week. With a cast around her left arm, I'd landed the job of a lifetime.

"I've heard Bisa doesn't like photographers in her space," I said, giving my best guess. "Bisa knows Regina, so there was some trust there. I hope she'll trust me too."

"Regina picked the right person for the job," Granny said. She motioned to the wall behind me where I'd hung a few street-life portraits I'd snapped around town.

We were all now congregated around my kitchen counter and I gave Granny's soft, wrinkled cheek a kiss for calming my nerves with food and moral support. The photos she admired were, in fact, the images that initially inspired Regina to hire me.

"Plus, there's a perk. Regina got me and Harry tickets to the opening of *All About Love*. She knows I haven't seen him in two weeks, and that I had to cancel his welcome home dinner tomorrow night because of the job," I said, delighted with Regina's completely unnecessary but welcomed bribe. "When

Harry left for his business trip, I made rezies for the night of his return at Ai Fiori. Instead, I spent my dinner funds on this week's wardrobe."

"I wish things were as rosy with my Hinge dates as they are with you guys," said Maria, rinsing her dish in the sink.

"You were going to take Harry to Ai Fiori? It should be Ai Fortune," said Granny, never afraid of a pun. She reached her hand over Maria's sponge to fill my espresso machine's water canister. "Harry's the one with the money. He should be taking you there."

"She's thinking about the *L* word," Maria said over the faucet.

"Ahhh." Granny broke into a mischievous smile and dropped her eyelid in a slow, impish wink.

"I'm not thinking about the *L* word," I said, but I was aware of our proximity and how much experience these two had in reading my face. I headed to my room to take off the dress.

"Yes, you are," Maria called to my retreating figure.

"Stop!" I said, my retort muffled as I slipped the gold silk over my head.

"And why not?" said Granny. "You're a beautiful woman. Especially when you put on some lipstick."

"And maybe a little more mascara."

"I'm a power babe," I said, returning in my next outfit, which got some applause, but I was having none of it. "I'm starting a history class in a few weeks to try out college again. With that, and my work, and Harry's work, who knows how much we'll see of each other? I'm not getting hooked on some guy. I only wanted a nice dinner. And whatever comes with dessert."

Honestly, I woke up and fell asleep with the name Harry Fellowes on my lips. The uptown man to my downtown life whose career as an art appraiser for an insurance company was a cover for his real work as an agent for the secret ACU. That's the Art Crime Unit. And yes, this was my boyfriend. A bad ass, international crime-buster disguised as a mild-mannered, albeit independently wealthy, insurance agent. I knew Maria and everyone else saw Harry as a good guy, but a trust-fund kid. They were nice about it and I kept my lips sealed about the rest. I'd promised.

As exciting as my impending job with Bisa was going to be, Harry was on assignment somewhere in Japan, tracking down the Cardinal, a thief who was almost as *larger-than-life* as Bisa. With a flair for drama that rivaled Bisa, the Cardinal left a red silk scarf hanging in the place of the paintings he stole all over the world to remind everyone that he could fly in and out before anyone could catch him. Of course, he hadn't met Harry yet.

The flip side of having a secret-agent boyfriend, however, was that from the moment Harry left for his assignment, we had not been able to contact each other. I felt bad that he'd be landing tomorrow night to a text that I was now going to be MIA. There were times I wished I had less of a work ethic, but I knew our night at Bisa's movie opening would make up for our missed dinner date.

"Looking good, ladies!" a man yelled at us from the sidewalk outside my studio's picture window.

"Watch your mouth!" my grandmother shouted loud enough for the block to hear. It was an impressive bark, made more so by the fact that a coffee mug covered her face. She looked over her rim as the guy hightailed it in alarm.

I took a step forward to pull a red, silk privacy curtain across the studio's display window.

"Vertebrae stretched; clavicles dropped . . ." Maria said as I lifted my foot.

"Head balanced." I finished her motto for a well-lived life on heels. She wore them every day as a paralegal at a law firm, and every night on the town after work. Even now, she wore platform sandals with her shorts.

Me? A simple black combat boot is my go-to. Someone once told me a pacifist has to dress defensively and I think they were onto something. Once, I wore my Doc Martens under a gown to shoot a wedding at the main branch of the library on Forty-Second Street. I'd wanted a perfect shot of the bride's spectacular train and decided to climb Patience or Fortitude, one of the enormous lion statues guarding the entrance of the monumental limestone building in Midtown Manhattan. Regina had grabbed my wrist as I'd readied myself to rock climb in a long, formal dress.

"Don't go for a Pulitzer," she said, leaning toward me with a genial smile pasted toward the crowd before I'd gone too far.

Working for Regina is a fine line between being both invisible to your clients while also going for the most original perspective a space has to offer. It's the opposite of what the paparazzi do.

I could tell their jobs were to holler and scream for the shot, given the scene around me as I now stood before the acclaimed Todo Amor, which was even more impressive in person than in photos. A Grecian-styled building with a subdued but regal limestone facade, its columned doors, at the end of the red carpet, were as stately as those at the Forty-Second Street library. The palatial structure was at the southern end of the island, and I'd arrived via the Roosevelt Tramway, the one that Tobey Maguire's Spider-Man hangs from to save both Mary Jane and other trapped citizens. The view of Manhattan's skyline was stunning on the short walk over, but the air-conditioned limousines that passed me looked more appealing as I pulled a rollie bag filled with equipment, some clothes, and emergency supplies across a brick sidewalk, arm jiggling behind me.

The hike was not long, but due to the heat, I arrived as if to a mirage in the desert and sucked in the humid, afternoon air, glad Granny had sprayed my hair three times this morning.

The first thing I noted about the grand house was how it appeared from afar to be a century old due to the recent planting of large, mature trees whose long limbs shaded entrance to the estate. These are the sorts of details I try to notice as a photographer. To succeed in any job, I needed a good sense of my surroundings as much as my subjects.

As I studied the house and channeled my foot pain into the universe, a man with a clipboard and an earpiece approached me.

"Staff is this way," he said, blocking my path. In a black suit, black shirt, black tie, and black sunglasses, he appeared as if he was trained to give his life to our president, but his attitude suggested he deemed Bisa to be more important than the commander in chief.

"I'm on the guest list. Liv Spyers," I said to clear up the confusion.

"I don't think so," the guy said.

"Really?" I'd tried being polite, but we were getting nowhere. I put my hands on my hips to signal I meant business, but I was getting anxious about the unceremonious welcome. "You assume I'm not on the list, just like that? You're not even going to check?"

"Exactly," he said. "And don't start with some big story. I've been sending fans like you home all day. I've been doing this job for twenty years. I don't need to check a list."

"This is crazy," I said, and pulled out my phone to call Regina.

I didn't like the direction of things between us. Regina definitively stated that I should be inconspicuous, but one or two paparazzi were looking our way.

"Don't make me ask again," he said.

"It's OK, Alfonz." A woman with platinum-white hair pulled into a tight bun, and wearing a cropped blue pantsuit, arrived beside me. She was a bit older than I, with winter-pale skin in the dog days of summer. A minimum of three phones pro-truded from her belt bag, and she gripped an iPad as if her life depended on it.

Alfonz, the security guard, stepped aside without further debate. I couldn't tell if his sudden indifference was a reflection of her or me or the stress he was feeling from the day.

"I'm going to guess by the camera around your neck and the fact that you're not clustered with the media over there that you're Liv Spyers" said the woman.

I nodded.

"I'm Kayla, Bisa's personal assistant, and your point person for the next couple of days. Here you go." She handed me a blue key card, Bisa's signature color, with the logo for the Diamond Blue Tour on one side and *All About Love* on the other. When Regina was going to run the shoot, she landed one of Todo Amor's coveted suites. Now, to my delight, I was its occupant. "You're in room 8. Only a very few of us are staying at the house. Bisa's family, as she calls us. Alfonz and I, plus her boyfriend, Dev; her manager, Ben; our exec from the record label, Shawn; and her stylist, Freesia. You're with the inner circle in order for these pictures to be a relaxed behind-the-scenes for the next two days and nights. It's very unusual for Bisa to invite a photographer into her home, but we trust this will be a rewarding exercise for all of us."

"Of course. I signed the NDA. It's all in the vault and you'll barely know I'm here. Unless Bisa wants me, of course," I said. It was all true. Bisa's team had made me sign a nondisclosure agreement that I wouldn't share with the world anything I heard or saw. The consequences of breaking my promise were spine chilling. Not only would I apparently never work again, but Regina Montague Studios would be sued to the point of bankruptcy, et cetera. My invitation to the inner circle came with many strings attached.

"Listen," said Alfonz as another attendant appeared and retrieved my rollie bag. "I need to ask you guys to move. You're blocking the entrance. People are coming."

Behind me, I heard a car door open.

"Oh, damn. Not this," said Alfonz, looking over us.

Kayla followed his gaze. I knew something was off because her face drained of the little color she'd had.

"I'm going to need that key card back," she said.

Before I'd even glanced at the newcomer, Kayla plucked my key out of my hand and gave it to Alfonz with a nod that seemed to contain five pages of unspoken instructions. From the nod he returned to her, I realized he understood everything. As for my room, *easy come, easy go.* Or, so I thought. Kayla was solving problems on the fly. To my surprise, she retrieved a new key card, also blue and sparkly, from a belt bag she wore. After pressing a couple of buttons on her iPad, she swiped the card through a small attachment at the top that looked like those devices people use to turn their phone into a cash register. I was cautiously optimistic there was an extra suite for me, maybe not as posh as room eight apparently was, but something up in that inner circle of the one-and-only Bisa. Before I could find out, I abruptly stumbled a couple of steps forward as someone bumped against me.

"Hey, watch yourself," I said with less volume but equal significance as Granny had used on our peeping Tom at my studio window last night.

I saw that my bruiser was surprisingly a petite, curvy woman, five-two at the most, with fabulously long eyelashes. A dusting of glitter sparkled against her dewy bronze skin. Her hair was pulled into a thick, high updo, with tendrils falling along her cheeks. She was objectively gorgeous. No doubt about it. Her outfit, on the other hand, was an interesting choice for the casual versus festive dress challenge. Opting for casual, she wore a bright orange T-shirt, with a deep-cut vee, and short ripped jean shorts.

In response to my warning, the woman turned to me and casually lifted her finger. She then reached out and touched the tip of my nose with a gorgeous blue-and-diamond-studded fingernail.

"Boop," she said.

This actually happened.

I didn't have a chance to zing her with a comeback because a buzz of excitement arose and cameras began to flash again. She turned toward the lights and took a few steps across the carpet, proving that she was the source of Alfonz's and Kayla's concern, and not one of the crazed fans Alfonz had been fighting off all day.

"Hello, all," she said to the media. "It wouldn't be a party without some family drama. I'm Anna Reyes, Bisa's sister. I'm here to hit the red carpet."

Cue excited cries from the media at the newest arrival of Bisa's inner circle.

"We'll all be getting to know one another better in the next couple of days," she continued, "but I'd like to start by saying how happy I am that Bisa, my wonderful, beautiful, talented sister, has reached out to include me in her celebration."

Questions for more details about Bisa's private family life thundered from all directions. I had to give her credit. She knew how to work a crowd. Anna waved a hand high above her head and strutted as if on a fashion runway across the carpet and to the front door, where two doormen, dressed in dark suits, let her in. Alfonz trailed behind with her key, glued to her every move.

"Well, that's a twist," Kayla said without expression. She handed me the key she'd made. "There's an empty storage room upstairs, next to room eight, at the end of the hall. I've put you there. It's large enough to store your stuff, take a break if you have time, et cetera. You won't be able to sleep here, but we'll provide a car to get you home and back each day."

Before I could answer, Kayla sped me down the red carpet toward Todo Amor's front door. Our brief walk was unexpectedly fearsome. Even though no one knew my name, I was with Bisa's assistant; so in case I was someone after all, the photographers casually turned their cameras on me. I'd never been on the receiving end of so many lenses. I knew their image of me would never be used for anything, but in that moment, I felt vulnerable and small against their flashes and clicks and zooms and snaps. I was impressed Anna worked the same walk to her advantage, even though I definitely didn't like her.

I quickly recovered from my paparazzi encounter when the cool air of Todo Amor welcomed me. Kayla, with a quick nod that I understood meant *go to your room*, disappeared, back to work. Alone, I found myself inside Todo Amor's grand entrance hall, a spacious atrium punctuated by thick Grecian columns. The room's walls were the same pale limestone as the exterior. In spite of its palatial size, the scent of coffee and breakfast flooded the room. Fortunately, considering the mouthwatering aromas, I'd eaten Granny's banana muffins before leaving for the day.

Before heading up a central, grand staircase to my newly assigned space, the photographer in me checked out the venue. Along the room's gray-and-white-checkered marble floor, a lush arrangement of candles and flowers formed a semicircle in front of the staircase. In this space, lounging areas mixed with high-top tables were placed here and there. This technique of creating intimate spaces within larger spaces reminded me of some of the weddings I'd covered this summer. I'd picked up some tricks on how to shoot these setups, which I could use in the morning's gathering.

I also nodded approvingly at the professional lights, which lit the room from above, as if we were onstage. I'd been concerned about how to take candid shots while toting an indoor flash, but I was thrilled to see I probably wouldn't have to. Bisa was making my job easy for me. Her guests liked to look gorgeous and she made sure they were.

The only sour note to the setting was Anna, who stood in front of a set of double doors to the left of the stairway. A man beside her wrapped his hand firmly around her wrist. The paparazzi had called him Ben Goldfarb when he'd arrived. From my job's dossier, I knew he was Bisa's manager and one of the house guests.

A stocky dude, with a belly that made his silhouette more of a square than a rectangle, Ben stood close to Anna and I could see he was speaking to her with an intensity that might make someone other than Anna back away. He stood out from the others in that he wore a leather jacket and a thick gold chain on what was at least a ninety-degree day in July. The room was air-conditioned, so the space was quite comfortable, but a few combed-back hairs were matted to his head like the *Before* shot in a Men's Hair Club ad.

I was dying to check out the rest of the who's-who, but I looked ahead, blasé, as if I belonged. It wasn't too hard because Felix Montgomery, who was the only real celeb on the guest list for the morning's get-together, was not around. I wondered if he was behind the door that Ben Goldfarb was protecting like a sentry. Instead, I ascended the grand stairway and focused on putting the least amount of pressure on my blister.

At the top landing, five sleek black doors ringed each side of the massive stairwell. Room 1 was to my left and the farthest from where I stood. The door was wider and the space between it and the next room was larger than the others. It was the star on the door, however, that confirmed this was Bisa's room. I smiled, thinking how these chambers would be easy to convert to classrooms when Bisa handed her building over to the City. In the meantime, she'd created a hotel nicer than any I'd ever stayed in.

Starting at room 5 to the right, I walked past the numbered doors until I arrived at a blank one next to room 8. As Kayla had instructed me, this was my abode for the next two days. Bisa's room was directly across the stairwell. Feeling both giddy and a bit silly that I was so excited to be standing where I was, I swiped the lock and opened the door as if I was about to enter a twelve-room apartment. I was greeted by a walk-in closet.

The space was no suite, but I'd worked out of smaller spaces at other jobs. Glad to find a light switch, I closed the door behind me. My so-called room included a stool, a coat rod with some bare hangers, and an extra dresser from one of the rooms that probably didn't need one.

My instructions were to start shooting at eleven and not before. I had time to spare, and still be early. Originally, I'd planned to luxuriate in my suite before the action began, but I sat on the stool and tended to my blister with some emergency supplies from my new camera's small bag, which I had bedazzled for the occasion. At one point, there was a knock on the door. I opened it to find a waiter outside with a conciliatory bottle of water and a drinking glass. He wordlessly handed it to me, looking confused to find someone in a closet. Bandaged and hydrated, I still had time before I was expected downstairs, so I sat back on my stool and leaned my head against the wall. I should mention there was no air-conditioning, so I was nodding off from the heat when the muffled sound of voices startled me.

I leaned into the wall.

"I specifically told you we would discuss this after the movie opens."

It was Bisa. I thought.

Her speaking voice was known to be melodic with its infamously husky yet gentle timbre. The voice I heard was tense. Too excited to even think about what I was doing, I picked up the water glass and placed it between my ear and the wall, to be sure. From the moment Regina gave me the job, I had anticipated this heart-pounding feeling, but the reality of being so close to one of the world's most iconic singers and entertainers was impossible to describe. All I can say is that my closet suddenly took on a mystical quality, as if I were backstage at Coachella.

"It's always about you, Bisa," Anna said.

The glass trick worked, by the way. Everything sounded clearer.

"Of course, it's about me," Bisa said. "These next three days are *literally* about me. Ask anyone. Go up to anyone on the street and ask *what are these couple of days about* and you know what they will say? *Bisa!*"

"And next week, everything will be about you for some other reason, but I need you to pay attention to me right now."

"That's not true," said Bisa. "Everything isn't always about me."

"Bisa," said Anna. "It is your gift and your curse. Don't apologize. It's just that you said you would invest so I could get the shoes to market. Things have evolved and now I need the money urgently. Like, right now. Sign a check and I'll be out the door."

"*Callate!* Enough already. Don't threaten me, Anna. I can't talk about a loan right now."

I knew I was listening to something private, but I couldn't pull my ear away from that wall.

"*Mentira*—you can't or you won't?"

"None of your business," Bisa said. "I've invested millions, several millions, into the next few days. Everyone is depending on me. You need to wait. Period."

"I can't," Anna said. "I don't care how much you spent. You are worth many, many millions. What I'm asking for should be a drop in the bucket. You don't trust me with it."

The room got quiet. I started to put my glass down when the voices resumed.

"You're right," said Bisa. Her voice had grown gentler. "I love you, but also I need to protect you, *querida*."

"Ouch," I whispered. I loved Bisa. I was fully into Bisa Mania. But this Bisa reminded me of my cousin Sandra. She has this way of making you feel bad about yourself under the pretense of her worrying about you. We're always really nice to her husband, Gary, for putting up with her.

"What about the last loan I gave you?" Bisa said. "One hundred thousand dollars. Where did it go?"

"Trust me. Asking you for money is the last thing I want to do."

The voices became muffled again, but I could tell the words were heated.

I heard the door open and slam shut and then open again.

"I'm warning you," Bisa said. "Do not come to this morning's reception. Unlike me, every person downstairs would rather see you dead than at my party. Ben made that clear. But I love you and we'll talk after the party tonight about how I can constructively help you."

The door shut again. Bisa was in a tough spot on what should be the start of an exciting three days. Still, I felt bad for Anna, which I'd never imagined possible less than an hour ago.

CHAPTER 2

I put on my shoes and wished I hadn't overheard one of my favorite pop stars fight with her sister. It didn't matter who was right or wrong. Families have their things, but at the end of the day, the bond is sacred. When I stood, my foot felt much better, but I wished my other bag would arrive so I could trade out my death trap Manolos. How did Carrie Bradshaw wear these all over town?

My new Leica camera was charged and gave me confidence I would manage my work, even with a gimpy foot. Regina had purchased the camera especially for the event and I'd experimented with it. I loved how the pocket-sized camera packed a punch. Its size satisfied Bisa's instructions for discretion; the features met my needs for professional-grade photographs; and the design screamed expensive and beautiful, two things that were a requirement among the crowds I was going to meet soon. Before I returned the gorgeous instrument to Regina, I planned to take it around town to capture some of the street-life portraits I love.

Ready to start working, I opened the door, stepped into the hallway, and fanned my hand through the much-appreciated air-conditioning. The door adjacent to me opened at the same moment. Anna stepped out and almost into me, once again, while she focused on her phone. She had made a quick change into a formfitting silver-sequined jumpsuit, which shimmered down to her shoes.

"Sorry," I said, trying to get around her while she blocked the space between me and the stairs.

She dragged herself from her screen and eyed me.

Ignore her; ignore, ignore, I told myself, but I felt her look me up and down. Sister to a star or not, I didn't appreciate the stare. I returned her negativity by looking her up and down, too; slightly unnerving, but two could play at her game. I was hoping our exchange wouldn't last too long when I suddenly noticed her shoes. I couldn't take my eyes off of them. Their silky Bisa blue hue and shining rhinestone design were captivating. It was the delicately chiseled block heels, however, which slayed me.

"Those look ridiculously comfortable," I said. My demeanor must have noticeably changed because Anna's dark glare softened. A little.

"They're easy on the feet and dazzling to the eye." She twisted her foot in each direction for me to admire them. "That's important in a shoe, but not in a grandma way."

"Exactly. Thank you," I said, glad I wasn't the only one with her philosophy.

"Alfonz tells me you're a photographer," she said.

I nodded. She looked at my feet and audibly tsk'd.

"Come in," she said.

I wasn't sure I wanted to hang out with Anna, especially given that I needed to get to work, but I wanted to see the room I'd almost had. I followed her into an HGTV *100 Day Dream Home*–worthy room, with a sumptuous bed, a full bathroom, a minibar, and a polished wooden table with cushioned chairs. Every detail reflected high-end and tastefully sleek décor.

"Alfonz says this was supposed to be your room," she said, heading to a large suitcase on her dresser.

"Family first," I said, trying my best to be a professional.

Anna laughed.

"You don't have to be so nice," she said. "Families usually make sure their guests are the ones who get the nice room. Kayla just wants to keep an eye on me, so she gave me a suite up here. The more I'm cooped up, the less she thinks she needs to worry about what I'll do. Between us? I like to rile up Kayla and Alfonz whenever I can. It's comical the way they cringe when they see me. I find it gives me a lot of power over them that I don't really have."

"Like the *boop*?" I said, addressing the elephant in the room.

"Exactly," she said, seemingly happy that I'd caught on so quickly. "Take off your shoes." She unzipped the suitcase. It was filled with nothing but shoe boxes, some of which she opened. "What size are you?"

"Seven," I said, peeking over her shoulder, and remembering the shoe business she mentioned to Bisa. Every shoe was more beautiful than the next.

"Here," she said, and handed me a box.

I peeled back lightly scented tissue paper to find a pair of shoes similar to hers.

"Take them," she said. "I know how it is. I'm an entrepreneur, too. You wake up and kick ass."

"And then repeat," I said.

We both laughed. I noted that whereas Bisa mixed only the hint of a Spanish accent when she spoke, Anna embraced her accent. And where Bisa's complexion was a sun-kissed tan, Anna was darker. Bisa was studied and staged to walk into any situation and connect with anyone. Anna was who she was. She seemed comfortable with that fact, too.

"I own a photography studio when I'm not at events like

this," I said. I sat in a comfy chair by her bed to change into my new shoes.

"I designed these shoes from start to finish. Hold on to those. Someday they'll be worth a fortune. Right now, I'm in a financing round, I guess you could say." She smiled brightly, something I hadn't seen. It suited her.

I stood, instantly feeling both sexy and able to run a marathon. I'd have kept the shoes even if they weren't going to be worth a fortune one day, but I believed her that they would. They were that great.

"My feet thank you," I said.

"In exchange, you promise to take some photos I want, whenever I ask you to."

I'd thought the shoes were a thanks, for the room situation, but I considered it an easy deal and accepted without a second thought. I held forth my Manolos to her for tradesies, but she rolled her eyes.

"OK, well, then, back to work for me, I guess," I said. "Thanks again."

"Don't thank me," she said, opening the door. "We made a deal, remember? You take photos I ask you to."

Before I answered, she closed the door in my face. She was a fickle one. Tossing my old shoes into my storage closet, I headed downstairs, now feeling tall and steady. About thirty minutes later, I was painlessly working the small party as waiters circled the room with delicious Puerto Rican–inspired breakfast bites, including what I learned after sneaking a couple were delicious mini *pans de Mallorca* and mini *quesitos*. About thirty people were gathered in the ringed party space. Some sat at the high tops; others lounged in the chairs. All piled their bites onto their plates, which were both easy to eat and left the guests free to schmooze, which seemed key. The high spirits and chatter bounced from the walls and down from the ceiling to make the gathering sound larger than it was. Champagne and mimosas were flying as people greeted each other with a shared awareness of how *chosen* they were to be at both the breakfast and the night's all-star Diamond Corazón party. While the night's fun promised to be a perfect blend of Bisa's upcoming Diamond Blue Tour and *All About Love*'s romantic theme, this morning's festivities carried an almost conspiratorial excitement in the air.

Across the room, I spied Felix Montgomery, Bisa's co-star in *All About Love*. I automatically twirled a piece of my hair, but in my defense, this was a man whose framed photo Maria and I had propped beside us during the days of sleepovers in my poster-filled bedroom in New Jersey. The star of *Man of Seven Faces, The Teller* and his Academy Award-winning *Moonshot Monty*. He was about forty years old now, but he had not one wrinkle or zit or visible pore. His makeup was a little heavy for my taste, but he carried it off.

Aside from Bisa's co-star, the gathering catered to industry people and their plus ones, or twos. It reminded me of the Oscar awards dinner that isn't televised. The awards are given for the less glamorous aspects of film that merit time, but not prime time. I supposed Bisa would need to be circling among the stars at tonight's party. This morning, she could give some attention to the powers behind the scenes.

The waiter who'd found me in the closet passed me with a tray of mimosas. I was hoping for another mini *pan de Mallorca*, but I took one of the drinks instead.

"Hang on," I said, and downed the glass, then replaced it on the tray with a sheepish grin. "I'm Liv, the photographer. From upstairs. I guess I'm steadying my nerves."

"I'm Miles. And, don't worry. You're not the first to polish one off today," he said.

I understood what he meant. There's a difference between people who drink because a party is the bash of a lifetime versus when they need one to get through a couple of hours. It's sometimes the challenge of the job for me. To make every party look like the bash of a lifetime. The mood was high at Todo Amor, but I also observed a couple of people who downed their drinks for more than good times. For example, Ben Goldfarb's smile was glued to his face, but his eyes furtively darted around the room.

"Liv." A hand rested on my shoulder from the step above me.

It was Kayla. I instinctively dabbed my lip for any traces of champagne, but she took a glass from the waiter's tray as well. She then gave him a look that sent him on his way. Kayla dripped with authority about how things should roll.

"Everything looks spectacular," I said, genuinely appreciating the room.

"Bisa will be arriving in a few minutes at the top of the stairs. You'll want to focus on her. And make sure to take a lot of pictures of Dev Anthony," she said, nodding her head toward the right side of the room. "Bisa's boyfriend."

I followed her gaze to Dev, who wore a Bisa-blue silk tie in honor of the day. Dev was talking to Ben at one of the high-top tables. Their heads bent toward each other as they conversed. Ben stopped speaking for long enough to ogle a beautiful woman with a crystal affixed under her eye like a beauty mark. I wondered if he thought his choice of a leather jacket made him appear younger. It didn't.

A man in a white T-shirt, which molded his sculpted pecs, joined us. He wore a pale gray linen blazer over darker gray pants that hugged his hips, and he smelled of soap. Nothing fancy. The pure soap you buy at CVS. The scent on him, however, made me want to go buy some. He wore a gold chain around his neck and a couple of thick gold rings adorned his fingers. He was a very put-together guy.

"Hey, Kayla. Looking good," he said.

"Shawnie," she said, a little color appearing on her cheeks in spite of the tight grip on her iPad and her immaculately restrained hair. "This is Liv Spyers. Bisa hired her to take photos for us. Nothing formal."

"S'up, Liv. I'm Shawn Jackson. Welcome," he said. "Bisa should have checked with the studio before she set up photos."

"Shawn manages Bisa's work at the music studio. The studio is also a big investor in *All About Love*," Kayla said to me. "He's in town from LA for the movie opening and to manage the concerts. Team effort, right, Shawn?"

"You're going to love the film and the soundtrack," Shawn said smoothly. "Bisa is magnificent. Don't worry about your photos, but she still should have been in touch with me. Just remember, the movie and music studios have rights to all materials related to the film."

"The pictures will be personal shots of Bisa's private events," Kayla said. "Remember, she's paying for all of this."

"Of course," said Shawn. "Forget I said anything. Bisa doesn't need to know I even mentioned it."

The two seemed to have forgotten I was there, so I checked the tables and other seating areas to make sure I hadn't missed anyone.

". . . I hope she isn't a nightmare. We don't need another fiasco, like LA," Shawn said, my attention turning back to them. "How could Bisa let her come?"

"She didn't," Kayla said.

I had a good guess whom they were speaking about.

"The powers above me at the label expressed concern weeks ago that Anna could do tremendous damage. They think any distractions from Bisa's sister will cost them millions when the tour starts this fall. I think—"

I didn't hear what Shawn thought of Anna Reyes, because the room quieted and the lighting magically switched to a warmer tone. A spotlight beamed toward the stairs above where Kayla, Shawn, and I stood. I followed the crowd's tilted heads and upturned eyes and realized that Bisa had arrived at her party. She was dressed in a tight blue gown that shimmered and sparkled under the light. If this was her outfit for the morning's meet and greet, I wondered what tonight would look like. She seemed in one breath to read the room. I had no doubt that everyone felt, as I did, that she was looking right at them and no one else. Her magnetic presence was so much stronger than anything I'd ever seen in a person. I suddenly understood the difference between we mere mortals and those with star quality.

I raised my camera and went to work, positioning myself at the bottom of the stairs.

"Hello, everyone! Am I late?" said Bisa with a huge smile.

The guests broke into applause as she began to descend, one sweeping step at a time.

"I'm so happy everyone is here," she said through a mic.

"Love you, Bisa!" someone yelled from the back.

"Love you, too, Melvin," she said, and threw a kiss across the room. "Listen, everyone." She stopped at a spacious landing midway down the stairs, but looked at us all as if speaking to an old friend in a cozy room by a fire. "The next few days are going to be wild and fun, and I wanted us all to get together before the machine starts running. I'm lucky to have my team staying here with me: Ben, Kayla, Shawnie, Alfonz, my security head, and Freesia, my stylist. Felix, you know I wanted you here, too, but he has his own people to host. And all of you here today, I'm sure you all have important things to do to prepare for the next few days. Like, where's Cyril?"

She waved to a youngish guy dressed in a hip-hop vibe who joyfully waved back.

"Can we give Cyril a round of applause? He's been in charge of the advance team, organizing everything for New York's *All About Love* release. He's been juggling agendas from producers and all of us crazy talent and the music label and dealing with every detail at the fabulous Radio City Music Hall. We're lucky he even made it today."

Everyone applauded Cyril and I could tell, movie executive or not, Bisa's appreciative words were a highlight of his career.

"Mostly, I want to thank everyone here for being the stars behind the star, or, in the case of Felix, the star who let me stand beside him."

Felix beamed across the room at the compliment. Everyone laughed and applauded him. Dev, Bisa's boyfriend, hopped up the stairs, two at a time, to join her.

"Hey, baby," she said, and gave Dev a warm kiss.

Bisa took her beloved's hands in hers. To everyone, Dev's appearance seemed spontaneous, but through my camera lens, I saw a different scenario. She acted surprised, but I noticed something else as I zoomed in on her. First, she had been expecting his entrance. Also, there was something about it that made Bisa nervous.

I shifted my lens to Dev. By all standards, he was a fit, attractive man in his midthirties. He sported the full head of hair and white teeth my granny loves. Dev was second-in-command at Lodha, the luxe watch brand, which I'd read was going to go public on the New York Stock Exchange in the coming weeks. The glimmer of a gold watch from under his shirtsleeve reflected his success. Like Bisa, his eyes drank in the room, but they were quieter in their gaze. Together, the intensity of the couple made them a perfect visual match. Both Bisa and Dev were gorgeous, and both were engaging, but Bisa brought the flash that allowed her to be the one in the spotlight.

"As you all know," he said to the crowd. His voice sounded comparatively quiet without a microphone, but it carried. He seemed of Indian descent and had a slight British accent, which I've learned, from other fancy events, meant he'd learned English, not American, a subtle but distinct difference. It was an accent that was much more proper than that of my British boss, Regina. "You need a good reason to interrupt Bisa when she's onstage, but I think—I hope—this is a good one."

While the crowd laughed over his jab at Bisa's diva-ness, Dev pulled his girlfriend's hands close to his lips. Then, he bent one knee and looked up at her.

"Snap," I said, along with the crowd's gasp of delight.

Bisa had another storyline, one with a personal element to it. My photos would fetch a fortune. Regina was going to be thrilled.

Playing the role of ingénue, Bisa's jaw dropped and her hand flew to her cheek. I photographed her joy, excitement, and fear. All seemed about right for this kind of moment, even if it wasn't spontaneous. Hell, if it were me, I might have nausea etched across my face as well. Dev reached into his jacket's breast pocket, and Bisa started nodding her head yes before the small black box appeared in his hand.

"Wait a minute," she said, and handed him the microphone so we could all hear him pop the question. As staged as I suspected the moment might be, there were tears in her eyes. She faced the crowd with a beaming smile. "I want everyone to hear this. And where's our photographer?"

The crowd laughed. Dev looked at the party with a cheeky deadpan expression. I waved, feeling as if I might break out in hives. In a fit of near delirium, I ascended a few steps. I'd told Maria I didn't expect Bisa to say a word to me, but an hour into the festivities, I was participating in her marriage proposal. I heard myself giggle like a teenage fan. I recovered enough to choose a side of the stairway so as not to block the audience's view while still having an excellent angle.

"I've been waiting for the right man to come along and I want to remember every moment of this," Bisa said, pulling the mic back from Dev before returning it to him.

The crowd's laughter turned to applause. Dev cleared his throat. His confidence was impressive.

"My love," he said. "They say New York is experiencing Bisa Mania. I have been suffering from this acute syndrome since the day I met you and I won't ever get over it. And so, from the bottom of my heart, I ask you. Will you marry me?"

Bisa took the mic back.

"The answer is yes, yes, yes, yes, and another yes," she said.

He put a ring on her finger that I couldn't wait to see up close. She screeched with delight, as loudly as any of us plebes do. It was a reassuring moment that Bisa was, in fact, human.

Dev rose from his knee and Bisa took his face in her hands. She planted a kiss on him that was worthy of the last scene of a romance film. The crowd hollered their approval and delight. I suspected the guests would be posting and tweeting their own images, so my work needed to be both outstanding and unique. Everything around me faded while I captured the intimacy of their joy for the world's next big news story.

"Hold the press!" a voice said loudly, breaking over the crowd.

Camera still glued to my eye, I panned up to its source. Above Bisa and Dev, the stairs were dim against the brightness of the spotlight, but I knew who'd spoken.

Anna began to descend the staircase and head toward the couple.

"Drink, everyone," Bisa said, and raised her hands to gesture that people should return to the festivities. If she hoped the crowd's adoring eyes would turn away, she was having no such luck.

"Listen up," Anna said to the room, clinking a big cocktail ring onto her glass of champagne to attract attention. She reached out to take the mic from Bisa, who resisted, but then gave in rather than make a scene.

From the expression on Bisa's face, I saw she would do anything to make her sister go away at that moment. Meanwhile, people looked at Anna, anticipating a toast. A few people raised their cell phones to film her, but I suspected the time had come for me to slink back down the stairs, which I did as delicately as possible.

Bisa and Dev were frozen with anxious smiles.

"I want it on the record," Anna said, "I love my sister."

A warm hum arose at the sentiment. Bisa looked relieved by the kind words and took her sister's hand. Kayla and Alfonz, who'd been inching toward the scene, stopped. I wondered if I should have stayed put as well.

"I know what's truly in her heart," Anna said. "She may be very attracted to Dev—I mean, look at him! Looks, money, brains. But he's not the one for her. No doubt, I'm embarrassing her by doing this in public, but at least someone said it. And now, when the wedding plans go off the tracks, you can all blame me."

Bisa waved her arms to a lighting booth set up behind the party's floral boundaries, and the spotlight switched off. The room's original lighting took its place. The guests awkwardly returned to the party.

I tried to retreat, but somehow misjudged the last stair's landing and stumbled a little. Fortunately, someone caught my imminent spill.

"I'm so sorry," I said.

"No worries," said a man in jeans, high tops, and a shiny blue hoodie. There was something natural, even affable, about him compared to the meticulously planned outfits everyone was wearing.

"Russell!" Anna said into the mic before dropping it. She was looking in our direction.

Anna dashed down the stairs, away from her sister, and over to where we were.

"I see you, Russell," she said as she approached us. "Don't go hiding. I *know* Bisa didn't invite you. How'd you sneak in?"

The party crasher next to me, aka Russell, gave her a genial wave.

"I'm so happy to see you," Anna said, throwing her arms

around the guy with a sisterly hug. "Fix this. Bisa has gone crazy—getting herself engaged."

"Let's go, peewee," he said to Anna. "Leave your sister to bask in her glories."

I realized I'd fallen into the artist Russell Bays. Also known as Bisa's ex-husband and the last person I would expect to see here. The days of the *will they/won't they* photos were well behind us, but I thought about their quick path to the altar, and their quick divorce two years later.

"You!" Bisa said. I hadn't seen her descend, but suddenly the woman of the week was standing next to me and staring straight at Russell.

"Congratulations," I said to her. My good wishes instinctively flew out of my mouth, and yes, I did feel giddy. I hadn't expected to say one word to Bisa, but things had changed. She had called me onstage. Freaking Bisa. I mean, who needed one of those suites upstairs to feel as if they were in the inner circle?

"Would you like to arrange some formal engagement photos for later today?" I said. It was bold, I know, but I was flying high.

"Are you *trying* to ruin my engagement?" Bisa said to Russell without acknowledging my presence.

I took a step back, but not too far back. As a newly-minted insider, I wanted to hear what was about to unfold.

"I missed you, too," said Russell.

"Did Alfonz let you in?" she said. "Did you bribe him with those candies you know he likes? You are ruthless."

"You're looking good, love," he said.

"I am not your love anymore," she said. "And you were never mine."

"He should be," Anna said.

"I was definitely her love," Russell said in a casual aside to Anna. "We all know that."

"Anna, go to your room. Please," Bisa said, seething, but trying to compose herself. "Russell, come with me. Now."

Bisa spun around and headed to a set of double doors that led away from the party. They were the doors I'd seen Anna try to open when she arrived.

"Follow her," Anna said to me. "Get some pictures. I want her to remember this."

"Yeah, I don't think that's a good idea," I said. I might have been invited into the action a moment earlier, but I knew when to call it quits.

"We made a deal."

I sighed. A deal was a deal, and I don't go back on my promises, but I was wary of this one. Ahead of me, the crowd enveloped Bisa with congratulations. I reluctantly followed, catching up to Russell, who lingered behind the adoring fans.

"Anna suggested I join you." My words swelled up in apology.

"I bet she did," Russell said with a laugh. "This should be fun."

"I'm not so sure," I said.

He was very calm for someone who was headed for a fight with his ex.

"I think I'd like a few pictures of me and the bride-to-be, too," said Russell. "And we can get Dev into a few."

This was not what I'd been thinking when I suggested we take some engagement photos. If I was heading into a family portrait right now, I had my work cut out for me. I added *dysfunctional family* to the job's profile.

CHAPTER 3

Bisa reached the double doors and typed a code into a small panel, after which the doors slid open and into the wall. An office, with a desk in its center that was about the size of my bedroom, appeared beyond them. The desk was glossy, black, and an oversized arrangement of flowers rested on one corner. She marched straight toward the imposing piece of furniture and stood to face us. I stopped at the threshold, but Russell grabbed my hand and pulled me in as the doors smacked closed.

"Is this how you want to play it, Russell?" she said, waving a hand in my direction while looking at him. She sat with hands clasped commandingly behind her desk. I slid against the wall, hoping to bump into a doorknob and make an escape, but there was none.

"I wanted a photo of the two of us on this memorable day," said Russell, tactfully leaving Anna out of it. "One day, in the future, when you're in bed listening to Dev snore beside his beloved watches, you can take it out and think of me."

"Who says you didn't snore?"

"Ha! You remember."

I wasn't sure what game Russell was playing, but he seemed to think he'd won a round. He walked to Bisa's ginormous desk, sat in the plush guest chair, and put up his feet on her workspace. It seemed like a bad move to me, but these two had their own rules.

"It's Liz, right?" Bisa said, recovering the warmth in her voice to acknowledge me.

"Liv, but everyone gets it wrong. It's so nice to meet you," I said, stuck to the wall. "I'm a big fan."

"I'm sorry my ex-husband dragged you in like this," she commented while touching her heart as if I was the most important fan in her life. "Let's add to our schedule those engagement photos. Kayla will find a time slot for us."

Holy Mary Mother of God. Get out of here. Stop!!! This is too much awesomeness. I could die. My mind, heart, and soul screamed inside me.

"My pleasure," I said.

"In fact, here's an idea," Bisa said. "How about a photo of my ring right now?"

She cast a victorious smile at Russell and raised her hand to her smiling face. I was one hundred percent a pawn of their game, but I did my job and began to shoot. The ring was an eye-popping sparkler with about as many carats as a candy ring pop, but it wasn't something I could imagine wearing every day, for the rest of my life, like in my pj's.

"It's a lot more impressive than my last one," she said to Russell.

"Which you said was the most beautiful gem you'd ever seen when we bought it from the sweet old man at the Villeneuve-les-Avignon Flea Market," Russell said evenly.

"Tastes can change," she said.

"Mine don't," Russell said. "Bisa, it's your instinct to dominate everyone and manage everything. We both know you could never do that with me. You made a big mistake, though."

"Russell, our marriage ended because of you. Because you can spend an entire day looking at a piece of string rather than pick up a paintbrush."

"What about how you play the same chord over and over when you're working on a new song?"

"That's entirely different," she said.

At this point, I returned to the wall and wished I could disappear. To the left of Bisa's desk was a door with an EXIT sign above it. The outside world was steps away, but miles from reach. To block out the two exes' as they kept at it, I distracted myself by envisioning the engagement photos I'd now been officially asked to take. I imagined a print of Bisa and Dev, smiling blissfully at one another, hanging on my studio's wall. Scratch that. I would spotlight the photo in my front-window display.

"Dev gets up in the morning," I heard Bisa say, "dresses for work, and throws himself into it all day. He does not analyze a thing. He holds himself to the same high standards I hold myself to. And he has big plans for our future. We're starting a line of Bisa Diamonds."

"I hold Dev in high regard as well. Which is why I asked Liv to join us," Russell said with a friendly but mischievous nod in my direction that brought me out of my engagement photo session daydream with a start. "You demanded my presence in your private office, but I don't think it's appropriate for us to be alone while Dev is outside, probably looking for you. That's how rumors start, right?"

"Why did you come to Todo Amor, Russell? To ruin my engagement?"

"I had no idea you were planning to marry that hardworking man who wants to sell diamonds with your name on them," said Russell. "I wish you every happiness. You deserve to be happy. I came only to tell you I have a solo show in SoHo if you have time to come."

Bisa looked down and flashed her ring finger to herself.

"Thank you for your good wishes," she said quietly. "And I'm proud of you, Russell. If I can come, I will."

"One thing. Now that I know about this engagement," said Russell, lightening his tone, "I'm going to need a room."

Bisa crossed her arms.

"We don't have any," she said.

"That's OK," he said. "I'll keep crashing the parties."

"Why, Russell?" she said.

"To make sure you're ready to be human," he said. "You won't be happy with anyone until you are. If not now, when?"

"Get out," Bisa said.

The office door opened and Dev walked in.

"Where've you been, babe? Don't worry about Anna. I'll handle her," he said, and then stopped short when he realized that Russell was with her.

Russell walked to Dev and gave him a bear hug.

"Congratulations," he said to Dev. "May you have better luck than I did."

Dev didn't have a chance to answer before Russell left the room.

"The door will shut behind you," Dev said to me.

"Of course," I said, and scrammed—but *out of the frying pan and into the fire*, as they say. I left to find Anna waiting for me, by a column not far from the doors.

"Did you take their photo?" she said.

I shook my head. Anna frowned at me, clearly disappointed.

"Anyway, I'm going in," she said.

"Maybe it's not a great time," I said, following her to the office doors. "Bisa's in there with Dev."

"That's fine with me," Anna said, and stepped around me. "What's the code? Never mind, I got it. It's always the same." Anna shook her head and typed in *four, three, two, one*. The automatic doors again opened and closed at Todo Amor's command center as if it was an alien spaceship.

I needed a moment to recover from my second brush with Bisa's family turmoil. I glanced at my phone, hoping to see a text from Harry, yet knowing he couldn't send one. His phone was off during his job out of an abundance of caution. The Cardinal was clever and the last thing they wanted, in case Harry's cover was blown, was for the thief to swoop in and steal a phone which contained personal information. Harry asked me to send him a line every now and then, however, so that he could read them when he turned his phone back on during the flight home, so I typed: **At Todo Amor! In less than 2 hrs . . . overheard Bisa and her sister fight, made what seems now to be a bad deal with the sister for shoes. Also lost my suite, so going home between gigs. Miss you & sorry again about tomorrow night's dinner.**

I felt calmer after I hit Send. My job came first and these celebrity shenanigans couldn't get in the way. Having reset myself, I became so engrossed in shooting the party I almost forgot about my awkward encounters with the world's biggest superstar and her family.

From shot to shot, I saw that in Bisa's absence, Shawn and Ben took over as the power players, while the main attraction was Felix Montgomery. Everyone made a point to congratulate the three men about the movie, the new songs, and, in general, grab some face time before leaving. The three men all eyed Bisa's office door at intervals. When the waiters began to serve little candies, always a sure sign at these kinds of events that the party is coming to an end, I climbed a few steps to get a final view of the room.

"What did you do?" Kayla said, coming up to me with a wild look in her eyes. I decided she was angry that I'd joined Bisa in her office.

"I'm sorry," I said. "But Bisa said she'll talk to you about booking time for formal engagement photos. Portraits are my thing, so I—"

"Alfonz said he saw you let Anna into Bisa's office?" she said, speaking over me.

"Oh, no, I didn't. Anna easily figured out the co—" I said.

Our conversation was cut short because the doors to Bisa's office slid open and Dev walked out, looking unhappy for a man who'd become engaged a short time ago to the world's brightest star. The doors shut behind him, but a moment later, Anna exited as well, with a spring in her step. Kayla flashed her eyes at me as if I still wasn't off the hook and disappeared back to work.

I hadn't let Anna into the office, but with Kayla's disapproval of everything I did, I now felt somehow responsible for what might have happened in there. I decided to look for Dev, to see if I could cheer him up with a few photos of him and maybe Felix Montgomery. As quickly as he'd left Bisa's office, however, he now seemed to have disappeared. I could not find him. I did see Anna at the far end of the room, by herself. She was cheerfully tossing back a flute of champagne, but then looked down at her phone and pressed it to her ear. I was surprised by an abrupt change in her expression: Her eyebrows dropped and she bit her lips. She looked scared. She was a changed woman from seconds ago. I couldn't imagine anyone scaring Anna Reyes. I was so amazed to see her in such a state, I raised my camera and took her picture. If she gave me another hard time, I'd look at the image to remind myself she wasn't as tough as she said she was.

As Anna spoke into her phone, she scanned the room as if the person calling her was not far away. Out of curiosity, I scanned the party as well, to see if anyone was talking to Anna. Half the remaining crowd was using their phones, so it was hard to tell. Looking back at Anna, however, I thought she spotted the person she was looking for at the far left of the room. Or maybe it was the right side and she was shielding her face. I wasn't sure. Either way, she dropped her phone beside her empty champagne glass on a high-top table and took a step back, looking from side to side like an animal calculating how to escape from a predator. She chose a path to her right, in the direction of the kitchen. As Anna sped away, I saw her phone was still on the table. I ran over and grabbed it. There was an open text still on her screen: **Time's up.** The screen then locked to a photo of her and Bisa doing a synchronized dance move.

I took off after Anna, because losing a phone is the worst thing ever. It happened to me last New Year's Eve at Maria's packed ball-drop-watching party. Instead of the Times Square ball drop, Maria had a piñata disco ball filled with those little airplane-sized liquor bottles. I wanted a chance to smack it, but I spent thirty minutes looking for my phone. I finally found it in the bathroom, but I missed the ball drop and everything. I did find a little mini vodka under the sofa.

Anna exited through the swinging doors that led to the kitchen as my favorite waiter, Miles, was coming out. He almost crashed into her, his tray wobbling, but he managed to keep its contents balanced in a feat of coordination. In phoneloss fellowship, I followed her.

"Excuse me," I said to Miles, who regained his footing in time for me to throw him off his game again.

This time, the food fell to the ground. We both scrambled to pick up little sweets and I followed him into the kitchen. Unlike the cool sophistication of the party, the kitchen was pure chaos as waiters scurried in and out to drop off and pick up trays. There was no sign of Anna, so I exited the back door. There were no paparazzi on this side of the building, but a few of the staff were outside for some air. Hot as it was, at least the river provided an occasion breeze.

In the distance, moving away from Todo Amor, I saw a woman in a glittering outfit on a Citi Bike, moving at an impressively high speed toward the bridge that connects the island to Astoria in Queens. Only in New York does a woman in a sequined jumpsuit drive over potholes on a bike. And I mean this in a good way.

I stopped to watch her retreat. She headed down a bike path, too far for me to call after her. I knew she'd soon be kicking herself about her carelessness, especially since she hadn't looked like she wanted to return any time soon. But since she'd have to come back, I decided to leave her phone outside her suite door.

Before going back to the house, I took a moment to appreciate the river. To my left was the Queensboro Bridge, one of the infamous cantilever bridges that are in so many tourist photos of the City. In contrast to its phenomenal steel, stonework and mighty size, the Roosevelt Island Bridge, a modest connector in a painted brownish color, ran parallel to it, farther north. I was thinking about the difference between the magnificent and the ordinary, and began to photograph the juxtaposition of the two steel structures, when I choked on my breath.

Something fell off the Roosevelt Island Bridge. I didn't have time to zoom in or take a second shot because everything happened so quickly. I thought I might be losing it, but whatever had fallen sparkled in the sun as it dropped. The vision looked exactly like Anna's jumpsuit. I looked around to find someone else who had seen what I'd seen, but no one was focusing on the unglamorous connector between the island and Queens. I took a few steps back and called out to the staff on break. They looked at me, but I wasn't sure what to say. I had a terrible feeling I'd seen something unspeakably horrible, but saying it aloud without being positive felt highly inappropriate. If I was wrong, I'd needlessly upset a lot of people.

Realizing I needed to take action, and quickly, I raced to the bike station, where Anna had presumably taken hers. I opened my phone to my Citi Bike app and swiped the lock of one of the three-speed touring bikes. I hiked my silk dress, glad for the slit, jumped onto the seat, and pursued, my camera bouncing uncomfortably on my chest as I did. Moments after I began to pedal, the heat waged war on my makeup. Worse, every strand of hair was reverting to its natural, unruly self. I huffed and puffed through the uncomfortable temperature, wondering how Anna sped at twice my speed or more. I realized she had taken a rare ebike, while I was on the equivalent of a golf cart at the Indy 500.

When I finally reached the bridge, I stopped to catch my breath. Some car engines hummed, but the bridge was mostly quiet. There was no sign of Anna. I grabbed my hair in a ponytail and pulled it back tightly. Anna could have already crossed the bridge by now, but my gut still told me I'd seen her fall in her unmistakable silver-sequined jumpsuit. I rechecked the arty photo I'd taken, but the shining mass had dropped so quickly, it was already in the water, without even a splash, by the time my shutter had snapped.

Still focused on the image, I enlarged a spot on the bridge itself, and noticed a shadow that might be another person looking over the railing as she fell. The camera's pixels weren't strong enough to clearly translate the image, since I'd taken the shot at a great distance and a tricky angle.

I lowered my camera around my neck, and then felt like knocking myself in the head. The indisputable fact was, her bike wasn't on the bridge. Facts were facts. If the bike was gone, Anna must have made it to the other side and kept going.

"Liv, what were you thinking?" I said aloud.

Anna was probably somewhere in Astoria by now, waving at onlookers who were admiring her outfit. I was about to pedal back and drink a huge glass of whatever they were serving, but before I did, something flickered on the bridge's bike path about halfway across the river. Too far to see clearly, I raised my camera again and zoomed in. An item blew in the river's light breeze from the bridge's railing. I didn't like what I saw. I pushed back onto my bike seat and began to pedal once more. A few black cars passed me on the vehicle lane, leaving Todo Amor. A couple of others passed in the opposite direction.

Halfway across, I got off my bike and stared at a wad of silver sequined fabric caught in the fencing along the edge of the bridge. With a heavy heart, I had no doubt that it came from Anna's jumpsuit. The idea that she had ripped her outfit violently against a fence without returning to Todo Amor seemed dismayingly unlikely.

"Are you OK?" an Uber driver called to me, slowing his car.

"Thanks, I'm good," I said, spinning around, surprised by his voice.

"You can't leave your bike here," he said. "Someone's going to hit it and get hurt."

He took off before I could ask him what he meant. My bike was right beside me, although he might not have seen it because of the divider between the bike and car paths. Nonetheless, the guy's comment was gnawing at me in a bad way. I took off my shoes and hoisted myself up and onto the thick divider, grabbing the edge of one of the bridge's steel girders for balance. Directly below me, I saw what the Uber driver meant. There was an abandoned Citi Bike lying in the car lane. An ebike model.

As I thudded back to safe ground, I held myself away from the median to protect my camera. In this difficult position, I noticed a small red spot on the ground. I touched it and lifted my finger to examine it. I'm not an expert, but I felt sure it was blood. I inspected the wad of sequined fabric again, and this time, I unbundled it to see the entire area of the cloth.

"What. The. Hell?"

The fabric had a blood stain on it. At my feet, I also spied a bedazzled blue fingernail, exactly like the one Anna had used to boop me. I picked it up, my pulse quickening. Everything suggested that Anna was in trouble, like falling off a bridge to certain death trouble. I might have passed out right there except for the distraction of an approaching limo. A woman I'd seen at the party, with a jewel stuck to the bottom corner of her eye like a beauty mark, waved and laughed through the sunroof of the car. The driver moved at a slow enough pace that she could enjoy her fun, at least across the lightly trafficked bridge.

"Look at that bike," she said. She pounded on the hood. "Stop the car. I want the bike," she said. The volume of her voice had picked up and there was a somewhat frenzied excitement to her announcement. "I found out today I'm going to be one of Bisa's next dancers. If I want the bike, let me have the bike. I'm celebrating my good news!"

The car stopped in defeat, followed by the back door of the car opening. The woman leapt out, at least shielded from traffic by the car, and dashed toward the bike. Her under-eye jewel slid down her cheek as she did, but she scrambled to catch it.

"Who leaves a bike like this, just lying on the road?"

"Don't," I cried out, but she waved a hand, as if I was unreasonably concerned for her welfare, and took off.

It's not that I didn't generally worry about her safety, but the limo driver stayed by her side, shielding her from other traffic. What I was raging about, however, was that she was absconding with evidence of Anna's last known place. I wanted to follow, to stop her, but I'd learned my three speeds didn't stand a chance.

Alone again, I had one more thing to do before I left. I tucked my foot into one of the iron railings of the bridge. Facing toward the water, I stared down from my perch, which was maybe ten stories high. Below me, I saw I was above one of the two massive piers that held up the bridge. The water shimmered in the sun around the pier below as brightly as Bisa's diamond engagement ring. The current was stronger than I expected, which made me dizzy. The railing was tall enough that I wouldn't fall over, but my distance to the water unsettled me. I raised my camera and took as many photos as I could but finally dropped my camera back to my neck.

I squinted, needing on a rare occasion to confirm something with my naked eye in what looked like a mid-sized fishing boat with a man aboard. I could only see the top of his bald head which was adorned with a star tattoo. I gasped when I finally registered why he was looking down. Lying motionless next to him on the open bow, I saw Anna Reyes in an inhuman contortion.

CHAPTER 4

When I stepped off the rail, I felt my body shivering, in spite of the heat. No one could survive a fall from my proximity to the water, not to mention the strength of the currents. I assumed the man on the boat was taking the body he'd discovered to the authorities, but I felt obliged to call the police as well. Between Anna's frantic escape from the party, her confirmed fall from the bridge, and even the blur in my photo that suggested someone else had been on the bridge with her, I was now convinced that someone must have killed her. As a witness, I needed to share my information.

Playing devil's advocate, I had to consider that Anna could have jumped from the bridge, but I found it impossible to accept that the woman I'd met earlier this morning was headed to such a fate. She'd had hope, both during her argument with Bisa and after she left her sister's office looking so triumphant. At the end of the party, she'd appeared scared, that was a certainty, but her flight on the bike seemed like an escape, not a death wish. Something changed with a single phone call. Something scared her. Amidst the lights and glamour and action of Bisa's world, it was almost impossible for me to imagine such a dark twist, but my visual clues suggested that quickly and quietly on a summer's day, someone killed Anna Reyes.

I fumbled for my phone to dial 9-1-1 but my hands shook so much I needed to use both to hold my device. *Breathe, breathe, breathe,* I told myself. I closed my eyes and inhaled deeply to stop trembling. It didn't help because I realized that although every fiber in me wanted to dial for help immediately, another part of me knew that what I had to add to the story could wait, for a short time, while something else took precedence. I felt I should share the horrible news with those at Todo Amor. I dreaded returning to the house, knowing what heartache was ahead for Bisa. Breaking the news would be horrible, but it would be better to hear it from someone who was part of the team than from the police who would likely be knocking on the door soon enough. I wondered who oversaw cases of bodies found in the river. Perhaps the man with the star tattoo would bring Anna to the coast guard. It seemed odd, actually, that the man had taken the body aboard rather than call the authorities from his boat, but I was beginning to understand how extreme shock could affect someone's decision making skills.

I decided to dial Kayla, glad I'd put her number into my contacts. She would know best how to handle the situation. If I could show her the crime scene as well, we could decide what the next steps should be.

"What's up?" Kayla answered.

"Please meet me on the Roosevelt Bridge. Something terrible has happened. I can't explain over the phone, but it's urgent that you come, for Bisa's sake," I said and hung up. I held on to the rail for support. I tried to block the image of Anna's twisted body on the boat, but the sound of the water below made it impossible. I don't believe in people haunting a spot, but if I did, that's what it felt like on the bike path. I studied the sinister space around me: the wired fence where I'd found the fabric, the small bloodstain on the ground.

I noticed the dirt and debris at my feet made a swirling pattern that did not match the areas ahead or behind me. I felt compelled to photograph them. I wasn't sure why I did, but I continued to shoot. I guess, somehow, I wanted to honor Anna at that moment, and taking photos was my way of doing so.

A couple of minutes later, a motorbike came up the path and stopped near me. Alfonz removed his helmet. He wasn't Kayla, but as Bisa's security guard, he probably knew the right people to call moving forward. My words a jumble, I blurted out what I'd seen. Alfonz listened. When I finished, he pulled himself onto the railing and looked below.

"Are you sure it was her in the boat?" he said.

"She wore a sparkly jumpsuit." Of course, it was Anna.

"Half the people here today were wearing sparkly outfits," he said "The Diamond Blue Tour is coming up. Her fans are crazy."

"I know I saw Anna," I said incredulously. What was this guy getting at? "And her bike was on the other side of the median for some reason."

Alfonz pulled himself up onto the divider in one motion.

"It's not there now," I interjected before he could cast further doubt on what I'd witnessed. "Someone took it."

Alfonz jumped down and scratched the back of his neck. I had the swath of Anna's jumpsuit in my camera bag, but I was becoming less and less confident in Alfonz's skill set as a security guard, or at least as an investigator.

"The jumpsuit was shining on the boat," I said instead.

"If it makes you feel better," he said. "The fish are running. My buddy Norman told me. The stripers have been teeming these last couple of days. Their underbellies are shiny. What you saw was maybe a pile of fish."

There was no way what I'd seen was a pile of fish. As I was struggling for words, Alfonz tapped at his phone's screen and raised it to his ear.

"Kayla, it's Al," he said, sounding grumpy over what he deemed a false emergency. "Liv thinks Anna fell off the bridge. There's no body, but she thinks some fisherman picked her up."

He listened quietly and then looked over at me.

"Kayla says Anna is there. She told Kayla she was going to take a nap."

I clutched the sides of my camera like a safety blanket, which I sometimes do when I get frustrated.

"Can she check Anna's room? You'll see she's not there."

Alfonz laughed.

"You think we're going to bother Anna? While she's napping?" he said.

My head was beginning to explode. Why didn't either of them believe me? I was the newbie, for sure, and I gathered these two were used to years of Anna's antics, but I was now worried that Anna had messed with Kayla and Alfonz one too many times. They thought everything was a ruse, created to frazzle them. At least when the authorities arrived with the news, they'd know I was right.

Alfonz held the phone in my direction.

"Get back to campus, Liv," Kayla said through his speaker.

A slight trace of camaraderie mingled with her impatient voice, as if I'd somehow joined the Anna Reyes Survivors Club that they'd been members of for too long.

The phone went quiet.

"I'm going to say this once." Alfonz put his phone into his pocket and looked at me with cold eyes. "Bisa has worked harder than you can imagine to create something the world will remember forever. On top of that, she's just gotten herself engaged. I'm not having anyone upset her."

"But—"

"But what?"

His question sealed my decision not to show him the piece of Anna's jumpsuit. He seemed much more likely to argue it was from a fan who tore their clothing, and, for all I knew, he might toss it rather than investigate. I was going to hold on to it for now.

"You said you followed someone you thought was Anna on a bike to the bridge," he said. I saw he was growing as uncertain of me as I was of him. "Why were you following her?"

It was one thing to withhold the sequined fabric, but another to lie to someone who could probably toss me right over the bridge with his pinky if he wanted. The thing was, along with the piece of jumpsuit, I had no intention of giving him Anna's phone. I still remembered the text, and Anna's frightened expression and desperate need to leave the mansion unnoticed. If he wasn't going to take me seriously, I'd share the fabric and my photos with the authorities.

I shrugged.

"I wanted to take her photo and she flipped out on me and left the party," I said. I prayed my face wasn't turning red as I made up my story. "I felt bad. I figured Bisa would want her to stay, even though things were tense between them, so I followed, hoping she would accept my apology and come back."

The muscles on each side of Alfonz's neck tightened and then relaxed. Something was bothering him, but maybe it was only me.

"You know you agreed that anything you see or hear remains private," he said.

"I wouldn't tell anyone about tension between family members," I said, upset but trying to keep it together. "In my family, the louder we yell, the more love we're sharing, you know?"

I laughed a little to lighten the mood, but Alfonz didn't crack a smile. I wondered what his family life was like. I imagined a little Alfonz getting his fingers rapped by nuns for slouching in his school chair and then coming home to a night without dinner for further punishment.

"Not only are you not allowed to share what you see, but

you are not allowed to invite the outside world into Bisa's life in any way. That includes stories like imagining you saw Anna fall from a bridge, when you have no proof she was even here. Kayla confirmed Anna has been at Todo Amor while you saw whatever you saw. Whatever happens with Anna, and anything can happen when she's around, you are not allowed to float crazy theories to the world. Not to the press, or your friends. And especially not to Bisa. As for the police," he said, as if reading my mind, "the City is working hard enough to make sure these next couple of days work smoothly. The forces are stretched thin as it is. You have no idea how complicated this enterprise is. Do you understand?"

It was my turn for my neck muscles to spasm.

"You mean, the police might turn a blind eye to the fact I saw someone, namely Anna Reyes, fall from this bridge to her death? Without even checking on whether a body has been found or whether Anna is actually in her room? Because for the next three days we don't want to upset politicians, or the City's economic boon, or unglue Bisa, or get bad publicity about the Reyes family which might haunt Bisa during her tour? Is that what you are telling me?"

"If that's how you'd like to interpret the situation, I'm not going to stop you," Alfonz said. "But I promise you, you're going to want to be careful about how you handle yourself. That's simply my friendly advice. There's a lot of money and a lot of powerful people behind the next three days and no one wants trouble from a nobody about something that's nothing. Trust me. The stakes are much higher for you, and your company, if you break the NDA. I believe that would be career suicide and cost your boss much more than she could ever afford in lawsuits."

I flinched.

"And then, there's Bisa's wild fans," he said. "You don't want them to turn on you. They can make your life, even your family's lives, a living hell. Your grandparents wouldn't want their key store cancelled." Alfonz had caught up on who I was, but if he was trying to bully me, I did not let it show. "I'm not saying this to scare you, but it's the truth. On Bisa's last tour, a fan fainted in front of her as she exited from an arena one night and accidentally grabbed Bisa's hair as she fell. Next thing you knew, the fans were picketing outside this lady's office about her disrespect for Bisa."

I remembered the story.

"As I said, it's always something with Anna," Alfonz said in a softer tone meant to comfort me. "You aren't the first one she's dragged into some sort of drama. Don't feel bad."

He pulled my bike off the railing and pushed the handlebars toward me.

"Grab a drink," he said, still holding my handlebars, "keep this to yourself. Kayla doesn't want to find another photographer right now, but I know for a fact she has many on speed dial who would never accuse Anna Reyes of jumping off a bridge."

He hopped back on his motorbike, leaving me with my three-speeder to wonder what had happened. I'd gone from watching someone fall to their death from a bridge, to a lecture on minding my place in the hierarchy of celebrity and politics. If I hadn't been so sure of what I'd seen, I'd have loved to believe the fish were running, as Alfonz had suggested. But my eyes are a gift and a curse. I'd seen what I'd seen, and I knew what I knew. Except, I didn't know how to proceed now that Alfonz had made it clear that I couldn't trust anyone, even the police. If the man on the boat delivered the body to the authorities, would the power machine running these next three days withhold the news about Anna for all of the reasons Alfonz had given me? I had to hope not. Surely, the authorities would arrive to Todo Amor soon. Meantime, I would check for myself that Anna was not in her room. The more proof I had that

I'd seen her, the easier it would be to make my case—to whomever that might be.

When I reached the mansion on my Citi Bike, I entered the way I'd left—through the kitchen. Kayla walked in at the same moment from the other direction. A couple of caterers gaped at my wild hair, but Kayla didn't look too hot, either. To begin with, her makeup, particularly her mascara and lips, had worn off.

"They're ready for you," she said, and motioned for me.

"Who is?" I said hoping the police had come through and that Alfonz was no more than a cynic.

Kayla's lips pursed and it was clear that whatever camaraderie she'd shared with me during our conversation on the bridge had vanished.

"The engagement photos," she said. "Chop, chop."

Taking Bisa's engagement photos was the opportunity of a lifetime, but I held my ground.

"Did you check on Anna?"

"Do you want to take Bisa's engagement photos?"

I remembered Alfonz's threat that Kayla had many photographers on speed dial. Dutifully, I followed her across the grand hall. Party planners bustled about, removing the morning's flowers and furniture so that preparations could begin for the night's main event, the Diamond Corazón. When we reached a set of doors adjacent to Bisa's office, I was happy to see old-fashioned doorknobs. My gut told me that an awareness of the exits in this house was important.

"I need my camera flash," I said as Kayla's hand reached for the knob. "It's just upstairs."

"You only have a minute," Kayla said, glancing up in the direction of my storage space.

"I'll be back in less," I said.

I hopped the stairs, and moved as quickly as possible, without running. As I passed Anna's room, I saw a piece of paper peeking out from under her door. I paused and knocked. There was no answer. I waited a few seconds and tried again. Nothing.

Since the balustrade of the stairs opened to the grand entry below, I didn't know if Kayla could see up to me. To be on the safe side, I left Anna's door and swiped the lock on my own *home-sweet-home*, which seemed more claustrophobic since my last visit. I picked up my drinking glass once again and leaned against the wall. I didn't hear breathing or snoring or music or streaming videos or anything through it, but that didn't really prove anything.

My rollie bag had been delivered, and I really did need some equipment for the photo shoot. I grabbed a speedlight flash and stand, a handy five-in-one light reflector to moderate any lighting situation, and a tripod. After a moment's debate, I decided my standard zoom lens would do the trick. All of my accessories would make the images from our session more formal than the events pictures. Pleased with my selections, I retrieved a small compact mirror from a stuffed toiletry bag I'd brought.

"Gorgeous, Liv," I said, and rolled my eyes.

I unleashed my ponytail and tried to do something with my hair, but any semblance of glamour I thought I'd achieved this early morning had vanished. I finally grabbed my hair tie and threw every strand that would cooperate back into a ponytail. I then took out some lipstick.

"OK," I said to my reflection. "You've got this."

I opened my door and covered the bolt with my two largest Band-Aids so that it would not click when I closed it behind me. My back to the balustrade and my equipment surrounding my feet, I raised my mirror at an angle that allowed me to see the grand hall below. In case someone saw me and thought my behavior was odd, I went through the exercise of applying my lipstick. Honestly, if there was ever a moment for the confidence that bright red lips can give you, now was the time. After casting the mirror in various directions and smacking my lips together, I saw Kayla seated on the bottom of the stairway, fully engrossed in her phone. That was all I needed to know.

With sweaty palms, I turned to Anna's door and gently tugged on the edge of the paper peeking out from it, a standard legal-sized white sheet. There were three words scrawled in a black pen on the page: *I'm watching you.*

The short note made me want to pack my bags and flee as quickly as Anna had. There's nothing good about a note that says *I'm watching you*, no matter how you slice it. The word *watching* kills any interpretation. There was no way the sentiment was supportive or caring. I also didn't like the fact that someone slipped it under Anna's door. This meant someone with free access to the second floor put it there. Aside from Miles the waiter and whoever delivered my rollie bag, only those from the inner circle had frequented the floor. If I was a detective, I would have called Anna's death an inside job.

I looked down the hall and across to the other side of the stairs, where Bisa's star hung from her number 1 door. No one seemed to be watching me. I knew I was pushing my luck, but I reached out to Anna's doorknob. I turned it, but, of course, without a key, it didn't open.

I was not deterred. Kayla, I knew, managed the key cards to the suites. She handed them out this morning, programming them with her iPad's handy key-making attachment. Fortunately, my family is in the key-making business. As a lover of the history of keys, and the mystique of the small metal in one's hand, my poppy has decried the key card movement since it started to become mainstream as far back as the late 1970s. A piece of plastic that could morph into a new key on the fly went against everything he believed in. That didn't mean, however, he ignored technology. He was, in fact, somewhat obsessed with these *key-bots*, as he nicknamed them, in a love-hate sort of way. Not a Saturday afternoon went by when he wasn't watching YouTube videos of his competition. This is why I knew Kayla was using the Montserrat 5600X key system. And it was also how I knew how to use it, if I dared.

I slipped the mysterious note back under the door, tossed my equipment bag over my shoulder, and continued downstairs to Kayla, who pointedly checked her watch when I reached her. Her exquisite timepiece, I noticed, was a Lodha, presumably a gift from Dev.

"Ready," I said.

Wordlessly, to punctuate her displeasure that I'd taken more than the given minute, she opened the doors to a reception room about the same size as Bisa's office, but decorated with lots of upholstered seating in sumptuous shades of blue, presumably in honor of her upcoming tour. The shimmer of jewel-like beads was everywhere, without apology. Only Bisa could pull it off so beautifully.

I used the time before the lovebirds arrived to set up my lighting and test different angles of the space, but every noise outside the room made me start. As time passed, and no authorities arrived at Todo Amor, I began to accept that Alfonz had been straight with me. At best, Anna was lying in a morgue and no one had identified her. Either way, Anna was no one's priority. Once I proved she was not upstairs, I determined to tell Bisa the news directly, even if it ended with my dismissal from the job. She would likely be angry that I hadn't told her before our impending shoot, but until I proved Kayla wrong, I'd keep my mouth shut. Alfonz's warnings had at least sunk in that much. I only prayed the police would come between the shoot and when I checked Anna's room so I would not have to be the bearer of such bad news. Until then, I had my work to help keep me in one piece.

Two oversized windows allowed a flood of natural light to pour in and would make for gorgeous photos. Unfortunately, I would not be able to take advantage of them. The party's setup was in full swing outside, but even without Bisa in her office or reception room, the workers kept looking through the windows to see her inner sanctum. Some went so far as to indulge in the all-time taboo of snapping a few photos of the client's private quarters. Usually, no matter how important the hosts or guests at a party, we service professionals keep our heads down and focus on executing our skills to perfection. With Bisa, however, there was no chance. The paparazzi, I realized, was only part of her never-ending invasion of privacy. Maybe this was why she'd only wanted one photographer from Regina Montague Studios.

I comforted myself that the loss of natural light for the shoot meant no one would see me when I dared to hijack Kayla's clever key-bot gadget. My confidence was growing that I could pull it off. Kayla fluttered around, making sure there were cold beverages and a few snacks. Feeling safe in the private chamber, she went so far as to put her iPad on the coffee table as she worked. I could not have hoped for more. Even the key activating swiper was still clipped to the top of her device.

Between pillow fluffing and flower rearrangements, however, Kayla still stood between me and my objective. With Bisa and Dev on the way, I knew if I didn't act quickly, my window of opportunity might close for good. The chance Bisa's assistant would leave her iPad unguarded again was probably zero so it was time to make a move. As Kayla leaned over to fluff the last of the sofa pillows, I reached into the drinks bucket, picked out a ginger ale, and shook the can before she could notice me.

"May I have this?" I asked her.

"Of course," she said, coming toward me. "Just leave the Diet Cokes. Bisa only drinks Diet Coke. She never drinks alcohol or juice or even other sodas. Just Diet Coke."

"Thanks," I said, and pulled back the tab.

As I'd hoped, the can exploded. Ginger ale spewed forth dramatically. I jumped back, my arm extended to keep my camera safe, but the liquid poured onto the hardwood floor in a huge puddle and Kayla's shirt was splattered.

"Oh, Kayla," I said. "I'm so glad I opened one instead of Bisa or Dev."

"Hurry," she said. "Get some napkins."

I put the can down and grabbed napkins from the snacks table. Handing a pile to her, the two of us fell to the floor to mop up the mess.

"Your shirt," I said, lifting my sopping napkins for more. "It's a mess. Why don't you dry off in the ladies' and I'll finish up here before Bisa and Dev arrive. I can also call the kitchen to ask for a couple of new Diet Cokes, in case the rest of these are ready to explode, too. And more napkins. We should divide and conquer."

"Thanks," Kayla said. Without an argument or even checking her fancy watch to see how close we were to Bisa's arrival, she rose from hands and knees. "I appreciate it. I'll be right back. Text the kitchen from my iPad, but be careful with it. Don't let it out of your sight."

She typed in her password, handed me the iPad, and off she went. I was alone in Bisa's gorgeous reception room, gloriously free, but not for long. I slipped my finger down to Kayla's text icon and typed *Kitchen*, followed by a request for supplies. This accomplished, I searched what seemed like a hundred icons that filled the screen. I saw some for the movie studio, the record label, a florist, a bank, Uber, Hulu, Netflix, Amazon, YouTube. Finally, I found the Montserrat app icon.

"Yes," I said to myself in celebration.

As I expected from the consumer market's most intuitive, user-friendly pass key system, four options appeared on the screen: one for security cameras, one for locks, one for keys, and one for alarms. I hit *Keys*. The directions from that point forward were simple. A list of rooms filled the screen, each of which I knew had locks with preexisting codes attached to them, and which the app tracked. Removing my key from my pocket, I swiped it across the attachment to erase the code that currently allowed me to get into the closet. Next, I touched the icon for room 8 and swiped again. It was that easy.

The success of my clandestine mission was a heady experience, but then the reality of what I'd done sank in. Technically, I hadn't trespassed into Anna's room. All I'd done was make a key. But if anyone found out, I would be in so much trouble. Unfortunately, from Alfonz's story about confusing sequins with fish scales to Kayla's story about Anna sleeping in her room, I knew I was the only one right now who would take the plunge to find out what had happened on that bridge.

I mopped up the last of the soda and dumped the soggy mountain of napkins into a small bin by the bar. The room smelled of ginger ale, but the floor was dry and not too sticky. I jumped at a knock on the door, but then remembered my order to the kitchen.

"Thanks," I said to Milo who held a tray of items I'd ordered. I brought them inside, refilled the drink bucket, and nervously readjusted the height of a reflector on my light pole.

Finally, I heard voices. Kayla opened the door and held it for Bisa, who entered ahead of Dev. I lowered my eyes, ashamed to look into Bisa's, knowing the pain that would soon follow in her life.

"Liv Spyers," she said, brimming with energy, as if I was the celebrity.

I confess, in spite of everything, I was flattered she'd gotten my name right. I found myself returning a smile. Being around her really was like a drug.

"Dev and I are so grateful to spend time with you in a more relaxing venue than earlier," she said, fluffing a perfect pillow.

"We can't thank you enough for carving time to photograph us on this special day."

"Yes. We'd love some pictures," Dev said without introducing himself. I guess he figured we'd done our meet and greet earlier.

The superstar wore an ivory satin pantsuit, which was traditional in concept, while also being super sexy with her low-cut camisole beneath, slits up the sides of the pants, and sequins sewn into the lapels of her jacket. I knew it was no coincidence she had packed the perfect outfit for marriage proposal photos. Dev wore the same suit and tie, which looked as pressed as it had earlier, if not more.

"Congratulations," I said.

"Let's move along so you don't tire yourself, Bisa," Dev said.

"Oh, Dev," Bisa said. "Always looking out for me. Liv? Over here. I like this spot."

She motioned to the sofa without skipping a beat. I knew they were on a tight schedule. However much she wanted pictures, we were on the clock.

"Kayla, what's the news on Anna? I don't like it when she goes quiet on me. Especially after her performance this morning," she said as Dev put his phone down and joined her.

I was taking some preliminary shots of Bisa to make sure the light was perfect, but her comment made me freeze. Pretending to check my equipment, I looked at the photo I'd just taken of her. The millisecond of an expression a photo can capture can tell you a lot about the real story. Bisa had sounded concerned about Anna, but a subtle lift in her eyes told me she was happy Anna had gone silent. Bisa was as comfortable with an Anna-free existence as Alfonz and Kayla were. The shock washed over me like the first wave against your body when you jump into the sea. Bisa, I realized, had motive.

I'd learned since I'd moved to New York that a crime of passion was a murder in which the killer is triggered to attack in the heat of the moment. There were big stakes ahead for everyone in the next two days, and Bisa was feeling the pressure of all of it. Anna's arrival had been a lot. Ben Goldfarb had strong words with her; Shawn Jackson had complained to Kayla about her; Dev Anthony was embarrassed by her during his proposal; and with Anna around, Alfonz and Kayla were distracted from their work. As Alfonz had pointed out, even New York City's economy gained from Bisa Mania. The combination, plus the pressure Bisa felt to pull off her concerts and movie opening, might have caused her to snap. Bisa probably had collected a few fixers over the years to take care of her messes. Maybe one of them was the blurry figure in my photos. Worse, Kayla and Alfonz might be willing to cover for their boss.

"Last I heard, Anna was resting," Kayla said, stone-faced and drying a chilled Diet Coke can from the ice bucket. She opened it as Bisa and Dev seated themselves on the sofa. Aside from holding a light meter to their eyes, I didn't have to tell them how to pose. They both arranged their clothes so there were no wrinkles and then turned to each other.

"Excellent," I said, staying as calm as I could. I shifted my light a tiny bit and began to shoot from my tripod. The couple looked into each other's eyes. Dev raised Bisa's hand to his lips. Bisa raised her left hand while they both snuggled to look at the ring. Dev put his arm around Bisa. In each frame, the couple radiated joy and love. Bisa played the role of the power babe who finally found her match. Dev was someone who would take care of her while supporting her artistic genius. Dev was a good model, too. I wondered how working in the watch industry required him to develop such skills. He was media-savvy, for sure.

His arm still around her, Bisa laughed as she leaned into Dev's shoulder, but the skin beneath her eyes tightened. Even through a pound of makeup, I saw her mind was going in all directions. She took her fiancé's hand and held it close to her heart. Dev leaned down and kissed her ring. I snapped away. For about five minutes, all everyone focused on were pictures. If I wasn't preoccupied by the fact that I might be photographing a murderess, Bisa and Dev were a beautiful subject. Since my specialty is portraits, this was a dream shoot.

Between the setup for each new series of photos, Kayla appeared with an iced Diet Coke with a straw in it for Bisa to cleanse her palate. Bisa never asked for one, but Kayla anticipated her boss's every whim. The only time our work halted was when Kayla and Dev's phones buzzed in unison. I lowered my camera and hoped it was the police.

"What's that about?" Bisa asked. "Is Anna awake?"

"No, it's catering," Kayla said as she studied her phone.

"I asked for extra champagne tonight," said Dev.

"We already ordered loads of champagne, Dev," said Bisa.

"Don't worry yourself about these little things," he said. "The news about our engagement has spread. People are going to want to celebrate, so I took the liberty. Now that I'm going to be your husband, I hope you'll trust me with things like that."

"Of course," Bisa said, but he had annoyed her. I didn't need a keen eye to see that. "You think of everything."

"I endeavor to," he said.

After giving his lesson on champagne, Dev was accommodating for the rest of the shoot. Finally, he put his arm around Bisa's waist and whispered into her ear. This time, she smiled.

"Do you think we took enough photos?" she said.

I realized the question was more of a statement. I lowered my camera and returned it to its bedazzled bag to clean up.

"I like that," Bisa said, and nodded toward my camera case. "Kayla, take a note of the bag. Those would sell for at least forty-five dollars. Make them a little flatter and, with a key ring dangling from them, we'll market them as phone holders. I think it would be a hit with the tween group."

"Got it," said Kayla. She typed the idea into her iPad.

"We make more money off merchandise than we do the albums when I'm on tour," Bisa said to me in a confidential manner, which made me feel, for better or worse, that I was in the inner circle.

"Let's keep our eye on Bisa's Diamonds," said Dev.

"One hundred percent," she said. "Diamonds, even cubic zirconia, are a perfect branding match."

"But to do it right, even the shoes will have to wait," Dev said, studying his phone.

Bisa nodded, and I wanted to scream *strike two!* for motive to kill Anna. In addition to being perfectly happy for Anna to be out of sight during her extravaganza, she would be just as pleased in the future not to have to juggle Dev and her sister's money-draining merchandising ambitions.

Our work done, Kayla handed Bisa her phone, which she'd held for safekeeping.

"Resting or not," Bisa said, staring at her screen and then swiping it, "Anna didn't wait to cash the check I gave her. Just pinged through twenty minutes ago."

"You gave her money?" Dev said. Was it me, or did he sound surprised?

"She's my sister, Dev," Bisa said, her tone slightly defensive.

Kayla gave me a subtle nose flare to confirm I'd wasted everyone's time earlier. Against everything I'd seen, Bisa was suggesting that Anna was alive and cashing checks. For a moment I questioned myself but then I decided: *Strike three!* With her knack of manipulating situations to get what she wanted, Bisa had it in her to lie like this without blinking. Plus, she had acting chops. She performed constantly on tour and was now about to start her career on-screen. I officially dropped my plan to tell her what I'd seen. I'd need a new agenda.

"If we're done for now," I said, "I'll spend this afternoon editing before tonight's event."

"Thank you," Kayla said on behalf of her boss, who had not

looked up from her phone. "You'll need to be here at nine thirty, the latest."

"Thank you, darling!" I heard Bisa say as I closed the door.

When I was back upstairs and behind the closed door of my closet, I first walked around in little circles, digesting the reality that Bisa was my prime suspect behind Anna's murder. My reasoning wasn't something that would fly in a courtroom, but through my photos Bisa had shown her hand without realizing it. After my final promenade, I downloaded everything I'd shot during the day and sent my file to Regina. We'd have a lot of editing ahead of us, and Regina had promised to help weed through them while I was still boots on the ground. I would also be interested in her perspective about the people I'd met today. She knew how to read a photo.

Next, I packed all of my belongings. I didn't trust anyone here. I had several hours before I was due at the Diamond Corazón party. There was no way I was spending them at Todo Amor in a closet. I needed a dose of reality and decided to hike it back home.

Lastly, at Anna's door, I knocked. There was still no answer. I looked down the hallway and then across the balustrade to the other doors. My waiter pal was delivering a tray of drinks to someone's room, but he did not seem to notice me. Everyone else was outside watching the party space come to life, or running around below me to transform the interior space into an ultracool party.

I swiped the lock. When I opened the door, I was ready to flee all over again. Instead, I stepped inside Anna's room and closed the door behind me.

CHAPTER 5

What was a tidy, new room only a couple of hours ago was now an absolute wreck. Anna's suitcase, once packed with exquisite shoes, was turned upside down. The boxes were all open, and shoes were strewn everywhere. The glittery, pale blue tissue paper that protected each pair was crumpled into little balls and littered the room. They looked like casualties on a battlefield. I imagined someone inspecting every piece of tissue from the shoe boxes, and then mashing the beautiful sheets so they wouldn't look twice at one. The lush bedding was bunched into the middle of the bed, the pillows were thrown onto a chair whose cushion lay on the floor, and the mattress was askew on its bed frame. Another suitcase, this one with clothes, lay sideways with the contents dumped onto the table.

One thing I did know. Anna had not made this mess. She would never treat her shoes this way. When she gave me a pair of her shoes, she'd lifted the box gingerly and handed it to me with the kind of pride a parent dotes on a firstborn child.

Someone had been here, looking for something, and without fear that Anna would return. I'd seen this kind of ransacked room scene in movies and television, but it was a whole other thing to be in a room where such damage has been done, especially after seeing the lifeless body of its occupant being hauled away on a boat in the river, like garbage. My legs felt like dead weight, but I stepped cautiously over the mess and peeked into the bathroom. Sure enough, her toiletries were strewn across the floor as well. Anna had something that someone wanted, which was odd given how desperate she had been for cash.

I wished I had an ally inside Todo Amor, but could not imagine who to confide in. Everyone was connected with Bisa and genuinely seemed to adore her. There was no way I would trust telling Ben or Shawn what I'd seen. Bisa was the source of their wealth and the celebrity-filled life they seemed to adore. I hadn't met Freesia yet, but anyone on the second floor was a suspect, even if not my prime one.

I remembered that Anna had trusted Russell. I decided I should, too. I hadn't seen him since his visit to Bisa's office, but he'd said he planned to crash her parties. I hoped he'd keep his promise. Until then, I was on my own. Anna was a pain in the butt, but I wasn't going to let her murderer get away with it. There were some high rollers around me, people who were used to getting their way all the time, even if it was for a Diet Coke they didn't know they wanted. That didn't give them the right, however, to use their power to destroy someone else. Murder was murder. And I am not a fan of partying with murderers.

For now, I was a one-person investigator. I began to take photos of the room, as if I was part of a forensic team. As I did, I realized there was one thing that everyone travels with, especially when running a small business, and that's their laptop. I had brought one with me to download my photos to Regina Montague Studios' server. Here, I saw no sign of Anna's laptop. The something that someone wanted might be on it, but why ransack the room as well?

"Anna, what did you get yourself into?" I whispered.

My body tensed as the sound of footsteps approached the door. Knowing how guilty I'd appear if I was caught in the room, I panicked and rolled under Anna's bed. I'd hit a point of no return.

I'd just made it under the bed frame when the door opened. I held my breath, trying to figure out how I would explain myself if I was found in this inescapable position. I also chided myself for hiding in the wrong direction, with my feet at the end of the bed. If I were the other way around, I might have seen who was there. After about five long seconds of silence, the door closed gently and the footsteps retreated. I didn't even know if they were made by a man or a woman, because the hallway carpeting muffled the footsteps.

Eager to escape this madhouse, I rolled back out from under the bed. I wiped the bathroom doorknob and everything else I'd touched, so that no one would discover my fingerprints and blame me for anything. Then, I scrammed with my rollie bag bumping and echoing down every endless step of the grand stairway. I was all but ready for something to jump out from behind one of the large reception room's columns when I finally hit the ground. I opened the front door and scooted past the doormen. Then I ran like the wind, my rollie bag jiggling my entire being in rapid fire along the brick sidewalk, until I reached the subway. Waiting for the F train to come, I paced the platform. After six minutes of holding my breath, I called work. If I was caught up in this crazy world, I would line up my own allies outside of Todo Amor. At least Regina had met Bisa over the years, and had rubbed shoulders with all sorts of celebrities. She would hopefully know the rules of a world in which not even murder was enough to stop the show from going on. Plus, she's also signed the NDA so technically I wasn't breaking any rules by talking to her. For a bit of a rebel, I'm still a rule follower, but Regina hadn't become who she was by sticking to them.

"Regina Montague Studios, this is Manjeet, he/him, please hold," Regina's personal assistant said.

I was left to listen to jazz that would appeal to both young and old clients. I suspected Manjeet didn't need to put me on hold. Lately, his new thing was to put everyone on hold before speaking to them. He'd decided that the busier Regina seemed, the more eager people would be to hire us. It was not a bad idea.

"How may I help you?" he said, back on the line.

"It's Liv."

He squealed.

"Sister, tell me everything," he said, sounding even more excited than Maria had last night.

"It's crazy," I said. "I just sent Regina my first batch of photos."

"She'll be thrilled. I'll make sure she sees the file," he said.

"I got great shots," I said. "And she will be happy to see I got an extra sesh in. Engagement portraits of Bisa and Dev."

"No!" Manjeet wailed with pure delight. My spirits lifted with his heartwarming and much-needed enthusiasm.

"Yup," I said.

"I'm looking now," he said. I heard his fingers fly across the keyboard. "Wait a minute, wait, wait . . . there! *Y-o-u* are about to be Regina's teacher's pet, although you already are."

I smiled at his enthusiasm.

"Can I speak to her?"

"She's out of commission. MIA. Even to me. She had a physical therapy session for her wrist this morning and she said it hurt so much she was going to soak in a bath all day and not to bother her. To make her point she's turned off her phone, her laptop, you name it. Very unlike her. If this accident doesn't get her to quit smoking, nothing will. And with the news that Bisa got engaged she's probably also brooding that she's not on Roosevelt Island with you."

Had I cracked a mirror without realizing it? Was seven years of luck hitting me all in one day? It was the only answer I could think of as to why I was having so much trouble connecting with the people I needed. Even Harry and half of the ACU, who probably knew some trustworthy people in higher places to call, were somewhere in Japan and under cover.

"Tell Regina I'm coming in tomorrow morning to see her," I said.

"It'd better be early," Manjeet said. "We're taking most of the day off to see the first of Bisa's concerts in the afternoon. How about Facetime? Aren't you working all day anyway?"

"I promise it won't take long. I need to see her about something too sensitive to discuss over the phone."

"Spill it," he said. "Is there some good drama behind the scenes? I want to know so I can tell my friends at bridge before the rest of the world knows. My street cred is very high there but this would put me over the top."

The train pulled up and I prayed the AC was working. Summer on the subway is brutal.

"Gotta go," I said as the doors slid shut.

Bisa's new building might inspire awe, but when I saw my small photography studio on my familiar street about forty minutes later, I felt like I was at the gates of heaven. I'd left a CLOSED sign in the window with details on how to contact me, and pin lights lit photos in my display window, but otherwise, the studio was dark. I bounded toward the paint-chipped iron gate between the sidewalk and my storefront as the sounds of a rickety window banged open.

"Did you meet Mateo DeLuca?" Granny leaned her head out from the second-floor window, where her bedroom was.

"Hi!" I looked up and felt another surge of comfort. "I won't see him until tonight, but I promise you'll have a photo of him by tomorrow."

"You want me to fix your hair? What happened to it?" she said.

"I know. I got it. Thanks, though."

Down the two stairs from the sidewalk, I opened my door and went straight for the fridge for a late lunch. I hadn't eaten anything other than some breakfast treats at the party, and my muffin and tea this morning to settle my nerves. I would've tracked down some Prozac, too, if I'd known what the day would bring. My cozy home, however, offered me something better than drugs. Leftovers. There is nothing like day-old chicken parmesan. I took the entire platter over to my desk and got comfortable.

Between forkfuls, I opened my laptop and then my photos. Over a hundred thumbnails filled my screen like pieces of a jigsaw puzzle, a mess that would eventually come together, piece by piece, link by link to shed new light on my prime suspect, Bisa. I opened a few images from the party but I didn't see anything unusual. I then studied the photos I'd taken of Bisa's ring, hoping I might spy something on the desk beside her that was an unexpected clue. I got nowhere. Finally, I turned to the photos related to the bridge. I found the photo I'd taken when I'd seen the fabric fluttering from the railing along the bridge. It had to have been taken moments after Anna died. I zoomed in on different areas, until I hit upon a small blot at the very end of the bridge. My interest had been the fabric when I'd taken the photo, so the background was blurry, but the shape looked very much like someone on a motorbike. It reminded me of the shadow I'd seen along the railing when Anna had fallen to her death.

"No!" I shouted, alone in the room.

My stomach dropped as I realized the figure speeding away was likely Anna's killer. I couldn't tell if the hazy image was a man or a woman. Even the colors blurred together to the point where there was nothing identifiable in what I saw. I couldn't believe it. I had a photo of a killer but couldn't see who he or she was.

I flipped forward to images over the edge of the bridge, before I'd seen the boat leaving with Anna. Since I'd held my arm over the railing, too queasy to focus, they were all over the place and all of them of water. I had no expectation I'd see anything enlightening. One photo finally caught my attention though. Taken at an angle I wouldn't have easily seen myself, it included a small concrete landing at the base of the pier holding up the bridge. I zoomed in on the landing and pushed away my leftovers.

"You poor, poor woman," I said.

I'm not a seasoned detective so that was my excuse for how I'd glossed over the fact that a woman who had fallen to her death into the depths of a mighty river was able to be recovered by one man on a boat. I guess I somehow assumed the fisherman had been in close proximity to Anna when she fell and he had been ready and able to pull her body aboard. That hadn't been the case at all, and of course, now that I thought about it, there was no way that scenario would have made sense. Her body would probably have sunk immediately. Fortunately, but sadly, my picture explained the real story of how the fisherman retrieved Anna's body. Her fall from the bridge had ended on the concrete landing. At its edge, I saw blood. The water was lapping against it and, most likely, the current had washed it away by now, but I had new proof that she had fallen.

I opened my browser and googled *woman found in East River* to see if anything had been reported. Nothing had. Where was Anna's body? I sighed and took my plate to the sink. When I turned back to my desk, contemplating another round of photo sleuthing, I saw something much brighter than the macabre scenes from Roosevelt Island. My heart went pitter-pat. The man who I was not taking to Ai Fiori's tomorrow night was unexpectedly opening my gate and stepping down my stairs.

"Harry," I said, racing to let him in.

I was totally stunned and also a little bummed he hadn't seen me when I looked great this morning versus now—a bike ride in the heat and a murdered woman later—but I threw my arms around him.

"I thought you weren't getting home until tomorrow," I said.

"Change of plans. I got home early and then I saw your text that you were coming home to change from a job working for friggin' Bisa?" he said, pulling me close, his dark curls and bright blues even yummier than I remembered. "As excited as I am to hear you're taking me to a big movie premiere Friday night with your new celebrity pals, I wasn't waiting that long to see you when I didn't have to."

His smile gave away how much he enjoyed his surprise appearance. I dragged him inside, popped him on my guest chair, and sat right on him so he wouldn't disappear again. Some might say I could have played harder to get—and I think I'd planned to be just that over my fancy dinner—but my adrenaline was so high from the day I couldn't stop myself.

His face, which I plastered with deep red kisses, was cleanly shaven and lightly scented. I felt the soft fabric of his summer suit. Lightweight, perfectly tailored. Places like Men's Warehouse don't realize how much a girl appreciates these kinds of details.

"For so many reasons, I wish I didn't need to work tonight," I said, pausing my smooches as the memory of my current dilemma intruded upon my bliss.

"I agree." He laced his fingers, solid and strong, through mine, slender and polished.

"And I hate to say this, but I'm torn about what to do with you right now," I said.

He wrapped his arm around my waist and pulled me closer.

"I'm completely happy with what you're doing right now," he said. "No complaints here."

"It's just," I leaned back from his wonderful face. "Does murder trump sex?"

Harry loosened his hold on me and tilted his head, but he could see I was serious.

"Is it a cold case?" he asked after a beat. He seemed hopeful.

I shook my head.

"I saw Bisa's sister fall off a bridge today. To her death. From the Roosevelt Island bridge. And I think Bisa was behind it, but I was dismissed by two people in her inner circle and then warned in great detail of the risks I ran if I report anything without an actual body to back me up."

"Damn," he said with a sigh mixed with a look of disbelief and horror. "That trumps sex."

I told him everything.

"I also checked and there's no news yet about Anna's body," I said when I'd finished. "But what if she's lying in a morgue somewhere and hasn't been identified yet? Who's to know?"

I stood up because it was too hard to be so near Harry after two weeks and be talking about murder.

"You know, people were talking about the Diamond Corazón party as far away as Japan. I wouldn't mind going to a party with music legends and movie stars."

I suspected he wanted to go because he was worried about me going back to Todo Amor after the day I'd had. I was twenty-eight years old and I'd been hustling through life long enough that I didn't need anyone to protect me, but I liked the sound of it. Not that I needed it.

"I'm sure we can slide you in, but you'll be jumping into murder and mayhem," I said.

"You don't scare me. And there's one person we can trust who has excellent connections while I'm investigating things with you," he said.

"Bernie's home too?" I asked, hopefully.

Bernie Andrews was not only the head of a covert global enterprise, the Art Crime Unit, but she was also Harry's aunt. She was a seventy-something old gal from Park Avenue who looked like she could fall over if touched, but in truth she had the spirit, and I sometimes suspected the strength, of the likes of James Bond.

"She came home with me." Harry confirmed.

"Can she check to see if the police or coast guard found a body?" I said.

"Definitely. And how about tracking Anna's Citi Bike activity today? You said that lady on the bridge took it, but we can track down its use to Anna."

"*We?*" I said.

"No reason to let a good team go to waste?"

I liked the sound of that.

Harry's phone pinged. He looked at the screen and furrowed his brow.

"Sorry. Work."

While he typed into his screen, I sat on the stool at my small kitchen counter and studied Anna's iPhone. The case was a simple blue. The battery was still almost full. I clicked it open. Her screensaver was one of her shoes. I realized how lucky I was to have received Anna's gift. Their designs were like works of art. If only I knew her password.

Harry looked up after a couple of minutes.

"Can I take you to an early dinner before you return?" he said with a smile that was mysterious in its own right.

"I will never say no to dinner, but I need to be dressed up. Where can we go that's fancy but fast?"

"I have a place in mind."

I reached into my rollie bag and pulled out the beautiful strappy number I planned to wear to the party. It was now a mass of wrinkles.

"I'll need a few minutes."

"That's fine," he said. "I have some work to do. You might have guessed from my return home without headlines of the Cardinal's arrest that Japan was a dead end."

Harry had been working overtime to catch his internationally renowned thief and I felt sad he'd struck out again.

"You'll get him next time," I said.

"I absolutely will. "Gotta go."

I watched him open the gate to my sidewalk. He took a right, but not before he gave me a wink. Above my studio, I heard one of my grandparents' windows open again.

"Harry!"

This time, my grandfather's voice called out to the sidewalk.

"Hey, Poppy," I heard Harry call up.

The guy had to go to work, but he still took a few minutes to talk about the Yankees. That is what I call the real deal.

CHAPTER 6

When Harry picked up me and my bundle of camera equipment in an UberXL a couple of hours later, I found him dressed in black tie, which is a style he pulls off well. He can wear that suit like I can wear sweats. I hoped for a cozy dinner to give me confidence that whatever was going on at Todo Amor, I would be able to both do my job well and follow up on the mysterious goings on with Anna Reyes. Given Harry's getup, I was expecting we'd head to one of those secret spots you hear about in town. The trend of hidden speakeasies was a fun one, and people sometimes dressed up for those. But that wasn't the case at all.

I was confused when the car instead drove uptown until it stopped in front of a building with banners down its side advertising: THE NEUE GALERIE OF AUSTRIAN ART. The banners canopied the street from pillars erected specially for the occasion. Other cars were pulling up, as well as ours, and people about four times the age of the average guest at Todo Amor were heading in.

"It's the museum's annual benefit," Harry said without further detail.

"Oh?"

I tried to smile like I was excited, but part of me thought he must be kidding. I studied the line of light scarves and linen blazers that draped over the rounded shoulders filing into the party.

"I promise, you won't regret it," he said. "You can leave your equipment in here. This isn't really an Uber. You can trust your things will be safer than safe."

I had no doubt he was right, but I bit my tongue and twitched my nose. Something was going on with Harry. And if there wasn't, I would need to explore the idea we weren't meant for each other after all. I wasn't ready for such dark thoughts, however—especially with the weight of Anna's murder. When we got out of the car, I did appreciate the banners floating across the street. A saxophone player stood on the other side of the avenue, by the wall of Central Park, and serenaded the city, his open instrument box at his feet in the late evening sun. I remembered a recent complaint I'd made to Maria that as residents in New York City we didn't visit sites as tourists might. I work so hard I don't take advantage of this kind of thing, so I decided that was the upside of Harry's dinner choice. I would enjoy the rock stars later.

The Neue Galerie was not as palatial as Todo Amor, but it was not a bad spread at all. Entering the museum, I could hear the guests' chatter from the second floor echoing below. We followed the noise up an elegant curving stairway. At the top, we reached a wide entrance to the museum's Main Gallery, where patrons were seated and steak dinners were being served. In front of the gallery was a long banquet table that showcased a few auction prizes. One caught my eye: *Item Number 3: Full-Sized Copy of Gustav Klimt's* Portrait of Adele Bloch-Bauer *in Oil on Aged Canvas.*

"She's gorgeous," I said.

"I agree. The painting is one of the most expensive paintings in the world," said Harry, my art expert.

He escorted me to two empty seats at a table by a floor-to-ceiling window at the far end of the room. We joined eight older guests at the table. I tried a few times to engage Harry in further talk about Anna Reyes, but he was more often than not in polite conversation with others at our table, repeating himself loudly since they all seemed to be hard of hearing. Finally, the sound of a microphone interrupted us.

"Good evening," said the museum's director, who proceeded to introduce the evening's auctioneer, a popular talk show host who bounded to the stage and took the microphone. He kept the crowd laughing and hands raised until a young couple made the final bid on the first prize, a trip to Aspen, to the cheers of their table, and then sold a walk-on in a new feature movie.

"Having fun?" Harry said to me. I almost felt like he was mocking me and I was about ready to leave. I'd still be an hour or so early back at Todo Amor, but an hour in my closet seemed more fun, even with murder in my orbit.

"Next on our list is a lovely copy of the *Portrait of Adele Bloch-Bauer*," the auctioneer said as two aides carried the canvas I'd admired inside and placed it on the dais.

"Shall we open the bidding at four thousand dollars?" said the auctioneer. "Thank you. Do I see forty-five hundred?"

One woman nudged her husband to raise his hand. Another husband nudged his wife to lower hers. Harry's eyes followed each bidder as if I wasn't there at all. After about a minute, an old lady in a fuchsia dress raised her hand. Then, a man with slicked-back hair, combed in perfect lines, raised his. The old lady smiled gamely at her new competitor, but the man met her bid each time. Finally, she shook her head.

"Sold!" the auctioneer said as a chorus of applause rose from the crowd at the staggering twelve thousand dollars *Adele*'s reproduction had fetched.

"I'll be right back," Harry said, and excused himself from the table.

As the museum's assistant rolled the canvas and dropped it into an oversized poster tube, the museum's lights suddenly went out. The gallery was completely dark. I turned on my phone's flashlight as the museum's security guards quickly entered our room and tapped a security panel behind the dais. They looked up at the ceiling as if expecting light, which never came. The auctioneer apologized for the glitch, but at each exit, police appeared to block the doors. They turned on their flashlights, but the result was chaos.

"What's happening?" someone began.

"Where's my heart medication?" another continued.

"I need to leave."

"Turn those lights off. I'm going blind."

A chorus of these and other slightly hysterical comments, both comedic and frenzied, flew around the room until the police turned off their flashlights. The guests applauded. I, however, had an art detective for a boyfriend, so I gathered something was up.

I smiled. Harry hadn't let me down. He'd taken me to work. I remembered his case of the Cardinal, a thief who flew in and out of his heists, often with spectacular flair, to make his mark and steal his loot. I kept my small beam shining and began to search the dark room, for what I did not know. I saw Harry outside of the dining room, at the top of the stairs. He held his hand to his ear and was speaking, but otherwise, his demeanor was calm. I found the whole thing very sexy.

Then, I felt something like a breeze fly by me. I turned my light to find its source and saw the man with the combed-back hair standing at the next table, by another floor-to-ceiling window like ours, and holding his auction prize. He opened the window not more than a few inches and slipped out to a narrow balustrade, closing the window behind him so as not to disturb the air temperature. I wasn't sure what he had stolen, but I knew I'd found the Cardinal.

I put my fingers to my mouth and let forth an ear-piercingly loud whistle, which got Harry's attention, plus half the room. Even the Cardinal paused from his escape. He turned to look at me for a brief moment through the windowpane. Frantically, I motioned to Harry toward the Cardinal as the thief grabbed one of the banners tied to the balcony, hopped over the stonework, and disappeared.

Harry took off like a shot down the stairs and I followed after him. I burst through the exit as the thief landed, gently as a bird, on the street. My eyes met Harry's as an army of men in blue from the NYPD circled the Cardinal. To my surprise, the thief looked at me with his quizzical stare one more time. I threw him a wave and walked to the corner to let the pros do their jobs.

"You show off," I said as Harry joined me at the corner with a satisfied grin.

"You make an excellent assistant," he said with a wink. With his arm linked through mine, he walked us toward a waiting car as the police behind us did their thing.

I liked the sound of being Harry's assistant. I didn't need a hero on horseback to protect me at Todo Amor. A little adventure on both sides was healthy for a couple.

"Happy to help, but I don't count that as a real dinner date tonight," I said, snuggling up to him in the back seat.

"Understood. Meantime, I'm sure you'd like the details. Turns out Japan was a decoy while the Cardinal was planning to hit the Neue. That's why I took the earlier flight home. We learned that the thief swapped out the original painting of *Adele* for the fake that was being auctioned off tonight. All he needed to do was make the winning bid and waltz past hundreds of people with his loot in his dramatic Cardinal style. The blackout was his plan B if we were onto him, which we were."

"So, this was take-your-girlfriend-to-work day," I said.

Harry smiled, but his phone pinged. He looked at his screen and furrowed his brow.

"What?" I said.

"It's from Bernie. She followed up on Anna. No one has reported a body found in the river."

I sat very still to let the news sink in. His phone pinged again.

"The bike," he said. "It was Anna's, too. She rented it. You were right."

We looked at each other, the seriousness of the situation hitting us fast and hard. Anna had taken the bike. Anna had gone over the bridge. Someone had taken her body. But no one had brought it to the authorities. Alfonz was wrong about at least one thing. The police weren't playing games dictated to them by Bisa Mania. They really didn't know about a body.

"Do you need to go to headquarters to tie up your case?" I said.

"It's Bernie's job now," he said. "I set up the trap and the catch. My work is done."

"Good. Now it's take-your-boyfriend-to-work day," I said.

We were on the Queensboro Bridge, which took us back around to the Roosevelt Island Bridge. It was about nine o'clock but the traffic for Bisa's party hadn't kicked in. I gazed out the window, quietly, at the East River.

"I think we should call the police now," I said. "We have proof that the abandoned bike was Anna's, and the woman I saw in the limo, with the jewel beneath her eye, can corroborate that. If we can find her. I witnessed the body being hauled away. And there's the mess in Anna's room with the ominous note that says someone was watching her. I wish I'd brought the note with me. I was so freaked out, I dropped everything and left."

"Let's get the note and then call the police," Harry said. "Bisa is going to be hard to bring down. Everyone is cheering for her. They haven't called it Bisa Mania for nothing. You have suspicious information, but it's arguably circumstantial. You don't want to lay it on the line and give Bisa the chance to make it fall apart."

"You're right," I said. "I'll get the note. Then, we'll call the police."

When we neared Bisa's Diamond Corazón, the party began to cast its spell on me. I was getting used to this kind of roller coaster of emotions. The Diamond Corazón was an indoor/outdoor event that showed off the New York skyline. The view was stunning enough as a backdrop for the evening, but for Bisa, that was just the start. Team Bisa had spent the day building a Bedouin-inspired world off the mansion. As a result, romantic tents with chairs and bars dotted the ground in a circular fashion. Large torches, lit in anticipation of the guests' arrival, gave a warm glow to the darkening sky. One large tent in the middle was a stage. This was going to be a party for the ages.

Alfonz would have had his work cut out for him with crazed fans trying to crash the party, but I saw the team had also anticipated this possibility. For the hundred or so groupies who somehow made it across the river, a couple of double-decker tour buses, the hop-on/hop-off kind, were waiting to take them around the island for a cinematic tour of *All About Love*. The tour concluded at the tram, where the fare back across the river had been paid for, and fans ended their night with an aerial view of Todo Amor, lit up in floodlights.

Guests were invited to arrive at ten o'clock, which meant in

NYC that they would arrive at eleven the earliest. The late starting time ensured the skyline would shine against the night, but it also implied that only those who really knew how to party would show up. At this still-early hour, Harry and I had the red carpet entirely to ourselves and we walked, hand in hand, to the entrance of Todo Amor. By the door, two men in black T-shirts that read SECURITY on the back were talking to the doormen. Alfonz was also in the group. He eyed me and nodded, then took a look at Harry.

"Who's that?" he said to me. "No crashers. If he's not on the list, he doesn't get in. No exceptions."

"Good. You're here," Kayla said, coming up from the rear. "Who's this?"

"My assistant," I said.

She looked Harry up and down, plainly skeptical. Harry didn't give off the air of a gofer. Or a party crasher. She was stumped.

"He's not on the list," Alfonz said.

"Well, put him on it and give them both all-access passes," she said.

Alfonz sighed, but did as he was told.

"Good news," she said to me as we put our coveted badges, which dangled from Bisa-branded lanyards, around our necks. "Bisa must have had a heart-to-heart with Anna, be-cause she's left. If you'd like, you can reclaim her suite. I made you a key."

I looked at Harry with a sinking suspicion that our plan to get the note had been derailed, and a growing conviction that Bisa was suspect number one. What had happened since I'd left?

Kayla handed me the key card and shoved off to the next thing on her list.

"Thanks," I said.

"In my work, this is what we call game time," Harry said.

"Welcome to Todo Amor," I said.

As beautiful as the outdoor setting was, the massive reception hall inside Todo Amor was transformed into breathtaking, Old Hollywood–style décor. The red carpet, where guests would enter, continued all the way into the party and up to a DJ stationed at the midway break in the stairs. The torches from outside repeated inside as well, and were positioned around the perimeter of the room. The professional lighting was programmed to beam a show of different colors moving like spotlights in search of a star. Guests would flow through Todo Amor's interior splendor, then to the party outside through large side doors, and back inside through another set of doors, both of which framed Bisa's private office and reception room.

"This is gorgeous," Harry said.

We walked around a velvet stanchion in front of the stairs. I nodded to the DJ, who nodded back, and we ascended to face whatever was now behind Anna's door. When we got to room 8, I swiped the key and gave it to Harry, since we now had two: the one Kayla gave us and the one I'd made before Bisa and Dev's portrait session. As expected, the recent explosion of chaos I'd found inside was now the picture of order. The clothes and shoes and tissue paper were gone. Even the flowery scent of the perfumed paper that wrapped Anna's shoes had left the room. The closet was empty. The hangers hung still. The bed was beautifully made. Seat cushions were returned to their original state. The letter, no surprise, was gone. Frantically, I opened my laptop. When I'd taken photos of the messy room, I'd still been holding the letter. Unfortunately, I had no proof of it.

"This looks like a professional job," Harry said. "I can bet you there's not even a fingerprint left."

"Do you think Anna's murder was a crime of passion? I

know that premeditated murders take planning, and a crime of passion is decided on impulse. If the murder had been carefully planned in advance, the killer probably wouldn't have made a mess, to begin with, right? Understanding what we're dealing with might help identify the murderer."

"I don't think you have enough information to decide. I mean, for the murder to be premeditated, someone would have had to lure Anna to Todo Amor and into a trap. Didn't you say everyone was surprised to see her?"

"As far as I know. And throwing someone off a bridge in broad daylight doesn't seem like something someone would plan," I said.

"But having a boat below to collect and hide the body does," he said. "That brings you back to a premeditated crime."

"It's time to unlock Anna's phone," I said.

I sat at the table. Harry pulled out a chair and sat beside me.

"At least the password is only four numbers instead of six. That means you have ten thousand configurations to guess from instead of one million," he said.

"It goes up that much?"

We both shook our heads at the enigma of math.

"I do know this. You need to think hard about what you know about Anna," Harry said. "People almost always use personal numbers—things related to their home address, childhood home address, Social Security number, phone number, pet's name, birthdays of themselves or loved ones."

"That feels like more than ten thousand options already."

I put my fingers against my temples and rubbed them, trying to think of what Anna might choose, but our paths crossed only briefly. I remembered her grumbling that Bisa always used the same password. Maybe Anna used the same one, too.

"Try *1-2-3-4*," I said.

He typed into the phone.

"Nope," he said.

I picked up my own phone and looked at the dial pad.

"How about the numerical spelling of Bisa or Anna?"

Harry typed again.

"Nope and nope," he said. "We might be blocked out soon."

I closed my eyes and thought about the woman I'd met. I looked at my phone's dial screen again.

"How about 7-4-6-3?"

"That's very specific. Why that?"

"It spells shoe," I said.

Harry tapped the screen and then looked up at me with a smile.

"Bingo!" he said. "You're pretty good with this. Our codebreaker at the ACU couldn't have done better."

"Remember that when someone accuses me of breaking my NDA with Bisa," I said. "I might be in the market for a new job before I know it."

"No chance someone's taking that camera away from you," Harry said confidently.

We looked at the log of Anna's recent calls. One was to Bisa—from the morning, but earlier than the time she arrived at Todo Amor. Once she had arrived, Shawn Jackson had made one. And one was from Ben Goldfarb. The last call, the one that had scared Anna so much she had fled, had no name attached to it.

"Should we call it?" I said.

"Are you sure no one knows you have this phone?"

"No one."

Harry put the device down and bobbed his knee a few times, then picked it up again and hit the number. I fanned my face, convinced we were about to be found out by a murderer.

The phone rang ten, then twenty, then thirty times. Harry eventually hung up.

"It was probably a burner," he said. "If it was the murderer's phone, they've ditched it by now."

There was a knock on my door.

"Liv?"

It was Kayla. I tossed the phone to Harry as if it was on fire and then opened the door.

CHAPTER 7

"Hi," I said to Kayla, who looked past me and into the room as I spoke.

"The people who built the tents outside reminded me we promised to take some photos before the party," she said. "They took their own pictures, but with Bisa, it's always a thing."

Harry was seated on the room's comfy guest chair. He had a pillow on his lap so that Kayla could not see Anna's phone, but I knew he was already trying to glean some information from it before we were required to go downstairs.

"I gave you an all-access pass because I trust Liv needs an assistant," she said to Harry, and then switched her focus to me. "I'll take it away as easily if I find he's only a friend you helped crash the party. We're running a strict policy against that."

"You don't need to worry," I said. "I'm completely professional and Harry is a great assistant—an up-and-coming photographer."

"It's true," he said, and put the phone in his breast pocket, with his hand covering it as he did. "I am."

Kayla dipped her eyes to her watch, which I understood was her impatient sign. I gathered my camera and flash, and we headed downstairs. She was ten steps ahead of us and gone before we'd hit the bottom stair.

"Did you see anything interesting on the phone?"

"She deletes her texts, which is not helpful, but there were a couple that came through today. All before you say she died. She didn't answer them. And no one sent a text after the time of death."

I shuddered for at least the second time that day.

"Who were they from?" I said.

We stepped outside and I raised my camera. The exercise was good practice for tonight when the guests arrived. I was able to test the lighting, which might be tricky given the flickering torches.

"Same people who called her. Ben, Shawn, Bisa—and Dev," he said.

"Dev sent her a text before she arrived? I can't imagine what he had to say." I handed Harry my portable off-camera flash. "I will also require drinks and foot rubs."

"At your service," he said, holding up the flash and following me.

"Everyone you mentioned is staying here," I said as I pressed the shutter for a burst of photos aimed at the empty stage. "They also all have suites upstairs, which would make it easy for any of them to slip a note under Anna's door."

"Shawn sent her a text that said he was looking forward to seeing her."

"That's also odd," I said, remembering how he'd griped to Kayla about Anna being invited. "He definitely acted like he didn't know she was coming."

Harry was doing a good job with the flash, so I moved across the grounds.

"Ben Goldfarb's text said he was done with her."

"That's not surprising. Or a secret."

"And to answer your question about Dev, his text said, *For the love of God, if you respect your sister, you will back off. You have no idea what she's going through.*"

I lowered my camera.

"He used the phrase *going through?*"

"I thought that was an interesting choice of words, too."

"*Going through* sounds more like Bisa has problems, not like she's busy with an exciting, multimillion-dollar extravaganza."

"Exactly."

"Good work," I said.

"Thanks, boss," he said with a smile.

Once the guests started to roll down the red carpet, we took up a spot at the entrance. I had an advantage over the paparazzi of capturing the delight on their faces as they entered the party. Even the most jaded superstar looked like a child seeing a balloon for the first time. With my camera lifted to my eye, Harry and I soon began to circle Bisa's all-star extravaganza. Bisa's event was several times larger than the benefit at the Neue. In comparison to the intimate affair Bisa hosted earlier in the day, I was now shooting an all-out bash. Through my lens, it felt as if I was watching a live-streamed version of the party. That was so much easier than having to make real eye contact with the invitees, half of whom still gave me butterflies, even though I was now used to jobs covering important people. Granny had been correct when she'd said that all of Hollywood would be descending onto Roosevelt Island. The room was saturated with power and glamour.

We worked our way through the crowd as they casually dropped news about projects they were working on, other celebs they'd bumped into, and their enthusiasm about the opening night of *All About Love* and Bisa's new creative output in music and film. Many flexed about concert tickets they'd scored for tomorrow afternoon's concerts. The room was so crowded we literally rubbed shoulders with famous directors, actors, comedians, and musicians of every genre. I got a great photo of Carl Withers, the newest superhero star, and rumored to be nominated for an Oscar for his latest performance, perhaps along with Felix Montgomery. He was handing a drink to none other than Mateo DeLuca, and, since a promise was a promise, I took an extra shot of Matty with my iPhone for Granny. I was breaking a professional code of conduct, but Carl kindly distracted his friend so he didn't notice me. He was a surprisingly nice guy. There were major musical celebrities, some of whom I'd thought were direct competitors to Bisa. I occasionally had a hard time not freaking out when spotting a new star. Harry, of course, was cool and collected through it all.

While my eyes and lens worked the room, I kept my ears alert for comments about Anna. Some conversations included Anna's less-than-flattering toast earlier in the day. News had spread. But otherwise, I heard nothing I didn't already know. I realized that I had more inside knowledge about Bisa and her sister than almost anyone there. I was naïve to think that these celebrities were a club or that their inside family dramas were part of shared confidences. This party was as much of a work event for them as for me. They needed their photos in the thick of New York's Bisa Mania. I needed to take their photos for my job. Bisa needed all of us to prove to the world that they should spend their money on her songs, movies, merchandise, and more. Everything about the night was transactional. We were all part of a well-oiled machine, each of us playing our parts, some of us having more fun doing so than others. Matty and Carl, for example, appeared to be having the time of their lives enjoying all of the extra champagne Dev had ordered.

Kayla seemed to be in the camp of those who were not having quite as much fun. There was an official events manager who was in charge of the night, but we hadn't met. This was a sign of how flat Kayla's organizational chart was. She was at the top of it and we all seemed to report to her. And she was everywhere. One minute, she was schmoozing with a fashion magazine darling, the next she was telling a catering waiter to refill his tray. No doubt she knew where everyone was, at every moment, including me. This was why I was not entirely surprised when she appeared while I'd slipped to a quieter side of one of the columns for a quick adjustment to my dress.

"Bisa will be arriving in twenty on the outside stage," she said.

Our hostess had not yet made her appearance and her guests grew more and more excited as time passed without her. I'd learned that Bisa's appearances were all about maximizing the bang.

"I hope Bisa is feeling less worried about her sister and can enjoy the night. Are you pleased with how things are going?"

Kayla was off before I got an answer. I was going to get nothing from the guests besides photographs, and nothing from Kayla, period. Harry and I followed her instructions to the outdoor space, where the tents were now filled with people.

"Let's go in here," Harry said, heading to a tent in front of the stage that, unlike the others, had a red rope across it and a security guard in front. "Looks like there's a bar inside."

"Great. We haven't properly celebrated your success in catching the Cardinal tonight," I said.

We entered a tent where about twenty people congregated on lounge chairs and at a bar. It took all of my self-control not to stare at a TV actor Maria and I had adored as kids on the first tween kind of show my mom let me watch.

"Two shots of Belvedere, please," Harry said, admiring the well-stocked bar.

We raised our glasses.

"One crook down, one murderer to go," he said.

I flashed my eyes, but no one seemed to have heard him.

"*Cent'anni!*" I said, giving him my best Italian toast. I downed the shot and appreciated the smooth warmth of the liquid as it washed through me.

"Laura, right?" I locked eyes with Shawn, the record label executive. "You're taking photos, right?"

"It's Liv," Harry said.

"No biggie," I said, even though it was my pet peeve when people got my name wrong.

Shawn tapped his fist on his chest and then made a little prayer tent with his fingers, leaning them toward me with a slight bow of his head.

"Liv, of course," he said. "I'm so sorry about that. I only wondered if you could photograph me with Bisa tonight. I need a good one for my office."

"Of course," I said. "Harry, my assistant, please meet Shawn, the music exec in charge of Bisa's music."

"It must be so wonderful to work with Bisa on this project," Harry said, catching on immediately that we'd stumbled across someone from the inner circle who might know something about Anna's fate. Bisa spun a tight web and it was possible any one of them knew what had really happened. "What was she like to work with?" Harry continued, raising his refilled glass in a sign of newfound friendship. "It must have been intense."

"Nah, she's a dream. No joke. And the truth? I've known Bisa almost my whole life," he said. By the way his chest puffed as he spoke, I suspected he'd dropped that fact to anyone who would listen.

"How'd you guys know each other?" I said, admittedly wowed that he'd connected himself with such talent since childhood. The man definitely knew how to pick a winner and I could see why he'd become so successful in the music industry. More importantly, if he'd known Bisa that long, he had to have insight into her family life. Shawn was my first opportunity to learn something about Bisa and Anna's lives. I wondered about the sisters and how their relationship could end with violence. Had it always been there?

"We grew up together as kids, in Ohio after they left Puerto Rico," he said. "Bisa used to sing in our local choir. I used to tell her, *Girl, one day you are going to be a star.* And she used to say to me, *Damn right I will. And you will sell all my albums.* I don't think it happens a lot in this world that a kid's childhood dreams turn out this way, you know? So, I need a picture of tonight. It's all coming together bigger than I could have ever dreamed."

I smiled, touched by his sentiments. I found it hard enough to run my photography studio, but people like Shawn and Bisa were working on a whole other stratosphere.

"So, you must have known Anna, too?" I said. "What were they like as kids?"

"They were two peas in a pod," he said, rolling the ice in his drink and keeping his eyes peeled on the people and action in the room. "Both of them, so talented. Bisa's always had a way of making things happen tho. Anna did her thing too and I'll give Bisa credit. She's always believed in her sister."

"That's awesome," Harry said and waved his glass to the bartender for another shot. It was a well-timed diversion to keep things light while I continued my interrogation.

I also outwardly nodded my mutual admiration for the siblings, but I wasn't so sure how much Bisa supported her sister. She gave Anna a hefty check this morning, that was certain, but her motive seemed to be less about believing in Anna's shoe business and more about making her go away. Anna, on the other hand, dished out tough love, like no one I'd ever seen. As tactless as her toast was, I got the feeling she was completely behind her sister and was genuinely committed to Bisa's well-being, even if there was a tinge of jealousy between them.

"It was wild, seeing Anna behave like that today," I said.

Shawn downed the rest of his drink. Something more than the usual Anna-is-a-problem anxiety crossed his face, as if the mention of her erratic behavior triggered concern he'd been trying to hide. That puffed chest sank and his smooth smile twitched, slightly, but enough to tell me he worried about Anna.

"What was Bisa like as a kid?" Harry said to change the subject. He'd clearly seen Shawn's agitation too and we didn't want to lose him.

"Yeah," I said. "Information like that sometimes helps me with my photos. I always like to capture the real person beneath the excitement of an event."

"That's excellent," Shawn said, recovering his charm. "All I can say is that Bisa goes for it. She'll do anything for the job, the sale, the pitch, so that it's right. She's been a professional since she was still playing in a sandbox. I remember, she once sold lemonade at the playground. Sales were slow, so she picked up a dead bird she saw by a tree and took it over. Charged an extra five cents for a peek at the bird. She made a fortune. I think of that to this day. Even bad publicity can help sales."

Shawn laughed at the memory.

"And Anna?" I said.

"Anna was a doll."

"So what happened?" I knew it was a touchy question but I went for it.

"Money happened," he said. "See you later."

He headed off outside with a wave and a holler to someone in the biz.

"He knows something," I said.

"He's certainly worried about Anna." Harry agreed.

At that moment, lights flashed across the outdoor stage. The DJ switched his music to a mix of Bisa's songs to give the audience a chance to sort themselves out. Bisa was about to make her first appearance of the night.

I was distracted, however, as Harry's phone pinged. He studied the screen and pressed his lips together, his nostrils slightly flared.

"Is everything OK?"

"I need to go make a couple of calls," he said without any additional detail. "I'll be back."

"Does Bernie have more info about Anna?"

Harry shook his head. He left the tent and pushed through the crowd without lifting his head from his phone. It wasn't his style to disappear like that, but I would need to wait for answers. Bisa was beckoning. I elbowed my way to the front of the stage, along with the other guests, and beelined toward a set of metal stairs leading backstage to where the view of both the performances and the audience would be best. Flashing my all-access badge to the security guard in front of the steps, I reached the quiet side of the stage wings.

At the other offstage wing across from me, Bisa was taking deep breaths to prepare herself for a performance. A woman with bright blond tendrils framing huge blue eyes stood next to her. She wore a bag that brimmed with beauty tools and was reaching for a contouring brush. I hadn't met Freesia, Bisa's stylist, who was also staying in a suite on the second floor, but I assumed that's who she was. I also saw Ben Goldfarb with her, and Dev by Bisa's side. I raised my camera and focused on the legend before her performance, wondering if it would be one of her last.

I got some good photographs, and Bisa seemed ready to take the stage when, all at once, Russell appeared. He handed her a rose. Dev looked like he was going to punch him, but Bisa beat him to it. She slapped him across the face, grabbed the drink Ben was holding, and downed it in one gulp. So much for Diet Cokes.

Unaware of the drama offstage, the tech crew moved ahead with the show. Beams of light hit the stage, and a thunderous chorus of sounds like cannons being fired replaced the music. Bisa took her mic from a stagehand by the curtain and waltzed onstage. I wanted to keep my camera trained on Bisa's entrance, but I cheated a little bit. I panned back to Russell for a peek at how he'd responded to such a hostile greeting. In true form, he looked victorious.

Back to work, I trained my view on Bisa, who was dressed in a slinky golden gown with a bustle that most women would not be able to stand in, forget walk onstage in front of people. She waved her hand across the crowd in both a theatrical and intimate gesture. Similar to this morning, it said, *Welcome to my home, which happens to be a stage.* One hand went to her ear and the other adjusted a mic in front of her mouth. By now everyone was in a frenzy to hear her voice, but she teased the crowd and waited to speak. It was like some kind of musical foreplay, and even the most blasé celebrities in the audience seemed to forget they were world-weary and reverted to their prior-to-fame selves.

"How's the party?" she finally said.

The crowd's applause and shouts increased a decibel. I was dying of excitement, too, and I heard myself cheering even as I was working feverishly to capture it all. I definitely had my work cut out for me. This was a moment where another photographer on the scene would have made a lot of sense. Everyone had an excellent view, but they still wanted to be front and center, which at least helped make the scope of my work easier. I remembered Maria's question about why there was only one of me. I knew Bisa didn't love to have photographers around, but now I wondered if, in some way, limiting the photographers helped her execute Anna's murder more easily. Perhaps this wasn't a crime of passion but one the was carefully premeditated. I focused in on Bisa, recasting every one of her features as that of a murderer. This was the job of a lifetime and my worst nightmare—all in one.

"I'm not good at speeches," Bisa said, and swished a bustle attached to the back of her dress. "But I do know how to sing, so can I sing you a song?"

"As long as it isn't from the new album," Shawn yelled out from the front of the stage. "The label and the movie studio will have our heads."

She gave him a coy smile.

"Shawn, nothing can hold me back when I have a song in my heart. And I will suffer the movie studio's wrath, although I love you very much, Cyril, wherever you are. There you are." She waved to the beleaguered exec who was clearly having a hard time exercising any control, not being in the inner circle. "I'm going to sing my song."

Cyril didn't look pleased with Bisa, but what was he going to do? Be the bad guy? Bisa dropped her head, her body straight and unmoving. I knew my photos were going to be fabulous because she made it so easy. A jazzy trumpet fanfare rang through the sky from music piped in from somewhere. A modern percussion beat joined in. Bisa slapped her hand on her thigh in rhythm.

"*It's all about love . . . love . . . love, sugar,*" she sang.

I couldn't believe it. I was listening to a preview of Bisa's new song. Murderess or not—this was big. I was keenly aware that I was seeing a private performance that, by the end of the week, would be blasting through everyone's AirPods. Every word was deliberate, punctuated with staccato, but blending all at once. Two dancers joined her on either side and Bisa ripped off the tight, full-length skirt so that only the bustle remained. The stagehand ran out to take it and then disappeared again. Bisa and her dancers broke into electric dance moves to a bongo and xylophone combo. Her energy reminded me of a shaken bottle of champagne—or ginger ale—that was exploding, but then she smiled playfully at the crowd and the music transitioned into a bluesy pop melody we were all familiar with: "Eye for the I," her biggest hit.

"Don't worry, Cyril," she cried out. "I'm saving the rest for tomorrow!"

On the other side of the wings, Russell was smiling and still rubbing his cheek, while Dev stood with his arms crossed and sulked. Felix had joined them as well, just in time for Bisa to bellow the final notes of her song. The applause was resounding. In lieu of a bow, Bisa threw her head back and reached her arms out as if trying to hug us all. Her chest rose and fell while she savored the moment. The dancers disappeared from the spotlight. Bisa looked back at us regular folk to resume her captivating gaze. I shifted my camera to photograph the crowd's euphoric response.

"The night wouldn't be complete without Felix Montgomery," she said.

Felix took the stage, holding a mic and a rose for Bisa. She took his flower and, unlike Russell's gift, she sniffed it and mouthed thank you. She bowed like an opera star as he stood beside her. Bisa again put her hand on her headset and adjusted it, which reminded me of Harry's similar communication device at the Neue not more than an hour ago. I wondered if he was OK. I checked my phone in case he'd texted with an update, but he hadn't. After closing such a big case, I'd hoped he'd be receiving congratulatory notes from his peers, but something unexpected was bothering him.

"Felix and I wanted to thank you all for coming tonight," Bisa said. "We are so thrilled *All About Love* will be released in just a couple of days, on Friday night. We are so delighted that

Radio City Music Hall will be hosting an over-the-top, old-fashioned movie premiere. In the meantime, I hope to entertain you all tomorrow with some songs from the movie in exciting pop-up concerts around town."

Over the audience's positive reaction to the week's events, she smiled at Felix, who raised his microphone.

"Bisa and I had a magical experience making *All About Love*, which is a love story between a successful but lonely science professor at Cornell Tech, situated not far from us here, and a young dancer who inherits an apartment in this usually very quiet part of Manhattan—"

"We had a chance earlier to thank everyone who made the film possible," Bisa chimed in. "Rob, it was an honor to work with you every day. You are a gift to film direction—no offense to Jefferson. I heard you were here tonight."

Jefferson Kincaid, the prolific film director, waved.

"Shawn Jackson, you and the studio were gracious every day and at any hour," Felix said with a knowing wink that everyone pretended to follow. Cyril, you and the studio are always the classiest folks to work with. And Bisa." He turned to his co-star. "I do believe you have a career ahead of you in film that will span the ages. I am delighted I was your first leading man. Working with you was a highlight in my career."

I assumed Felix came with a big ego, but he expressed what seemed to be genuine humility with his co-star. Both looked quite pleased to be in each other's company. The acting legend and the diva might not be the kind of friends one usually makes at work, where you overhear each other's private conversations over the flimsy partitions of cubicles in the office, but they worked together for three months. Felix had to know something about Bisa's personal life.

I decided to join the more exciting side of the stage's wings, where I could take some photos of Bisa and Felix after their speeches and infiltrate the power players at work. This was one of those moments where my camera gave me the confidence I needed to go anywhere and do anything. While the stars' jokes and laughs and acknowledgments continued on stage, I slid from my perch, through the crowd, and up the stairs to stage left. Or was it stage right? Either way, I was walking right into Bisa's hot zone to see it in action and up close.

"I'm glad I found you," Ben Goldfarb said by way of a greeting when I reached the top of the stairs, and making my arrival easier than I expected. "Please make sure to get a photo of me with Bisa and Dev tonight."

"Of course. And when Anna returns," I said, "we can get a group shot. I'm sure you're close to all of them."

"My dear," he said, pinching his lips in disdain, "I would rather throw myself under one of those tour buses outside than take a photo with Anna Reyes. Anyway, she's left."

"I heard. And I didn't get any good photos of her today. I hope Bisa won't be angry."

"Bisa will not be angry," he said with confidence. "Anna is a complete heartbreak for Bisa. Among my long list of responsibilities when it comes to Bisa is to protect her from Anna's idiocy. And I'm quite motivated. A happy Bisa is a wealthy Ben."

He smiled as if he'd said something very clever, so I smiled back. In truth, I wanted to spill something that left stains on the leather jacket he still wore. Who says things like that?

"You are a lovely thing," he said, eyeing me up and down. "Don't forget to get that photo of me with Bisa and Dev. Family is family."

He returned to his prime spot to catch the rest of Bisa and Felix's comments.

"Family is family unless one member of the family is an inconvenience," I said, and muttered a few more things about Ben.

Russell appeared at my side and gave me a sympathetic nudge.

"Don't let him bother you."

"Where've you been?"

"Playing with string, painting a little, generally killing time," he said.

I thought about how comfortable Anna had seemed with Russell. Part of me considered that he was someone I could trust, but, still, I didn't know if I was ready to share my worries with him. Although he genuinely cared for Anna, it was painfully clear he also still loved Bisa. And love can make people do crazy things.

A could of yards away, Ben, Shawn, and Dev applauded as Bisa and Felix left the stage. Bisa went straight to a bottle of champagne on a makeshift backstage bar. She lifted it up and then gulped the bubbles straight from the bottle.

"Darling," Dev asked with a shocked expression, "what has gotten into you? You don't drink."

"I will tonight," she said to Dev, but she was looking at Russell. "I'm a human, flesh-and-blood person with feelings. Isn't that right? And this is a celebratory night, so I'm gonna celebrate!"

She took another swig, and Ben slid to her other side and gently took the bottle away.

"You have to be up bright and early for your rehearsals," Ben said, sounding as if he was talking to a child. "It's a big day tomorrow."

"Oh, Ben, you worry too much," she said. "That's what Anna always says. Where is she? Why did she come all the way here and then disappear on me?"

Bisa looked at the bar and lifted a bottle of tequila, which she downed before Ben or Dev could pry it away. I cringed at the thought of the two liquors mixing together. It was going to be a tough morning rehearsal for Bisa. If this is what guilt looked like after killing a sibling, she was nailing it.

"Have you spoken to Anna since this afternoon?" I asked

Russell as Bisa's charade continued. I searched his eyes for a re-action.

Russell searched my eyes right back.

"Do you know something?" he said.

I felt like a spy during a war, trading secrets. It was thrilling and terrifying.

"I'm not sure," I said.

Russell looked around, as if nervous to continue our conversation.

"Come with me," he said, and pulled my arm.

"Wait a minute," Ben said. "I wanted a picture."

"Me too," said Shawn.

"I'll have her back before you know it," said Russell.

"Hold on," Bisa said.

She walked toward us and I could see she was a lightweight. When she reached us, she smiled at me and poked Russell in the shoulder, somewhat reminiscent of Anna's booping of me.

"See, Russell?" she said. "I can party and have fun and marry Dev."

"Suit yourself," said Russell. He grabbed my hand. "Come on, Liv. Let's check out the fans in front of Todo Amor. Bisa loves her fans so let's get some pictures of them. And the bus tour is a one-in-a-million idea. The media aren't allowed on it, so you can take some inside shots."

"That's a splendid idea," Bisa said with a hiccup.

It actually was. I couldn't argue, but I also couldn't help feeling I'd once again been played by these two. I followed Russell, nonetheless, with Bisa's inebriated blessing.

A cluster of tourists milled around a stop for a tour bus behind a barrier across the street from Todo Amor. After a few moments, the sound of large tires rumbled down the street, and the waiting fans craned their necks as a double-decker red bus, with NEW YORK SIGHTSEEING emblazoned across its side, pulled up in front of us.

"It's here," a man holding a cup of Dunkin' Donuts coffee said to a woman who was moonbathing on the grass.

Before I stepped onto the bus, I heard my name. I turned to see Harry, who, I'd thought, was in our room. I wanted to talk, but I couldn't let the opportunity to talk to Russell pass.

Instead, I waved.

Russell waved.

Harry slowly waved in return.

CHAPTER 8

The bus tour screamed Disney ride. A guide greeted us with saccharine smiles, while a trailer for *All About Love* played on small screens above the seats. I walked down the aisle with Russell ahead of me. The bus was packed, but we found two seats toward the back, where Russell offered me the window.

"Can't," I said, and raised my camera. "I need the aisle so I can shoot."

It was a handy excuse. I didn't know what I was in for with this guy, and the aisle felt much safer than being trapped by a window. I hoped I'd made the right move by coming with him.

"Gum?" he said, taking a pack of spearmint from his jacket pocket.

"No thanks," I said.

I took a few photographs and then sat down beside him as the bus doors closed and the vehicle jolted forward.

"I don't really want gum, either," he said. "It just felt like a nice way to break the ice. This is an awkward situation we're in, wouldn't you say?"

A new recording began with the tour of the sites we'd shortly see from *All About Love* and the behind-the-scenes stories we'd soon hear about the making of the film.

"I'm not entirely sure what the situation is," I said.

"I'm worried about Anna," he said. "And it seems like you are, too."

I nodded my head.

"Why?" he said.

I looked past him and out the window as we passed the crumbling ruins of a building I'd only ever seen from a car while speeding along the FDR in Manhattan. I now learned from our guide that the old wreck was once a smallpox hospital, otherwise known as the Renwick Ruins, and was considered one of the most haunted places in America. I remembered how I'd felt the bridge was haunted today. I wanted to trust Russell, but I wasn't ready to show my cards to someone I didn't know.

"Why are you worried about her?" I said instead.

Russell looked out the window as well, as if trying to decide what to share.

"At the heart of this," he said, "I'm worried about Anna's drug use."

"Anna does drugs?" Of all the things people had complained about Anna, drugs had not come up.

Russell shook his head.

"Not anymore," he said. "She's been clean for a year, but I heard she stormed out of Todo Amor today. I don't get it. You wouldn't think it from her toast, but Anna adores Bisa. I haven't spoken to her in a while, but the Anna I know would do anything for her sister. And she wouldn't show up today, only to turn around and leave."

"You think she's back to using drugs and wandered off?"

"I don't want to, but I can't think of any other scenario that makes sense. Bisa's too busy to look for her, and no one else will bother, that's for sure. They're thrilled she's MIA. They're the ones who probably plotted to get her off the island, to begin with. I don't trust any of them."

The bus had turned north toward the other end of the island, where most of *All About Love* had been shot. To our right, we passed the bridge Anna had fallen from. The timing once again made me feel haunted.

"When you say *they're* thrilled Anna is MIA, who exactly do you mean?"

"Dev, Shawn, Ben," he said. "Alfonz. Even Kayla. She hates to see Bisa in any sort of turmoil. Kayla's the biggest enabler of all. That group has Bisa believing she's a goddess and that she's in control, but bit by bit, they've taken the reins and she doesn't even realize it.

"Anna sees it, though, and usually makes it her job to alienate anyone working for her sister, but for some reason, she connected with you earlier today. Why?"

"Long story, but she gave me a pair of shoes," I said. "From her collection."

Russell smiled.

"She has some prototypes? Good for her," he said.

I guessed he really hadn't seen Anna in a while if he didn't know that her shoe business was progressing.

"And she wanted Bisa to loan her money," I said, venturing a little further into sharing what I knew.

"Did Bisa lend her the money?"

"Yes, but reluctantly. First, I overheard them arguing before the party. Anna said she needed a loan immediately. Bisa said she wasn't liquid enough to give one to her. But during the engagement photo session I had with them later in the day, Bisa mentioned that Anna had deposited a check from her."

"How did Dev respond?"

"A bit peeved," I said. "Although he seems to have a chip on his shoulder when it comes to Bisa. I mean, she's the superstar. She created everything. But he acts like he knows what's best for her."

"He's an insufferable snob," Russell said.

I laughed.

The bus stopped in front of an unremarkable low-rise building.

"This is where they filmed a love scene that you will all soon come to love yourselves," the tour guide said. "It was filmed last spring, and as the story goes, Bisa was allergic to the pollen and she almost sneezed on Felix Montgomery as he went in to kiss her. Fortunately, it was friends-and-family day. Mr. Montgomery's aunt was there and had some Sudafed, which Mr. Montgomery took to her trailer. After that, filming started up again and the script was changed to make a small character at the end of the film have the name Trudy, in honor of his aunt saving the day."

Everyone ate it up.

"Bisa's not allergic to anything," Russell said. "That is the worst junket story I've ever heard. I bet Shawn came up with that one. Felix probably doesn't even have an aunt."

"Bringing up Dev really got to you, huh?" I said.

Russell crossed his arms, aware that he'd been caught.

"They're all a bunch of controlling sycophants. All but Anna. She is a true believer in her sister."

I appreciated that he spoke about Anna in the present tense, but it broke my heart, too. I doubted Russell had killed Anna, and I suspected he would be in pain when he found out.

"Is that why they're so threatened by Anna? Because she sees through them?" I asked.

"Yes and no. There's a dark side to Anna, too. I was with her when she was at her worst. I was the one who drove her to rehab. Those drugs, they changed her. They unleashed a hunger in her that I don't think anything or anyone has been able to satisfy."

"You seemed surprised Bisa gave Anna a check today. Why?"

"You heard it straight from Bisa," he said. "If she says she's genuinely low on funds, I believe her. Bisa gets maniacal when she's putting a tour or any kind of production together. She will risk anything, even her fortune, to make sure she creates something spectacular and unforgettable. You know? And usually it pays off in the end."

"I get it. I took a risk and left my job at Starbucks to follow my dreams," I said, keenly aware of the difference, but I needed a splash of the real world or I was going to lose it. "Do you actually think Bisa would put her entire fortune on the line?"

"It wouldn't be the first time," he said. "On her last tour, she insisted on fireworks outside every venue, after every show. She had to cover the expenses and insurance for the entire tour, even though the after-show endeared her to new and old fans, while probably helping to sell thousands more albums."

"I wonder, then, why she'd lend money to Anna if she has none," I said.

"I agree. In spite of the risks she takes with her own money, she'd never spend what she doesn't have," he said. "It doesn't sound like her at all."

"Maybe Bisa is more reckless than you realize," I said.

"Reckless, no. Judgmental, yes. Bisa despises other people's shortcomings and failures, since she strives for perfection in everything. But really, she's an artist. I wish I could remind her of that fact."

This guy was a goner when it came to Bisa, but everything he was saying convinced me more and more that Bisa had orchestrated Anna's death. The check and her claim that it had been deposited was no more than a cover to show she loved her sister. Meanwhile, the people who were enabling her were only too happy to turn a blind eye.

The bus came to another stop, but when I looked through the window, I noticed we were not at one of the tour sites. The driver opened the doors and a security guard boarded.

"Liv Spyers," he announced firmly.

I felt my phone buzz as well, but did not dare answer. Instead, I stood and raised my hand.

"Don't worry," Russell said to me. "This has Bisa written all over it."

The guard walked down the aisle. In his wake, the customers of New York Sightseeing fled.

"Ma'am," said the cop, "please get off the bus."

I quickly followed, thankful that Russell joined me.

"Everyone can get back on," said the police officer.

The crowd looked disappointed, but filed back on for the rest of their tour.

"How can I help you?" I said, but the guard walked to a security car and opened the door.

"You're needed back on campus," he said. "Bisa is in your suite, waiting for you."

Russell laughed, which I found annoying, but we got into the car and suffered the short ride back in silence. When we pulled up to the side entrance, I didn't wait for the guard to give me any instructions. I opened the door and headed straight inside.

It was now nearing two o'clock in the morning. In the last twenty four hours, I'd stumbled onto a murder, helped Harry catch a thief, and dealt with all kinds of nonsense at the Diamond Corazón. I should have been exhausted, but I was on fire.

"Hey, Carl," I said to the star, who was now slumped on a sofa and watching the light show above him, as I headed for the stairs.

"Hey, Liv," he said, to my surprise.

I marched up the stairs toward my suite. Infuriatingly, the door was ajar. I pushed it open.

Bisa was sitting on my bed; Harry was next to her. An empty bottle of champagne was nestled between them. Harry wore an expression of wonder and drunkenness and shock. He made a motion to me with his hands, passing his fingers across his neck. It summed up my thoughts perfectly.

"S'not what you think," he said. "She came in here crying, so I comforted her."

"You're here," Bisa said, not looking at all as if she needed to cry. "I met your lovely assistant. He's a doll and very sexy, too. Don't you think? Dev was so smart to order all that extra champagne. I've been drinking it all night. He's so thoughtful."

Harry stood, unsteadily, and smiled before rolling into the chair beside our bed.

"I'm being wild, Russell," she said, throwing her arms into the air. "What are you doing with my photographer? Why'd you kidnap her?"

"Tha'z what I'd like to know," Harry said, raising his hand to Bisa for an air high-five motion, which she tried unsuccessfully to return.

"Liv'z a little sweetheart, who takes lovely pictures, and she's going to help me make lots of money with them, so don't upset her, Russell," Bisa said.

She stood up, but immediately began to stumble. Russell caught her in his arms. Harry took the opportunity to fill the vacancy left behind in the bed, shoes on and all.

"I've got this," Russell said about the superstar in his arms.

"I've got this," I said, and motioned to the bed.

I closed the door and turned to Harry. After two weeks apart, we were in a room that had been ransacked earlier after its occupant had been murdered. It was not the ideal place to have a reunion, but there was no way I was getting Harry's deadweight home. Accepting our fate, I climbed in next to him.

"Did she at least say anything that would incriminate herself?"

"I tried, but she jus talked about that Russell guy. I dun love her, you know," Harry said, eyes closed. "Dun worry. An' anyway, I know that dude'z an artist, but I'm the guy for you."

"Yes, you are," I said, and patted him on the arm while I looked at the ceiling. "Russell said Anna had a dark side. I wonder if she went too far and that's why she needed the money. All the more reason for Bisa, the perfect goddess, to keep her distance from Anna. And if she planned to kill her sister, she could have written the check, knowing full well that Anna would never have the chance to cash it. Russell said she never would have written Anna a check if she couldn't afford it."

"That'z nice," Harry said. He rolled over and put his arm around my waist like I was a big teddy bear and lightly snored in response to my detective work. I kissed his forehead and got up to return to my day job.

"Livvvy," Harry said when I reached the door.

He dragged one eyelid open.

"Th'Carnial broke out of his jail cell n'scaped."

He pushed his head into the pillow and fell to snoring. Harry worked for months on his arrest. He was out for the count, but I hugged him hard. And three hours later, when the last of the guests from the Diamond Corazón left, I pulled off my dress, rolled over next to him, and closed my eyes. A heavy sleep crept over me. I fell into dreaming that I held a billowy, blue sash on a string that carried me around town.

CHAPTER 9

Exhausted as I was, I began to feel restless in my sleep and soon gained enough consciousness to feel that Harry's large body was entirely curled around my smaller one. When multiplied by a factor of about ten due to the complete lack of muscle tension after his bender with Bisa, he felt like a thousand pounds. The room was air-conditioned, but not enough. Eventually, I admitted to my still half-sleeping self that I was more awake than asleep and forced one eye, then both, open. I looked out at a sleepy summer dawn and checked the time to find it was only about an hour past when I'd fallen asleep. The only drink I'd had at the Diamond Corazón was my shot with Harry, but I felt as hungover as if I'd drunk the whole bottle. My entire body ached from hours and quite possibly miles of walking last night.

I lifted Harry's arm, like someone afraid of waking a sleeping baby, to enjoy the very quiet light peeling through our window before my eyes shut again.

"Hi," I heard a tired voice in my ear.

I was about to return an equally sleepy hello when Harry bolted upright.

"What time is it?" he said.

"Five thirty." I wasn't ready to budge.

Harry lay back down. I heard him rub his head. The change from rhino weight to a more human heft signaled to me that he wasn't going back to sleep, but the dead quiet that followed surprised me. I rolled over and threw my arm over him, eyes still shut in spite of my adoration of the man.

"I'm sorry about the Cardinal," I said.

Still, no answer. I rubbed my hand across his morning stubble.

"I was hoping I'd imagined it," he said. "He could be half-way across the world by now. Six months of work out the window because one of the officers at the correction facility left him uncuffed in a room for literally one minute."

"The Cardinal earned his name," I said.

Harry sighed.

"Too soon, Liv," he said.

He lifted my head from his chest and lay it on the pillow next to me. He then turned the water on in the bathroom sink; now I was awake.

"Is there anything I can do?" I said as he returned with a wet face and sat on the cushy chair instead of rejoining me. His eyes were red and his hair stood straight up. If he didn't look so sad, I'd have called it comedy hair.

Harry slid his eyes in my direction from his saggy stare at the floor.

"I should go clean up and then check in with Bernie," he said.

"Should we reconvene later today on both cases?"

"Looks like you can work with Russell," he said. "I'll leave you two to it."

I wanted to throw a pillow at him. Was this man actually sulking because I took a bus ride with Bisa's ex-husband? Did he not remember that I'd literally found him in bed with the superstar? I knew Bisa arranged the scene to irritate Russell, but if anyone was going to be mad, it should be me. I shook my head and dropped it back on the pillow as I realized he didn't remember his part of the night. Still, I wasn't pleased to be accused of skipping off with some guy I barely knew.

"Let's get some coffee from the kitchen," I said, pulling my feet over and to the floor and throwing my dress back on again. "I can't fight without a coffee. You have an unfair advantage."

"Fine," he said.

We were literally wearing the same clothes from last night when we headed downstairs. I felt I was on a walk of shame, but so be it. I didn't bother to put on my shoes and at least the limestone stairs cooled my aching feet. With the prospect of coffee and some TLC for my toes, I brightened a little, but I was still ticked off by Harry. He should know me better. Implying I was off with Russell was low. I huffed, almost forgetting my offender was still next to me.

Since the party ended so late, the general décor was still set up. The caterers had swept and the space downstairs was tidied up, but the aroma of drinks and dancing and celebration lingered in the air. As we limped wordlessly toward the kitchen, I noticed two people asleep on one of the party sofas. I grabbed Harry's forearm and stopped.

"It's Bisa and Russell," I said.

Harry looked at the passed-out figures. Russell was sleeping sitting up, with his head thrown back against the headrest. Bisa lay across the rest of the sofa, her knees curled to her midsection and her head resting comfortably on Russell's thigh. I watched Harry's face and my mood lightened. He stood in stunned silence, likely replaying the night in his head and coming to the parts he'd forgotten. His mouth dropped, his sulk vanished, and he closed his eyes.

"I'm so sorry," he said.

"Hey, you two," Russell said, yawning deeply. "Good party."

He looked down to see Bisa on his leg and touched her hair. She looked up at Russell.

"Hello," she said in a deep, husky voice.

A smile crossed her face and then quickly faded.

"Anna," she said, sitting up.

Not what I expected, but maybe the horror of what she had done was sinking in. I dragged Harry with me and sat us down on the sofa beside theirs.

"What about Anna?" I said.

Bisa looked at me and squinted. Then she looked at Harry. Once again, I witnessed the face of someone who remembered things that made them want to cringe. We were a motley group. Harry rubbed his eyes; I rubbed my feet; Bisa rubbed her head; Russell looked at all of us, amused. Bisa pulled herself away from Russell and waved a weary hand.

"Where's my phone? Nothing good can happen until we all have some coffee."

She found her phone tucked into a cushion and texted an order to someone. At five thirty in the morning. I thought how poorly that kind of request would go over in prison. Maybe Bisa did, too, because she buried her face in her hands and sucked in a sob as Russell rubbed her back.

"Liv, I told Bee you were concerned about Anna," he said to me.

Harry rolled his eyes, still a bit peeved by my bus ride, I guessed. It was sort of cute. Russell noticed, but didn't say anything.

"Show her, Bee," he said. "She might be able to help."

Bisa looked up at me, her makeup a mess, and unclenched her fist to reveal a wire-thin, circular band. I leaned forward to see it more clearly, that's how nondescript it was. Even Harry put aside his hangover, huffs, and humiliation to lean in. Our mutual interest at least made me wonder if we were in some kind of cease-fire amidst our cryptic morning fight.

"This is Anna's," she said. "I found it when I was in your room last night."

"About that—" Harry said.

"As I was leaving, I saw it under the table," she said. "It's our sister ring. She has one and so do I." Bisa flashed her pinky and I saw she, too, had the little piece of wire around her. "When I got my first paycheck as a singer, I bought one for her and one for me. It has a little diamond in it."

Harry and I narrowed our eyes for a better look. The room was still half lit, but I noticed the tiny chip. Bisa's first diamond.

"We swore we'd always wear them," she said. "There's no way Anna would leave Todo Amor without hers. And if she had forgotten it by accident, she would have noticed by now and contacted me. I think something bad has happened to her."

She choked on a sob again. Russell responded with tenderness and genuine concern. I wasn't as taken in by the act. Since she was my prime suspect, I considered that Bisa might have kept the ring in order to weave this story. On the other hand, no one had raised concerns about Anna, especially after Bisa had announced that Anna had cashed her check. There was no real need for her to tack on the missing-ring story.

"Did Russell tell you I was concerned about Anna?" I said, speculating my investigating prompted these new details.

Russell shook his head.

"Bisa was the one who brought it up to me. I explained to her that we took the bus ride to discuss Anna." He flashed Harry a look as he said this. I sensed Harry's shoulders sag in further embarrassment. What a night we'd all had.

"Anna has a history with drugs and Russell's worried she's sliding backward," Bisa said, and threw her head back into her hands. "If I'd known, I never would have loaned her the money. She wasn't even supposed to cash the check until next week. That was our deal. I gave it to her yesterday as a sign of my confidence in her, but she understood I needed some time before she cashed it."

"I noticed her arrival here shook everyone up yesterday," I said. "Shawn said the music label was afraid she would cost them money. You must have been very stressed."

"Anna has no sense of business, and she's outspoken, but she'd never do anything to destroy my work," Bisa said.

"What about Los Angeles?" I said, remembering Shawn's reference to something that happened there with Anna.

"That was nothing more than an accident. She fell down the stairs one night and landed on me a couple of years ago," Bisa said. "I sprained my ankle and had to take it easy with some dance moves for a few days, but if it had been worse, I would have had to cancel some concerts. She was on drugs back then. The real problem these days is just that she spends money on the finest materials for her shoes without any thought to the bottom line. I've tried to work with her, connect her with accountants who could help, but she's too proud. Honestly, it had been so long since she'd asked for a loan, I'd started to relax. I convinced myself she was learning on her own. Now, I don't know what to think."

"If Anna couldn't cash the check until next week, you must be tight on funds," I said. I decided to delve a little deeper into Bisa's financial situation. "Is that why you hired only one photographer?"

Bisa nodded.

"I knew I could trust Regina to understand my vision and capture the photos I wanted," she said. "And she would trust me to pay her based on royalties from media sales versus a flat fee. I'm down to the penny at this point, managing my cash flow. I may know better than Anna how to manage a bottom line, but when it comes to my work, I am willing to bet on myself every time. All or nothing. I didn't get to where I am by playing it safe."

The theory I'd floated last night, that she'd hired only one photographer in order to make her job of killing her sister easier, was off the table.

"Does Dev know?" Russell said.

"No, and don't you tell him," she said to Russell. "Don't ruin this for me. Dev is reliable and a grown-up. And he puts me on a pedestal."

"I'd have thought enough people put you on a pedestal that you might want someone honest when you get home at night," Russell said.

"Liv." She ignored Russell and looked me in the eye. "If what Russell says is right, I'm worried that Ben Goldfarb is behind her relapse. When Anna hit rock bottom, it was because he supplied her with enough coke to knock her out for days. If Russell hadn't found her, who knows what might have happened? Ben always said that Anna found his stash, and Anna's never denied it, but now I'm wondering if he left it out for her to find. I know he can't stand her, but how far would he go?"

I watched Bisa roll the small ring across her fingers and then slip it onto her pinky, above her own. I was becoming more certain that if Bisa had killed her sister and cleaned out her room, she would not have advertised the discovery of the ring. As convinced as I was that Bisa had the greatest motive to get rid of Anna, I realized I'd been following the wrong suspect. I'd once accused a police detective who'd thought Regina had killed someone of doing the same thing, focusing on one person instead of the big picture. I had to be honest with myself if I wanted to prove that Anna had been murdered. Bisa did not kill Anna. I looked at Harry, who gave me a nod in agreement. He knew what I was thinking. It was time to be straight with Bisa. Time to bring the story to light and hand it over to the authorities. I could see that she wouldn't let the Bisa Mania machine stop her.

I reached into the pocket of my dress for Anna's phone. I hadn't let it out of my possession since I'd found it.

"Where did you find this?" Bisa asked. She reached a visibly shaky hand to take the phone from me. She eyed me suspiciously, and I could see the trust we briefly had between us was gone.

"Anna left it behind yesterday. I saw her leave Todo Amor after her meeting with you. After speaking on the phone, she absently put it down and quickly left."

"You didn't tell me this last night," said Russell.

"She didn't know whom to trust," Harry said.

"Tell me what happened," Bisa said. "Tell me everything."

"I saw her leave," I said. "I followed with the phone. A short time later, I saw someone in a sequined jumpsuit fall from the Roosevelt Island bridge. I'm so sorry to tell you any of this."

Bisa softly moaned, then shook her head.

"Why didn't you tell me?" Russell said, ashen. "Anna would never have done that."

"Stop, Russell," she said, grabbing his arm like her life depended on it. "Anna can do a lot of crazy things, but suicide is not one of them." Bisa started to wring her hands. No one was a good enough actor to fake the agony that spread across her face. I was afraid to show Bisa the piece of jumpsuit, for fear she might become hysterical.

"I think you should call the police," Harry said to her.

Bisa shook her head.

"I can't," she said. "Not yet. They will make a huge story of this, and for all I know, she threw a bag of sequined fabric over the bridge and is holed up somewhere working on new designs. Or relapsing. She shouldn't have to deal with the press if she has."

"I saw her body," I said, my eyes on the ground, unable to watch her grief. I realized I was squeezing Harry's hand beside me. "A man had fished her out and took her away on a boat. Alfonz tried to tell me I'd seen fish scales from a successful fishing trip, apparently the stripers are teeming in the river right now, but I am very certain it was her."

"No," Bisa said forcefully, shaking her head. "It wasn't her. I'd have heard by now. Someone would have told me." I knew a drug addiction was easier to swallow. Bisa needed time to accept what had happened. "Alfonz didn't tell me anything."

"I have some other evidence." I hated this.

Bisa raised her hand for me to stop. She couldn't hear or see more. She took a deep breath, her eyes closed. When she opened them, she was a changed woman. The vulnerable and grief-stricken family member was replaced with the chief executive of the Bisa empire.

"I want to look into this carefully before we jump to conclusions. The minute I go public, I'll lose control of finding out what really has happened to my sister. And worse, the media will take over, and who knows what will happen to her? I'll tell Alfonz to look into it first."

"I wouldn't do that," I said. "When I told Alfonz yesterday, he brushed me off with the fish theory."

Bisa looked like I'd stabbed her.

"To be honest, I don't know you, and I don't have a good track record with photographers. You see someone like me, who has a big personality and is always in front of the crowds, but that doesn't mean I don't want my privacy, too. And yes, I send mixed messages. I want privacy, yet I put you across the hall from me, but that doesn't mean I trust you more than Alfonz, who has worked with me for over a decade."

"I understand. And I gather you put me across from you to keep an eye on me, and not so that I could have an extra peek at you. But I spend a lot of time watching people as part of my job. Like yesterday, I could see that you and Dev already planned the proposal ahead of time. It was no surprise."

"Is that true?" Russell said.

She nodded.

"That was insightful. What else did you see?" she asked.

"That Anna was scared when she left Todo Amor. After she answered her phone, she looked across the party as if trying to find someone. I think she saw that person, because that's when she fled."

"You think one of my guests scared her?"

"I think she's suggesting one of them might have killed her," Russell said with frightened eyes.

"But that's ridiculous," Bisa said. "I know she riled up a lot of people, but who would murder her? Oh my God, I told her yesterday that people wanted her dead. Maybe I scared her off."

"I don't think you did," I said. "I saw how Anna looked at you before she made her toast yesterday. She admired you and would do anything, even make a fool of herself, for you. She loved you."

"Thank you," Bisa said, and took my hand. "Did you really see that?"

I nodded.

"Bisa," said Russell, "I understand how you want to control the narrative and pull the strings, but you need to call the police."

"Not yet, Russell," she said. "If Liv is right and Anna was killed, then I'll be able to get to the bottom of this better than anyone. Quietly and privately. No media, no headlines, and no way for a killer to know I'm looking for him."

"And how are you going to do that?" Russell said.

"I have a team right here I trust," she said.

Russell buried his head in his hands in pure frustration. Ironically, for a guy who claimed Bisa could never control him, he was at least still following Bisa's lead and not calling the police. I guessed Anna's death was an exception to his rule.

"I fear someone in this very fragile ecosystem that you have built might have gone too far," Russell said.

Bisa raised herself up and breathed deeply, as I'd seen her do before taking the stage last night. The world she'd worked so hard to create was crumbling around her on what should have been the apex of her career, but she didn't fall apart. The fight in her was taking over.

"Liv and Harry, I'm adding to the scope of your job. Regina will be paid for your additional services. You will be my eyes and ears. Russell, go to your gallery. You have work to do. Liv and Harry, please join me at rehearsal this morning, in addition to the concerts this afternoon. Please, will you two join me? At least until we have a better idea of what has happened to Anna?"

"You have work to do, too," I said to Harry. "I've got this. At least for now."

"I can ask someone else to help at work," he said. "At least for a day or two."

"But time is everything for you and I'm here already," I said. "I'll be fine. Between me and Bisa, we'll get the job done."

"Amen," Bisa said. Sad as she was, she smiled at me genuinely for the first time since we'd met.

Harry stood, still holding my hand. As we walked to the front door, we heard a new set of footsteps joining our dawn breakfast. Dev was walking down the stairs.

"Bisa," he said without a glance at the rest of us. He reached out his hand. "Come upstairs. I don't know what got into you last night. I have a feeling you were behind it, Russell, but Bisa is no longer yours."

Bisa stood and raised herself to her full height.

"I'm no one's possession, Dev," she said.

"You know what I mean, my love," Dev replied. "Come upstairs. You have a huge day ahead and we need to get you ready to leave for rehearsal in the next twenty minutes."

Dev reached his hand out to his fiancée. Reluctantly, she took it. As she passed Harry and me, she gave Anna's phone back to me without a word.

"I'll meet you at rehearsal," I said. Not that I was expecting Bisa to give me a lift, but I also needed some time to digest this morning's meeting. I was quickly discovering that I needed to counterbalance every celebrity-filled drama with some *me* time.

When the couple passed, Harry gently pulled me close to him.

"I feel like an idiot about last night," he said.

"Good. That's not a bad thing to admit, every now and then," I said, and kissed his stubbly chin. "But I need you to strip down and hand me that shirt. I can't go around town in this dress. In all the excitement last night, I forgot to pack a change of clothes and a toothbrush."

The striptease helped me forgive him. He gave me his shirt and put his jacket back on, over his bare chest. It was a great look. Russell met us at the door and the two guys headed out of Todo Amor as Harry called an Uber. I wondered what the conversation would sound like on that car ride.

The coffee arrived. I lifted the service for four and carried it upstairs, where I found a toothbrush and change of clothes waiting for me at my door. Inside my room, I unfolded the items to find a pair of black, Spandex leggings and a Diamond Blue Tour t-shirt. I wondered if I'd inherited a pair of Bisa's leggings. If so, Maria was going to literally die.

Photographer that I am, the first thing I did was fall into the comfy chair and open Anna's phone. My number one suspect was now my main ally and I had a new list to investigate in the murder of Anna. I quickly realized, however, that Anna's photos weren't going to get me anywhere. Her interest in photography extended as far as photos of shoes and food. That's it. There were no photos with friends, no screenshots. She also didn't seem to have any social media presence, which I thought was odd, given that she had shoes to brand and sell, but maybe that would come next. I hit the icon for her Notes app.

My breathing quickened as I saw the first page. I knew I had to meet Bisa, but I also decided she would forgive my tardiness given what I was seeing. Shawn's name headed page one, and below it was a number with a dollar sign: *$50,000.* I wondered if Shawn had given Anna money for her business as well as Bisa. If so, Bisa was right. The woman went through money fast and furiously. And Shawn would never see a return on his hefty investment.

I flipped to the next page of notes. This one listed *Ben/ Burt* up top. This time, the page listed smaller sums of *$15,000* in eight rows. The next page's headline was one word: *Debt.* The page was otherwise empty. I wondered if Anna erased the page after Bisa wrote her the check, or if Anna's grasp of numbers was so bad that she'd never bothered to fill it in.

I looked back at the page listing Ben's investments and wondered about the name *Burt* beside it. It was only about six a.m., but I took a risk and called Maria.

"Oh my God, oh my God, oh my God. How's it going?"

"It's pretty all-star," I said. "And pretty crazy."

"You sound like you're saying crazy, like *Shutter Island* crazy, not like I made out with Carl Withers crazy."

"That pretty much sums it up," I said.

"What's wrong?" Her voice shifted to concern.

"I need help," I said.

"Do you need me to come to Todo Amor? I can be there in twenty. *Shutter Island* didn't scare me at all."

"No," I said. "I need legal help."

"Are you in jail? Is that why you're calling at this hour?"

"No," I said, and laughed in spite of myself. "There's a guy here who I think is bad news, like *really* bad news, but I don't want to raise any red flags, at least until I'm sure."

"Oh," she said with a hint of disappointment that my call wasn't more dramatic. "OK."

"His name is Ben Goldfarb, but I think to some people, he might also go by Burt," I said. "Or maybe Burt is a different person, I don't know, but I'd love to know what you can dig up on Ben."

"Like a lawsuit?"

"Anything, I guess. Can't you run those things that tell you what his history has been, where he's lived, if he's had any lawsuits or car tickets and stuff?"

"Sure," she said. "What's up with him? Who is he?"

"He's Bisa's manager," I said.

"Liv," she said, exasperated. "What do you care about Bisa's manager? If you're trying to get me to feel sorry for you, it's not working. I am going to spend my morning reading a client's tax returns for the next five years."

"I never feel sorry for either of us," I said.

"Me neither," she said. "And, for you, I will get up early and check on this guy."

"Love you," I said.

"You too."

Coffee or not, I was still running on very little sleep. I jumped into a cold shower to wake myself up. When I got out, I walked back into the suite with a towel wrapped around me.

There was a man with slick-backed hair, combed in perfectly straight lines, seated in my chair. He was none other than the Cardinal, although he was smaller than I remembered. I could imagine how he might be able to sneak in and out of spaces easily. He sat on his heels as if ready to spring into action at any given moment, but his eyes were glued to mine and

I couldn't break away from them. I'd already made eye contact with him briefly last night, before he had disappeared, but our current staring match was on a whole other level.

"Hello," he said, the first to break the ice.

"Hello," I said to Harry's thief.

"We meet at last," the Cardinal said to me.

"We do?" I said, my heart pounding.

CHAPTER 10

Harry and his team at the Art Crime Unit believed their elusive thief was halfway around the world by now; yet somehow, he was here in my suite at Bisa's Todo Amor. If the media lingering outside only knew, the headlines that followed would be for the ages.

Questions lit every part of my brain, but I could not speak. The obvious one was, *why was he here?* The only answer: He saw some value in me, enough to track me down, which was eerie and mind-boggling in itself. I didn't like his choice of words—*at last*—either. As Harry's girlfriend, had the thief been spying on me? Did he plan to use me as leverage to get out of town? I had a big job and a murder to solve. There was no time for me to be kidnapped as well.

"You don't think I believe the Neue's little security team brought down the Cardinal," he said, referring to himself in both first and third person. "I've known about your secret Art Crime Unit, and how you've been on my trail for months. And I've known you all upped your game. You, madam, came so close in LA that I had to create an entire decoy in Japan. You've cost me a lot of money."

It hit me. When we'd made eye contact last night, I'd given a mighty whistle to alert Harry that I'd spotted the Cardinal. I was the only guest who'd had my eyes on him. Ergo, he thought I was Harry. Or, he thought I was the ACU agent who'd been tracking him down all these months. He mistakenly thought he'd made me.

Harry's entire career as an agent for the ACU depended on him being undercover, playing the role of himself: He was the wealthy heir of an old New York family. His parents died when he was fairly young. His aunt Bernie raised him. Harry and Aunt Bernie, who appeared to be no more than a Park Avenue matriarch with a penchant for parties, rolled through the world of old money and art collectors, with Harry posing as an appraiser for an insurance company. Harry's cover was even better than I imagined. In the Cardinal's eyes, my scrappy, whistle-blowing persona seemed like a much better fit for an undercover agent.

All to say, if Harry's identity was revealed, his days at the ACU would be over. I decided, therefore, that I would play the part the Cardinal had assigned to me. I could juggle three balls as well as two. I added secret agent to my résumé. From waking up with my boyfriend in a murdered woman's room to conversing with a world-renowned art thief, this is how things seemed to roll with me and Harry. As long as we had some nights to binge the latest shows, I could live with it.

I thought of the game of chess that formed the basis of Russell and Bisa's relationship and decided to try it out for myself. The best I could do was keep the Cardinal on his toes and guessing until I could alert the ACU about this new development in their manhunt.

"How'd you find me?" I said, raising my chin and tightening my eyes as part of my new persona. "I'd think you'd have much more interesting things to do than visit me after escaping last night. I don't even get a day off?"

The Cardinal laughed.

"From what I can see here, you never take a day off. You

have your aliases. I have mine," he said. "Although this one is brilliant. I should remember it for one of my next heists. Who would imagine the ACU's biggest agent was moonlighting as a photographer for Bisa's big visit to New York? As for finding you—I saw your picture online. Your one mistake was to let fans take your photos on a hop-on/hop-off bus last night. People post pictures of those sorts of things. Unfortunately for you, I, too, have Bisa Mania."

"I can get you an autograph if you want to wait here," I said.

The thief tilted his head, somewhat like a bird.

"She's already left through a side entrance from her office," he said. "No paparazzi there."

I felt bad that Bisa couldn't even leave through the front door of the mansion she'd built, but that was another story.

"I guess you dropped your guard, once you thought I was imprisoned," the Cardinal said, absently tapping my windowpane, "but seeing as I've escaped, I'd like to have a chat. We're both professionals at the end of the day."

He had me at a few disadvantages for a business meeting, but one was more pressing than the rest.

"Would you mind if I changed?" I said, still dripping wet. "This is a little awkward."

"Fair enough," he said. "But don't think you can call your troops here in time. I'll be long gone before anyone arrives. And I guarantee you can't catch me twice."

To prove his point, he sprang from the chair to the desk, halfway across the room, in a catlike leap. This guy was freaky.

"Gotcha," I said.

"Never."

"I see what you're doing," I said, channeling Russell's verbal jousting. "The pun on *gotcha*. Very clever. Give me a minute. Take a loop around the mansion if you want."

"Already did," he said. "The art is hideous. Shawn Jackson's room is the most interesting. Looks like he was hoping he'd have a guest with him, the way it's set up with peonies and two champagne glasses and a Tiffany box. Not a ring box, but a dazzler, nonetheless. And as for Freesia, the hair and makeup lady, I might be in love. Her aesthetics are quite pleasing. Do you know her room is next to Bisa's? The fiancé's room is two down from hers. I don't think that's a good sign for their future."

I knew he was trying to rub in how he'd been able to tour Todo Amor so easily, and right under my ACU nose, but his intel was a gold mine I decided to take advantage of.

"Did anyone have boxes and boxes of shoes?" I asked. "Someone here has some of Bisa's sister's new shoes and they're supposed to be fantastic. I wouldn't mind a pair."

"No shoes," he said, "but the security guard has some dubious taste in clothes. All black. Every single thing."

"Out of curiosity, does anyone have drugs in their room?"

"A stiff, by the book agent all the way. I hate to disappoint you, but I didn't notice," he said. "That's not my thing. And who can tell in this place if there's any snuff, right? The only room that looks like a drug user lives in it is the manager guy's. What a pigsty."

Bisa had said she feared Ben gave Anna drugs once before.

"Amuse yourself," I said. "I'll be back."

I locked the bathroom door and then dressed in the clothes that had been left for me. Bisa's leggings were very flattering, and I threw Harry's shirt on over my concert T-shirt, tying the bottom for a little style. After a quick hairbrush and ponytail, I decided the Cardinal could wait a few more moments and applied my red lips. I stared at my reflection and considered what the Cardinal had shared. Shawn Jackson had some sort of romance going on, but no one had mentioned it. He was keeping it a secret. I remembered Kayla's blush when I met him.

When I opened the bathroom door, carefully, I was happy to see the thief had climbed off my table and to its chair. I joined him and clasped my hands in the same way Bisa had when facing Russell yesterday. I realized it was not only a no-nonsense gesture, but it kept my hands from shaking.

"We'll keep this quick," he said.

So far, he was speaking my language. I had a photo shoot to get to.

"I'm aware your disguise is significant to your career," he said. "Without it, who are you? What would your future be? At best, you'll be a paper pusher for the ACU, but we both know you're cut out for more than that. The shrewd expertise you demonstrated last year in Ireland with the capture of my colleague, Frank Jones, was superb."

I tried to look appreciative of his compliment on my past work, but I had no idea who Frank Jones was or when Harry had a job in Ireland.

"What are you driving at?" I said, hoping to look as shrewd as the Cardinal expected me to be.

"A deal. I'll keep your identity a secret," he said. "And you leave me alone. I'll even retire if that eases your conscience. I'm a wealthy man, as you can imagine. I'll buy a villa somewhere in Europe, preferably by the sea."

"I don't think so," I said. Who did he think he was kidding? Did he actually believe that Harry would fall for that? "Your last heist was a flop. You were arrested and the painting was saved. There's no way someone with as big an ego as yours would be willing to end on such a low note."

"But I escaped," he said. I caught the wounded pride in his voice.

"Not good enough," I said. "You get off on the heist. To some degree, we all do."

The Cardinal sat back and studied me. I swallowed, hoping I hadn't gone too far with my last line. What would he do to me if he realized he'd made a mistake about who I was?

"You're lucky," I said, committing to the part. "Your arrest would have been all over the front page if it wasn't for Bisa Mania. Trust me. I can make or break what the world thinks of you."

The Cardinal shifted his jaw as if he was cleaning out a piece of stray food that had been caught. I knew I was the stray food in this metaphor, but I held his gaze.

"Bottom line," he said, "we have a deal or I reveal your identity."

I had to give this guy credit. He was a genius. He also, even for a brief moment, needed Harry's help. I knew enough not to let the opportunity go to waste. The best I could do for now was buy time, and maybe develop a friendly rapport. And as long as I was multitasking, maybe I could mine the brain of a criminal while I was at it.

"Coffee?" I said.

"Black," he replied.

I poured.

"Putting our deal aside," I said, placing the cup in front of him and returning to my seat. Now that I knew Bisa had not killed her sister in a fit of passion, I wondered more about the man with the star tattoo on his head. "I have a question you might be able to answer for me. Say, for example, someone was thrown off a bridge. Would you say the murder is premeditated if someone was below to scoop up the body before it sank?"

The Cardinal tilted his head in his quirky way.

"Why would someone want to retrieve the body after throwing it into the water?" he said "If the body sank, no one would find it. The perfect crime."

He had a great point, but Anna had landed on the concrete landing. Even still, wouldn't it have been easier to shove her body into the water? I concluded the man must have been a good Samaritan but it still didn't make sense that no one had reported the body, at least according to Bernie.

"Premeditated or not," I said, playing devil's advocate with myself. "Who would you use to clean up the mess?"

"Obviously, a mob connection would be the most thorough," he said. "Because a death like that is usually mob-related. A regular joe doesn't throw someone over a bridge. If this is your way of threatening me, you need to do a much better job."

"OK, truce," I said, realizing I'd inadvertently threatened the Cardinal.

The Cardinal removed a red scarf from his pocket and wiped down his cup.

"I see I can't fool you," I said. "And . . . you're right. My heart is in the chase. I'm not a desk guy. But you're asking me to throw away my principles."

"You could say it's for the greater good," he said. "You'll be free to capture the copycats who will come after me."

"This is a significant proposal you've made. You're going to have to give me a little time to decide," I said, standing firmly and extending my hand, which he declined to shake. "How can I contact you?"

"I'll contact you," he said. "To keep the playing field fair."

Out of nowhere, the Cardinal threw something over my head. Instinctively, I looked and saw it was his signature red scarf. When I turned back, he was gone. The window was locked. I hadn't heard the door open or close. I even looked under the bed, but he was gone.

I flew as fast as the Cardinal to the chair where I'd left my phone and called Harry, but there was no answer. The story was too unreal for a text, so I drank another cup of coffee and this time called an Uber. Regina could reimburse me. I needed to get to Bisa's rehearsal pronto, and then meet Regina before the afternoon's concerts. Things had changed since yesterday. Bisa was no longer my suspect, but I was still wrapped up in

Anna's murder and disappearance. This was above my pay grade and I welcomed whatever help Regina could offer.

The Cardinal had said one thing that I found very interesting. Why would anyone want to throw someone off a bridge, where the body would immediately sink and all evidence would disappear, and then retrieve the body? This seemed to be a critical question to understanding Anna's murder.

I was about to try Harry again when my phone buzzed and Maria's name appeared on my screen.

"Liv?" Maria said.

"Did you find something about Ben already?"

"Oh, yeah," she said. "I have answers for you about this guy. He's sooooo creepy."

I braced myself for Maria's update.

"Turns out," she said, "that your Ben Goldfarb was Burt Goldman until about twelve years ago. The Ben you know is a successful talent manager with a solid track record and a successful career. Burt Goldman, however, was a con man. He worked as an agent booking acts for cruise ships and skimmed hundreds of thousands of royalties off the top. He was sentenced to five years in prison, but only served three, got out early for good behavior. When he was released, he changed his name to Ben Goldfarb."

"That's insane," I said.

"I know. I'm dying to know what tipped you off about him."

"I'll tell you the whole story when I see you."

"There's more?"

"It's a doozy," I said. "I've got to go, though. Bye and love you—and thank you!"

I was thankful I had a photo shoot ahead of me, even if I was on no sleep, with enough caffeine in me to feel like I was having a heart attack. With it, I saw the world in a way that always answered questions. Without it, I was lost.

* * *

The address I had was on Broadway, a few blocks up from Union Square. I love the Union Square food markets, plus the best Barnes & Noble in New York City is nearby, so I had a general idea of where I was going. The buildings always looked to me as if they were once factories, but many of them had architectural flourishes that seemed too glamorous for such use.

The entrance to the building was small and unassuming, and nothing like the red-carpet greeting at Todo Amor. Somehow, a couple of paparazzi had discovered the location of the early rehearsal and were lingering outside, hoping for a shot. They drank coffee and looked at their phones, lifting their heads briefly when I approached, and then returning to their business. Inside, the lobby consisted of an old linoleum tiled floor and a lone security guard on a stool behind a modest podium. Alfonz stood by the door as extra security. Neither of the men looked at the other.

"Hey," I said to Alfonz.

He nodded.

"She's OK," he said to the building's guard. "She's going to five."

I rode the elevator to five and found studio 2. It was a little after seven in the morning, but even before I reached the studio, I heard voices and chords of live music on a piano and a couple of bangs on a drum. I opened the door to a full cast of characters for the afternoon's shows. About ten dancers in casual dance attire were stretching and leaping and twirling. A pianist, drummer, and guitarist chatted in the corner of the room. A full craft table was set up with breakfast food and drinks. Bisa stood to the side, in conversation with a man I soon learned was the choreographer.

I was amazed at how professional Bisa was after the conversation we'd had this morning. The vulnerable, sad woman I'd spoken to was replaced by someone with energy and focus. She seemed able to put her heartbreak on hold. Watching the dancers and musicians, I understood that Bisa's commitment to a successful launch of her film and its music extended not only to those pulling the purse strings, but also to an entire company of performers. She was the CEO of a huge enterprise and a true leader. If only Anna had been able to execute her vision in fashion, these two would have been a formidable team.

My camera raised, I started shooting—partly because it was my job, but also because the space was marvelous. After walking these streets dozens of times, I realized there was a world above I never appreciated. The studio was an enormous loft-like space, with a ceiling that must have been twenty feet high, with lots of windows that were almost the height of the room. The shades were pulled down for privacy, but sunlight still beamed into the room from the cracks between the shades and the window frames.

Bisa watched her dancers, made comments on their moves, and reviewed her sheet music with the pianist while also belting out octaves to warm up. Her voice was so beautiful, people applauded. After a few minutes, the man with the clipboard approached Bisa. They both conferred for a moment and then nodded to each other. Bisa walked over to where her stuff was piled on a couple of folding chairs and took a drink from a water bottle.

"OK, people," the choreographer said, clapping his hands loudly to get people's attention. "Let's take it from the top."

The dancers also put their warm-up gear on chairs, took their own sips of water, and then returned to the middle of the floor in a formation they clearly knew by heart. The choreographer looked to the musicians and gave them a beat with a wave of his hands. Bisa was by the piano and made a few comments, then took the floor as well and stood center stage.

"OK," he said. "Everyone? A five, six, seven, eight."

At eight, the musicians began to play, Bisa began to sing, and the dancers did their thing. I felt like I was at a Broadway show or a private concert. I couldn't stop photographing the gorgeous moves of the dancers. Bisa's focus and the obvious joy she was feeling as she perfected the performance she would soon give were profound. I now understood entirely what Russell had meant on the bus last night. Bisa was an artist to the core. The merchandising, the pandering to industry people, and whatever else she did so well were icing on the cake. I felt as if I was seeing the real Bisa for the first time.

The opening number was a medley of Bisa's songs. I assumed this opening and a similar closing would be part of every show, with one of the three new songs dropped at each location. Billed as pop-ups, the concerts were each only going to be about forty minutes long, but I could see already how exciting they would be. At intervals, the choreographer would shout a special-effects cue—"Smoke machine begins now"— so that the entourage kept pace with other theatrical elements that would be happening onstage.

In about the middle of the performance of a second number, the door opened with a loud pull and bang, but Bisa and the dancers didn't break from their focus. I, however, did. I looked over to see who would be so rude as to walk in before the number was finished. It seemed fitting that Ben Goldfarb was the culprit. He talked on his phone for at least five steps before hanging up. This morning, he'd traded his leather jacket for jean shorts, a T-shirt that said BEACH MODE across the front, and a Diamond Blue Tour baseball cap.

I was surprised to see Dev behind him. I would have thought he'd understand Bisa's rehearsal space was like a sanctuary. He wore shorts as well, although everything about his outfit was tailored, from the crease in his shorts to the button-down linen shirt he wore. As Bisa had said to Russell, he was quite a grown-up.

The dance troupe was spinning and leaping and at times lifting Bisa above them like the goddess she was. It was hard not to watch, unless, it seemed, you were Dev and Ben. The two men huddled in whispered conversation. I wanted to punch them both.

CHAPTER 11

"Let's break," the choreographer said.

The strict order of the room immediately relaxed. The dancers went back to their chairs and drank water, put leg warmers back on, even though it was a hot July day. One dancer lay on the ground. Another rubbed his calf. Two others sat across from each other, their feet touching, and pulled each other by the hands in a circular motion. Bisa touched her toes and stretched as well. No one dared to bother the troupe. Although they were on break, they were still at work.

I took a few more photos and meandered toward Ben and Dev. I finally planted myself a few feet in front of them in hopes of catching some of their conversation, but they continued to speak in hushed voices. They'd found folding chairs in the corner of the room, so it was tricky to step too far back without them realizing I was eavesdropping. Accepting I'd made no headway with this strategy, I decided to face them head-on.

"Good morning," I said to Ben. "I didn't get your photo with Dev and Bisa last night. Maybe we could do it this morning?"

"I'm busy right now," he said to me with barely a glance in my direction.

"What's up?" Bisa said, coming to my rescue as she patted her face with a towel and radiated energy.

Both men stood. Dev took a step to be closer to her, but did not kiss or touch her.

"How's it going?" Ben said, getting right to business. "Did you work out the kicks and jumps or whatever for the smoke machine bit?"

"We're good," she said. "It's going to be a great show."

"The JumboTron at Liberty Island is now working and the lighting challenge in the Bronx is fixed," he said. "You can Zoom with them to make sure it's perfect, but people are already gathering there. We have extra security."

"I've invited Liv to join us. Make sure we have room for her with travel. Liv, be back at Todo Amor at noon."

They went back and forth a bit about the business of the shows and I'll admit I felt a little silly standing there. I finally took a step or two back, but Bisa shifted her body so that the circle widened and I was still in it.

"Dev," she said, "can I speak to you privately, honey bun?"

"Sure," he said, his hand on her butt as they walked toward the other side of the room. Bisa glanced at me over her shoulder once and then kept going. Ben was now stuck in his little corner with me. I was glad. I had a whole lot of questions for this guy.

"When we get to the venues, Alfonz will show you where you can and cannot stand," Ben said by way of small talk. "I'm glad you're coming. As you know, I've been watching you."

He winked.

I pressed my lips together to keep my composure. *I've been watching you.* The note wasn't for Anna. It was for me. And it wasn't a threat. It was a come-on. I was originally supposed to be in room 8. Ben must not have known Anna was given my room instead. Ben smiled and seemed pretty cocky about the whole thing. I guess as Bisa's manager he had some street cred. Women might see him as a way to get to her.

"Ah, yes. Thank you. By the way, I hear you've been investing in Anna's business. Giving her monthly checks," I said by way of a comeback.

Ben's smile vanished.

"Does she have you giving them to her, too?" he said. "She works fast. What did you do?"

"I see, Mr. Goldman," I said flatly, things becoming clearer, "you're being blackmailed."

"You know?" he said. It seemed as if months of anger were now being vented at me. His tone made my body tense. "I've done everything for Bisa. I've cleaned up messes she doesn't even know happened. I've fended off leeches in this business that would eat her alive if they could. I find the deals. I make the deals. I take care of Bisa. And it's my privilege to do so. Trust me, I know that. I did one thing wrong. I didn't tell Bisa the truth about my past. Bisa isn't the kind of person you can go back on. She can't stand any kind of deceit."

"Which made you decide not to tell her about your alias, and now you can't come clean," I said.

He sighed. He seemed relieved in some way to have gotten things off his chest, but his anger still festered.

"I've been hoping Anna would use the money to work on her fashion business. I'll get royalties when those shoes sell. At least I'd get some of the money I've given her back," he said. "She's a horrible woman, but she's very talented. She just can't pull the trigger. Plus, she resists all help. She wants to show Bisa that she can be her own star. Idiot."

"Not so much of an idiot," I said pointedly. "She got you to 'invest.'"

"I don't know why she told you, but since she did, the deal is off," he said. "I'm not paying her another dime, and I won't pay you either, if that's what you're after. I'll tell Bisa myself. And if she decides to fire me, good luck to her. People who pretend to be her friends will use her for every cent they can get before she even knows what hits her. But for the love of God, let's get through the next two days first, OK?"

He didn't give me a chance to answer. Instead, he stormed across the room to the craft table and piled three donuts onto a napkin. Given the diet restrictions of everyone else in the room, I was glad to see that someone was eating them.

I'd actually learned a lot from Ben. I now understood the confusing messages. Only the text, **Time's up**, was meant for Anna. The note was meant for me. And Ben was not an investor in Anna's business. She was blackmailing him for ten thousand dollars a month since she somehow found out about Ben's past. I had a feeling she knew how much Ben protected Bisa, however. Knowing her fierce loyalty to her sister, Anna probably would have used the information to have Ben fired if she didn't think he served a genuine purpose for her sister on some level. Unfortunately, I forgot to ask one important question: Where was he when Anna was killed?

The band started warming up again and I noticed the choreographer approach Bisa. When they finished, she grabbed a last sip of water and walked over to me.

"Did you find anything good?" she said.

I nodded.

"Excellent," she said. "I knew this was the way to handle this. See you at the concerts later."

I nodded as she lined up to run her dance again. It was hard to leave such an exciting bit of magic, but I had to get over to Regina's.

It was only a quick subway ride on the express train before I was in the elevator heading up to Regina's studio in Midtown.

I tried again to call Harry before getting on the train. Harry texted me back to see if I was OK. I told him to come see me at home in an hour.

Regina Montague Studios was nestled right in the middle of the high-end world she catered to, but once I stepped off the elevator, the atmosphere changed substantially. The hallways were covered with gorgeous ten-foot images of some of the most famous events she'd covered, from presidents to socialites to rock stars. At the end of the hall, I could see Manjeet at his desk, juggling calls, letting them ring thrice, and carrying on conversations with anyone in the office who passed his desk. I arrived to find him dressed in a light linen shirt in an ecru shade topped with a pale green bowtie.

Manjeet cared for Regina the way Kayla did for Bisa. He didn't go as far as feeding her soda all day, and he'd campaigned to get her to stop smoking, even before she fell off the bike and learned the hard way. But he also was her best man at her wedding to her wife, Donna; and when Regina's business almost fell apart, he showed up to run the switchboards, dry her tears, and cover for her when things got tough.

"Your Highness," he said to me when I reached his desk.

"I have arrived," I said, kissing him on each cheek as was his custom. "Is Regina ready for me?"

He opened the door to Regina's office, where she sat behind her desk, pointy heels resting on her desk and a cigarette in her mouth. She was looking at a stack of photos with a magnifying glass, likely making sure the prints were perfection for a client. When she saw me, she motioned to a chair.

"I've been so jealous for over twenty-four hours, you little wench," she said good-naturedly. "What's the scoop?"

Manjeet pulled up another chair so we were both across from her. Whereas Kayla would have emptied Bisa's overflowing ashtray, Manjeet would have none of it. He adored his boss and the company he worked for, but he also *called a spade a spade.* If Regina wanted to live around ashes, it was her problem.

"First, the bad news," I said. "The reason Bisa hired only one person is that she's pretty broke."

Regina let out a horsey laugh, followed by a cough.

"No joke. She told me herself," I said. "She's poured everything into the next couple of days and the Diamond Blue Tour. Our paycheck is going to be all about the royalties. Bottom line, those engagement photos were a big break for us."

"Good girl," she said.

"But there's more," I said. "Not good. That's an understatement."

"Oh, good God, what else? I love Bisa, but I hate working with divas. They always diva things up and there's no end to the drama."

I jumped into what I'd seen on the bridge and how Bisa asked me to be her eyes and ears. When I finished, I looked at both Manjeet and Regina, who were speechless. A first for both of them. Finally, Regina stubbed out her cigarette. She didn't pick up another.

"Bullocks," she said. "Our paycheck relies on you getting photos the media will want to buy. Meanwhile, Anna's been killed and Bisa has you running around to investigate? You'll be lucky if you get anything else worthwhile with all this other nonsense. Thank God for the engagement photos or I'd have to say good-bye to buying that new Jacuzzi in the Hamptons."

"I'll get the photos. Don't worry. The big question is, why did someone throw Anna off a bridge, but then wanted to hide her body rather than let her drown?"

"That's a real Sherlock Holmes of a twist, isn't it?" Regina said.

"There's Ben, the former con man who is now her manager; there's Shawn Jackson, the longtime family friend, who represents her music at the reord label; and there's Dev, her fiancé, who would probably love to get rid of his crazy, future sister-in-law, especially with Bisa heading on her tour. He's keen on starting a branded jewelry line for Bisa. It might be his way of segueing from watches to a broader product line. But he'd be coming up against Anna's fashion endeavors and there's only so much room for merchandise before the market is saturated. According to Bisa."

"Who else is in the sanctum sanctorum?" Manjeet said.

"There's her assistant, Kayla. She didn't like Anna, but she adores Bisa, so I can't imagine she'd kill her sister. That's a risky show of loyalty," I said. "But there's also Alfonz, the security guard. He brushed me off quickly at the bridge. I haven't met Bisa's stylist, Freesia, but she didn't seem to have any connection to Anna. And, for the time being, there's Felix."

"Felix is too much of a lamb to kill anyone. Let's look at the photos," Regina said. "Manjeet, bring me the stack you already printed. Let's figure this out so you're safe."

Manjeet pushed an envelope already on her desk toward her. We lay the pictures across the table. They did not account for everything I'd taken, but there were enough that, laid out as they were, I could start to piece together the big picture. Regina and Manjeet stood back and let me study them. After a couple of minutes, I tossed some photos aside I deemed unhelpful, including the proposal. I was more interested in wide-lens shots where I could explore my suspects' interactions.

"Maybe you're right about Felix," said Regina. She pointed to a photo where Felix was looking up at Bisa like a puppy dog while Dev was proposing.

"Poor Felix," said Manjeet with hand to heart.

"I don't know how a crush makes him a suspect," I said. "Why kill the sister of the woman you hold a torch for?"

"Revenge that she didn't love him back?" Regina said, but she looked doubtful even as she said it.

I added the photo in the discard pile. After dismissing other shots, I picked up a photograph I'd taken after the proposal, when Russell and I were following Bisa to her office. The picture was print-worthy in that it captured the excitement of the engagement, but it was also perfect in that it showed most of the party as if in one tableau. I hadn't noticed it then, but Kayla was at the side of the frame, following with her arm raised and a Diet Coke in her hand, straw and all. I shook my head at the unerring loyalty she had for her boss.

"Oh my God," I said, freezing.

"What?" Regina and Manjeet said in unison.

I pointed to the other side of the photo, to the back of a man who was bald with a star tattooed atop his head.

"That man," I said. "He was on the boat that picked up Anna's body."

"That's it," Regina said, also shaken. "We're calling the police."

She picked up the receiver to the office phone. I pressed the button to hang up.

"We have no proof of a body, no picture of the boat with her on it, and nothing in this pile is giving us those answers. But we're making progress. Give me a little more time. Let me ask Bisa if she knows this man."

"You'd better be on your toes at these concerts," Manjeet said.

CHAPTER 12

I hoped to see Harry when I arrived home, but he hadn't arrived yet. I saw from half a block away that my grandparents' stoop was empty. Before passing their stairs to get to my studio, I popped in to check in on them in their store. They weren't believers in AC, so the window was open and an oversized fan oscillated across the hot, sticky store. Granny was fanning herself behind the counter, but the two seemed at peace with the heat.

"Livia," Poppy said, lowering his *New York Post*, "how's your big job?"

I was so happy to hear him ask the question. His memory was fading fast, but a new drug he was taking was helping significantly. Little things like remembering I had a big job were a huge step forward, even if he didn't remember the details of what the job might be.

"Did you get me my personal photo of Mateo?" Granny said.

Poppy clicked his tongue and shook his head.

"I don't get what she sees in him," he said to me. "Especially when she has a looker like me at home."

Granny laughed and rubbed his shoulders.

"I didn't say he was an upgrade, Antonito," she told him.

"Rosa, no one could ever be an upgrade to you," he said, sweetly.

"I see you two are having a good day," I said. "Need anything?"

"No, but I have *pizzelles*," Granny said, lifting a tin from behind the counter and offering me her homemade Italian cookies. What the store lacked in cool air, Granny made up for in baked goods.

"Here he is," I said through a mouthful of cookies while finding my photo of Mateo for her.

She eagerly leaned against the counter to see, while Poppy went back to his paper.

"I can't believe it," she said, putting her hand to her mouth. "You were with him?"

"What do you mean, I was with him? How do you think I got the photo?"

"I can't believe you were with all of these famous people." She took my phone from me. "Look, Antony. Liv was with celebrities. Is that Mick Jagger in the background?"

I was smiling so hard that my cheeks began to hurt. Perhaps I'd acquired my interest in the backgrounds of photos from her. She always had a creative way of looking at things. When I was little, she taught me how to read by browsing through toy catalogs with me, pointing out pictures and the names of the products below. She joked how I could spell *Barbie* before I could spell my own name.

"I'll send the photo to your phone," I said.

"How?"

Poppy lowered his paper.

"She can never find things when you send them to her," he said. As poor as his memory was, he was more tech-savvy than Granny. "She says the AirDrop doesn't work."

We went back and forth for a few moments on how to send the photo, until I did the whole thing myself and saved it in her photos. Heads together, we looked at Mateo one more time before I had to get downstairs. Granny was delighted, but I took her phone from her.

"Hang on," I said.

"Did you erase it?" she said.

"No," I said.

I zoomed in on the photo where Granny claimed to have seen Mick Jagger. It was not Mick Jagger, but next to his doppelganger was a man who interested me. Again, I only saw the back of him, but it was the man with the tattooed head. He'd come back to Todo Amor for the Diamond Corazón after absconding with Anna.

The photo reminded me how much work I needed to do. I refilled a pitcher of water for them from the kitchen and hopped downstairs. At my gate, I stopped. Something was very wrong. I'd left my red privacy curtain pulled across my studio window, but one of the photos was askew. It hadn't been that way when I'd left.

I reached into my bag and grabbed the pepper spray Maria had given me for Christmas. It wasn't the coziest Christmas gift, but she pointed out that the longer I stayed in New York, the more trouble I seemed to stumble upon. I hadn't reached for it once, but occasionally Maria made a surprise inspection to see if I had it. And once or twice, on a very late return home, she grabbed her own and reminded me how lucky we both were to have them. I loyally carry it with me. I was glad to have it now as I pulled it out and slowly turned the key to my studio door.

It was one thing to have walked into Anna's room to find it trashed; it was a whole other thing to find my own place, my sanctuary, trashed as well. Tears sprang to my eyes. My kitchen shelves were open and my small file cabinet behind my desk, containing client files and prints, was overturned. The cushion on my guest chair was ripped.

"Who's here?" I said raising my can of spray for protection.

My breath became shallow. I listened hard for any sounds coming from my bedroom or bathroom. I don't know how long I stood at my entrance, but finally, my body began to unclench a little, while my arm remained raised with my weapon.

"What the—" a voice said behind me.

I screamed and turned, my finger hitting the top of my pepper spray. All at once, a hand grabbed mine and pulled it away from my body. Another hand wrapped around my waist and pulled me close.

"Are you OK?" Harry said.

I put my finger over his lips and motioned for us to speak outside.

"I don't know if there are bugs in my studio," I said.

"Why would there be bugs?"

I told him about my meeting with the Cardinal. He began to pace the sidewalk as I spoke, interrupting me here and there with questions, mostly to confirm that his name never came up. When I finished, he sat on my grandparents' stoop. Then he stood up again.

"And he didn't say when or where he'd be back to speak to you again?"

I shook my head.

"This is unprecedented," he said. "I mean, he's the most flamboyant thief I've ever come up against. He loves to make a statement, but to go after an ACU agent to strike a deal? And, of course, to top off this craziness, he decided you were me. He's not the complete genius we thought he was."

"It was my whistle, at the Neue," I said to clarify the mix up. "It's very effective. And I looked that guy in the eye like his days were numbered. Maybe that's why he's so scared now. Sometimes I can give a very scary stare down. I think it might be genetic."

"I think I saw it this morning," he said.

Harry ruffled his fingers through his hair until it stood up straight again. Whereas I'd thought his messy locks were funny this morning, they perfectly summed up the situation now. Chaos.

"Time to see if my thief or your murderer made the mess," he said.

"That's a line I never thought I'd hear," I said.

"I don't think you need to worry about the Cardinal bugging your place," he said as we walked back inside. "To be honest, I doubt he would ransack your studio either, especially after he met with you in such an oddly civilized way. He's clever with sleight of hand and quick escape, but his interests have never been high-tech."

"He has an Insta," I said. The one tech-savvy thing in the thief's life had given me away, but I'd learned from him a few things about Bisa's inner circle and how they lived, so I wasn't complaining.

Harry checked my room and bathroom, confirming I was bug-free, and did his best to straighten up. I did an inventory of the studio and was at least relieved to see that my standing flashes and the camera I depend on, when not using Regina's Leica, hadn't been destroyed. After a few minutes, we sat on the edge of my bed. Harry put his arm around me.

"Someone trashed Anna's room, looking for something," Harry said. "Maybe they think you have it."

"Why?" I said. "I haven't been home since we went to the party last night and found out we had Anna's suite for ourselves. It's not like I could have found something in her room and stashed it here."

"The murderer made a mistake," he said. "They killed Anna and realized after her death that they didn't get something they wanted from her. Do you think someone was looking for the phone?"

"No one knows I have it, unless Dev overheard us this

morning. But if he was looking for Anna's phone, I don't know what for. The texts are garbage, the photos are shoes and food, and the phone calls are nearly nonexistent. The text he sent her was fairly benign too. He asked her to leave Bisa alone but he didn't threaten her in any way. What if there was someone else on or near the bridge who saw me?" I said. Exhaustion washed over me. "There were a couple of cars crossing. I wasn't looking to see if someone was watching me."

"Do you mean the killer thinks you have something of Anna's from the murder scene?"

I reached for my tote bag, which I'd dropped with a thud when I entered. From inside, I retrieved the bloodstained fabric and the fingernail. I lay them out on my desk and we studied them like scientists looking at Petri dishes.

"Maybe there are fingerprints on the jumpsuit," I said. "Or maybe these are real diamonds on the fingernail?"

As an expert in fine art, which often included jewelry, Harry only needed to glance at the sparkly gems to confirm they were not diamonds. He went over to my kitchen and opened a drawer. He came back with a box of Ziploc bags and put each piece of evidence inside one.

"Give me the phone, too," he said.

He got another baggie and I put Anna's phone in it.

"I'll have my office test for fingerprints," he said.

By *my office*, he meant his auntie's thirteen-room apartment, which served as her home and as cover for the Art Crime Unit's headquarters in America. One could say, in a way, she was living and working out of her home like I was. We shared that in common on a much different scale.

I yawned, my lack of sleep catching up to me. I wished I could lay my head on the pillow but it was ten o'clock and I had to be back at Todo Amor by noon rather than meet the crew on Liberty Island at one thirty when the concert began.

"At least you're not hungover," Harry said.

"That, my dear, is called consequences," I said, straightening his hair. "Now you know not to get in bed with a hysterical pop star who has a bottle of champagne."

"It was two bottles," he said. "Did you say that the Cardinal has an Instagram account?"

"That's how he said he found me," I said. "I was following Bisa Mania. Why?"

"Just thinking. I'm not sure yet."

I could see the wheels were in motion. I lay my head on his shoulder while we both digested the whirlwind of mysteries surrounding us.

"Harry," I said. "Do you think it's strange that my clothes are scattered, but unlike my kitchen, my dresser drawers are closed and one closet is closed?"

I opened the dresser. Nothing had been touched. The closet was the same. Whereas one had been ransacked, the other was intact.

"Whatever the intruder was looking for, they must have found it in my room and left before they needed to look in these other places."

Knees to the floor, I looked under my bed and then under the piles of clothes around me.

"Do you see anything?" Harry said.

"Of course." I lifted my head from under my bed. "The shoes Anna gave me. They're gone. That must have been what they were looking for."

"Are you sure?" he asked.

I nodded.

"But it makes no sense," I said. "They left the shoes in Anna's room. They were everywhere. Why would they take mine?"

Harry folded his arms and leaned against my doorjamb, equally puzzled.

"Were the shoes she gave you from a special box?"

"Not that I could see, but maybe they were somehow special. Maybe she was hiding something important about those shoes by giving them to me."

"Do they look any different from the ones you saw lying about her room?"

I shook my head. My alarm rang. It was time to get dressed and head back. I wished I had said I'd meet at Liberty Island to buy myself another hour or so, but there was no arguing with Bisa's plans.

"Are you coming with me to the concerts or laying a new trap for the Cardinal?" I said.

"Hopefully both," he said. Harry pulled me to him with a little nibble on my ear. "Our reunion has been a little different than I expected."

"I have a little time before I need to get going," I said.

I leaned in to give my crime partner a kiss. His lips reached mine for one glorious moment and then both of our phones rang. Mine, on the bed, lit up with Bisa's name. I sprang from my bed. I could hear Harry laugh quietly as he found his own phone. I went into my studio to give him privacy.

"Hi, Bisa," I said, my voice embarrassingly happy given our shared concern about murder.

"Did Kayla call you with travel details about the concerts?"

"No," I said. "But maybe Ben didn't tell her the instructions you gave him this morning?"

"I don't know who or what to believe anymore and it's killing me," she said. "These people are the closest I have to family outside of Anna. I just keep praying you're wrong and that she's alive and is going to come back through the door and bother me with something new."

"Don't worry," I said. "I have people, too. And I trust them to help. You need to focus on the concerts."

"We'll be travelling by helicopter," she said. "See you at Todo Amor in an hour."

The roof, as I should have guessed, worked double-duty as a

helipad. I understood Bisa's desire to build her mansion away from massive crowds she could not control. Not only could she leave by a side door, she had a roof, to boot.

"You have enough copters for everyone?" I said. "Including the dancers?"

"I have a different group of performers at every stop," she said.

"That's a lot of rehearsals," I said.

"What do you think I've been doing all morning?"

How did she do it?

"As you know, Liberty Island will be first. With security checks before the audience heads over, the island should be very safe."

Bisa sounded like she was reassuring herself as much as me with her last comment.

I only had an hour to get ready. I opened my closet door and pulled out my combat boots.

CHAPTER 13

I'd never been on a helicopter before and very rarely fly at all. We drive everywhere. We drove from New Jersey to Disney World when I was little. When I returned to Todo Amor, without Harry, who needed to download with Bernie, I quickly realized that getting Bisa to Liberty Island was like a military operation. Two choppers waited for us on the roof. Everyone wore their all-access passes like soldiers wear their stripes. Kayla was already there when I arrived, speaking with the pilot. Bisa, her stylist, and a man, whom I did not recognize but seemed important, joined them. Bisa's stylist, Freesia, stood behind yellow tape at the roof's entrance. I was eager to talk to her. She didn't seem to have a personal connection to Anna, but she was the only member of Bisa's handpicked family I hadn't met.

Kayla walked up to me.

"You'll be flying in *Chopper One* with Bisa. Sit in the co-pilot seat" was all she said before she walked behind the yellow tape as well. She did not look happy and I wondered if I'd taken her coveted spot, flying with her boss.

Bisa and the man I hadn't yet met were already boarding with Alfonz, so I followed a woman in a bright yellow vest to join them. I was glad the blades weren't spinning before we boarded. In every movie I've seen with a helicopter, the blades are whirling in a head-chopping fashion. The interior of the cabin was small. I stepped up to my seat, and noticed the man had attached an IV to Bisa in the back seat.

"Vitamin and energy drip," he said in answer to my curious expression.

Bisa was in another world, her eyes closed as the liquid dripped into her body. There was a headset on my seat, but she already had hers on. Her breath was measured. It was as if she was putting herself into a trance. Once we all had our headsets on, the pilot gave us perfunctory instructions on seat belts and safety measures. I realized about halfway through his speech that the instructions were primarily meant for me. Bisa and her vitamin man flew like this often, but I couldn't contain my first-timer excitement.

My enthusiasm momentarily vanished when we took off, straight up. The turbulence was terrible and I assumed we were going to need to abort flight, but we didn't. The chopper gained altitude as we rocked up and down, back and forth. I closed my eyes until we finally evened out. When I opened them, I was floored by the view. All of Manhattan was before me. I felt as if I could reach out and touch the buildings. I photographed everything and still couldn't get enough. The chopper headed south, past the tip of Manhattan, where the Freedom Tower stood. Even from my height, I was sobered by how many names I knew filled the memorial where each of the Twin Towers once stood.

The helicopter swerved to head out over the water to Liberty Island, where the Statue of Liberty stood. Straight below, at the tip of Manhattan, I saw hundreds of people lining up to take one of two ferries that would bring people to Bisa's concert. I realized how easy it would be for someone like Bisa, or any superstar, to forget the simple everyday things, like waiting in line, or scalping tickets. We were literally above everyone, and Bisa, seated right behind me, was pulling all of the strings. I decided she needed someone like Russell, who reminded her what it was like to be human, to make mistakes, and to forgive others for not meeting her standards.

The helicopter hovered for one moment above the crowd. I could not hear their cheers, but I could see the upturned faces, the bodies jumping with excitement, and arms raised as if she was, in fact, a goddess. Bisa waved, even though it would be impossible for anyone to see her. She loved her fans. Any fatigue or worries took second place to the bond she had with the people below.

We continued out to Liberty Island, where a stage was erected at the tip of the star-shaped base of the statue. I'd never realized Lady Liberty's base was a multi-pointed star and that beautiful parks surrounded her on the small islet. The park grounds on each side of the statue would serve as the arena, and there were, of course, multiple booths that would sell food, drink, and Bisa merchandise lining a concourse behind the statue. The concert might only last forty minutes, but Bisa knew her guests would come early and leave late.

The helicopter landed at the farthest end of the island. The turbulence was light and I'd gotten my sea legs. When we disembarked, security surrounded us and took us down the concourse to a staging area. Bisa walked with a combination of swagger and military precision. She had a show to do, people to inspire, and T-shirts to sell.

Behind us, I heard the helicopter take off again to make space for the next one to land with Kayla, Ben, Dev, and Freesia. When we reached the performance area, we were greeted by dozens of stagehands. The equipment was locked and loaded. The light and soundboard area was set up and the technician was running through his cues. The once-broken JumboTron Ben had mentioned at this morning's rehearsal was running the trailer for *All About Love*. Bisa's band members were riffing on their guitars and drumming a beat to get warmed up. Some invited members from the media were seated in a press area and Bisa waved to them.

"I've got to run a sound check and then I'm excited to talk with all of you," she said to the press with a friendly wave. When she turned away from them, she wrung her hands. Her fear of the media was strong.

I climbed the stairs behind Bisa and stood offstage while she did her sound check. A black curtain encircled the back and sides of the stage. Behind it were three makeshift structures that served as a lounge for the guests, Bisa's dressing room, and the performers' green room. The view upfront, however, was spectacular and I ventured as far as center stage. Standing behind Bisa, I photographed her as she faced the New York Harbor and the empty seats below, which would soon be filled with fans.

"This is a restricted area," a voice said from beside me.

I lowered my camera to a guy in black shorts, black knee socks, and a baggy dark gray T-shirt. He also had a camera and an all-access pass. I scanned the stage and realized that there were two other photographers and two other guys with video cameras, all of whom looked similar. Immediately, I realized they were the official concert photographers.

"You're not allowed to shoot onstage," he said in a friendly but firm voice.

"Gotcha," I said. My job was to keep an eye out for offstage happenings, not shoot the concert. This was Shawn's territory.

When I returned to the sidelines, Kayla was coming up the stairs with Ben. I knew I'd taken her seat on the helicopter ride over, and I didn't want to make enemies with her. If anything, I hoped she could shed more light on the group staying at Todo Amor. I went over to the craft table and picked up a chilled Diet Coke and a straw. I saw her visibly stiffen, but then relax as I walked toward her with my soda outstretched.

"I know you like to have these ready for Bisa," I said, and handed it to her.

"Thanks," she said. "It's her main vice. She works so hard on her body, her business, and her music. I like to think I can give her something to make the day go by with a little less stress."

"I've never seen anyone work harder," I said in agreement. "How does she have so much energy?"

"She rides on passion," Kayla said, looking at her boss with admiration.

"How do you keep up?" I said.

Kayla laughed and dropped her tight-shouldered, chin-up posture.

"I do what it takes," she said. "It's not always easy, but I try to ride on her fumes. She has a lot to share."

"I'd be on drugs," I said.

Kayla nodded, but didn't say anything. We both looked as Bisa walked to different parts of the stage for a light check.

"You must feel better now that Anna is gone," I said. "I don't know your little family, but she seemed to add stress. And I'm sorry about yesterday."

I took a photo of the river in hopes that my words sounded lighter than their meaning if I was doing something else while I said them.

"I notice you photograph almost everything," she said, and snapped open the Diet Coke. "You should have taken a photo of the boat. You could have proven to yourself that it wasn't her much sooner. If Bisa hadn't told me Anna was taking a nap, that would have been a huge scare."

"Thanks for being cool about it," I said, even though she wasn't. "Did you find it weird that Anna left? She seemed so excited to be there."

"Honestly," she said, "I wouldn't have known she left. Her room was a pigsty. Shawn told me."

Shawn. The guy who was waiting for someone to share his room with. Was he the person who opened Anna's door when I was hiding under the bed?

"There's a lot that goes on in this gang," Kayla said. "Allegiances shift. Agendas change. The only thing everyone shares is love for Bisa and the money machine."

"Including you?"

Kayla laughed.

"I wish," she said. "For those guys, the more Bisa makes, the more money they make, too. That goes for Anna and now Dev. He's convinced her to start a jewelry line he'll manage. He's going to make a fortune for Bisa, but he will profit, too."

I went back to photographing.

"With everything you have on your plate, it was kind of bitchy of her to come and go like that," I said. "And it's weird, Anna left her things behind, especially her shoes."

"That's Anna for you." She sighed. "But the party planners brought a professional cleaning crew to have on hand. That's how the house looked so good this morning. They're pros. They were in and out of Anna's room in no time. You lucked out."

I lowered my camera and looked at her with a smile. During our conversation, her shoulders had tensed again and her white bun seemed to have tightened. She looked pretty strung out and I felt bad for her.

"I hope Bisa gives you a couple of days off before the Diamond Blue Tour," I said.

It was a lot to expect others to share the same focus and passion for your own work. Russell accused Bisa of this flaw, but she either didn't have the time or space to agree with him.

"I meant to ask you," I said. "When I was looking at my photos last night, I noticed the coolest looking guy. He has a tattoo of a star on top of his head. Do you know him? My friend, Maria, and I have been thinking of getting matching tattoos. We've known each other since we were five."

In truth, Maria was avidly opposed to body art.

Kayla shook her head.

"I think I might have seen him, but I didn't know who he was," she said. "He had to have been on the guest list to get in, but he wasn't someone I know. He was probably a friend of someone's."

Kayla raised the Diet Coke and looked ready to tend to her mistress.

"Gotta go," she said. "And, Liv, don't worry. I'll add you to my speed dial of photographers for the future. It isn't often that Bisa bonds with anyone outside our group. When I see it happen, I take note."

"Thanks," I said. The compliment gave me a thrill. Briefly, I imagined my future where one of my idols trusted me. I was so glad Bisa wasn't the murderer.

Bisa waved and I did, too, but her greeting was aimed at someone behind me. Mortified by how my fantasy life and real life had clashed so awkwardly, I stepped to the side and hoped no one had noticed.

"Brenda!" Bisa said. "It's so good to see you. I'm sorry I've kidnapped your husband for the last couple of days. Oh my God, is that Vicky? You've gotten so big."

I turned to see who merited this special greeting in the midst of last-minute preparations. I wasn't surprised to see Ben. He wore pressed linen pants, a loose-fitting linen shirt, and dark sunglasses. His appearance screamed successful family man, but I remembered his flirtations. I felt sorry for Brenda and Vicky, who stood beside him with dopey grins.

"She wants your autograph," Ben said, pointing to Vicky.

"*Dad!*" Vicky said in exactly the same way I would have reacted.

"Let me take a group shot," I said.

Ben looked at me, and for a millisecond, a scowl crossed his face.

"You're just everywhere, aren't you?" he said.

Bisa stood among the family and put her arms around Brenda and Vicky. Ben stood to the side of his wife.

"Brenda, you look gorgeous," I said in solidarity. "OK, everyone, say *cheese*." The women, including Bisa, said *cheese*; Ben did not. He did not take directions well. I decided Ben did what Ben wanted. Period.

After a few photos, Ben led his family to front-row seats. An usher appeared with Diamond Blue Tour T-shirts, warm pretzels, and bottles of water. The women put their shirts on over their summer dresses. They were part of the support team, even if on the periphery. I was pleased to see Ben heading back to the stage area. I had more questions for him and it would have been hard to question family man Ben and get straight answers.

Before I could approach him, Freesia waved and joined me.

"I hate helicopters," she said.

"It was my first time," I said.

"I know Bisa asked you to join her, but I was hoping to get here before Dev," she said. "He has a way of taking over. I've never seen anything like it. He once convinced her to change her hairstyle right before she went onstage. We'd spent weeks perfecting it so she could dance and sing and even sweat in a way that would work with the stage and theme designs. And then, *poof*, he arrived three hours before the concert and everything changed."

"Was it good?" I said. "That could have really backfired."

Freesia puckered her lips and crossed her arms.

"I guess," she said. "Actually, it was cool. But I'm saying he's very directed at getting what he wants in Bisa's orbit. She always took my suggestions and it threw me. Just saying. I'm praying he doesn't interfere today. There are too many things going on in the next five hours to change hairstyles on a dime."

"Fingers crossed," I said.

Dev didn't like Anna's aspirations to start her shoe line. He didn't like that Bisa supported her. He wanted to raise Bisa's brand to diamond status, while Anna was reaching out to Bisa's core audience. He bought champagne, changed hairstyles. What else would he do to manage the life he wanted with Bisa?

Freesia started to tap a hairbrush onto her palm as she watched her client. She noted where the sun was shining, and the wind was blowing, and how it would affect Bisa's performance.

"People!" A man, in all black and wearing pants on this hot day, took center stage at the front and spoke through a mic so that everyone could hear through the speakers. "The first ferry is leaving the station. Performers, please head backstage. Tech, please finish your work as quickly as possible."

Immediately, the backup dancers I'd seen this morning, plus a juggler and a man on stilts, and someone pushing a rack of hats that looked like large diamonds, all left the stage. Bisa and Freesia beelined to her dressing room, already talking about a change in lip color. I joined the group in the green room, where I found Ben and Alfonz. Ben sat on a sofa. Alfonz stood between the guest lounge and a short hallway that ended with Bisa's dressing room. I chose a chair closest to Ben. He glanced at me and audibly huffed and then moved to another chair at a table. I counted to five to steel my nerves and then crossed the room and took a seat at the other side of the table.

"Hi," I said.

Ben laid his phone down and stared at me, right in the eyes. Everything about his thick, tense neck, the redness in his face, and the way his fingers gripped the table, as if he needed to hold on to something or he might take a swing at me, dared me to stay seated. I, in turn, placed my camera across from him and clasped my hands, Bisa-style. I knew that with Ben, the only way to get what I needed was to bully the bully.

"You have a wife," I said.

Ben sniffed. His cheek twitched as if my words were a minor annoyance, like a gnat.

"What do you want?" he said. "The note I gave you was harmless fun. That's how it works with us. When we're in the middle of concert time, the world extends only as far as the concert. And in this bubble, we occasionally live differently than we do in everyday life. You should understand that."

"I don't understand that, but I do get you hit on me, and if I were a different sort of person and had sucked up to you, I might be very upset right now."

"I paid Anna, I'll pay you," he said. "But this is all on you. If you make waves, you risk putting this entire operation into chaos. People will lose their jobs; you will lose yours. Is that what you want?"

"No," I said.

"How much? Give me the note and we'll call it even," he said. He even opened his wallet and pulled out a check. I wondered how often he bought off people if he had bank checks in his back pocket.

"Actually," I said, "I don't want a penny. I just want you to answer me one thing."

Ben put away his wallet and sat back in his chair. He no longer gripped the table and his heart attack shade of red subsided. He stretched his legs in front of him and smirked. His phone buzzed, facedown on the table. His hand tapped the table, but he didn't answer. He was too busy smirking at me.

"What do you want to know?" he said.

"Do you remember what happened after Dev proposed?"

He sighed and leaned forward, his elbows on the table.

"I don't have time for this," he said. He put his hand on the phone, but didn't lift it.

"Tell me," I said.

"Anna made that moronic speech. Bisa banished her to her room. Russell, and I think you, followed her into her office.

Dev stood on the stairs, looking like a dope, so I ran up the stairs to congratulate him. When others saw me, they came up to congratulate him as well."

"Was Shawn one of the people?"

Ben looked up at the ceiling. His jaw clenched and I worried his impatience would overtake him.

"Felix did, along with his date," he said. "That dummy, Cyril, from the movie studio basically tiptoed over with some other guy in a baseball cap, he's so intimidated by Bisa. There was a weird guy I didn't know, with a tattoo on his head. Freesia was there. She even went over to shake Dev's hand. I didn't see Shawn, actually. And there was a woman with a diamond underneath her eye. That's all I can remember."

"Why was the tattooed guy there?" I said, thrilled at the chance to find out about this mysterious man.

Ben smiled and lowered his eyelids.

"So, that's what this is about?" he said. "Some guy? I think you should have taken my check. I don't know who he was. Kayla might. I thought he was with the staff or tech team, so I was surprised when he went up to Dev."

"One more thing, and then I will sit as far from you as possible," I said, ignoring his snide remark.

Ben didn't look like he hated me anymore, but he did seem desperate to get rid of me. In this one short conversation, there was a good chance he'd make sure Kayla took me off her list of photographers, but I didn't care. Honestly, I hoped Ben was the murderer. Everything about him got under my skin.

"Where were you after Anna's meeting with Bisa at the party?"

"I was at the party," he said, and shook his head like I was dumb and it was time for me to go. The gnat had gotten too close to him.

"You weren't there," I said. "I have a photo of everyone in the room, but you left."

From beyond our little offstage world, I heard the piped-in music become louder. The audience exploded with cheers. Similar to last night, the music transitioned to the sound of cannons. As it did, Bisa's dressing-room door opened and she walked through the room and to the stage. Alfonz was beside her and Freesia followed. No one spoke to her. She was *Bisa the Superstar* right now and everyone could feel it. Except, maybe for Ben. I kept my gaze on him so he knew I wasn't distracted. I wanted his answer.

"Where were you?" I said again.

"Let's just say you're not the only one I was watching."

I smiled to put him at ease.

"I see things, too," I said.

"What the hell is that supposed to mean?" Ben raised his hands in an offhand dismissal of my comment.

I'd heard the woman with the bedazzled eye on the bridge say she'd assured herself a spot in the chorus for the Diamond Blue Tour. Only Ben had the credibility to make that promise. Of course, he never would have backed it up. Ben had given me a characteristically credible alibi, but it was one that I would need to check.

I stood up. He sniffed a laugh and picked up his phone.

The sound of the audience was growing louder and louder by the moment. I left for the stage.

Dev passed me without seeming to notice. I was surprised he wasn't watching his fiancée. Bisa was starting her first set. Her new song was next. The pulsating rhythm that began threw the audience into a near-frenzy as I neared the action.

"Psssssst." I heard a whisper, which was followed by a tap on my shoulder. Manjeet and Regina popped in front of me. They were both wearing their Diamond Blue Tour T-shirts and, to top it off, each had a blue cocktail in hand. We mouthed silent cheers of excitement as if our voices would be heard above the music and the crowd.

"What are you doing here?" I said, thrilled.

"I still had my all-access passes," Regina said. She wasn't allowed to smoke, but she had an unlit cigarette in her hand for comfort. "I'm putting the perks of my job to good use."

"We also decided to help and we may have come through," Manjeet said.

Our excitement about seeing each other eclipsed the thrill of Bisa's new song, which was hard because the music was fantastic.

"We did a little sleuthing for you. I should say, Manjeet did." Regina patted Manjeet on the back.

CHAPTER 14

Onstage, Bisa finished her song. The crowd started to chant for more. I knew Bisa wouldn't let them down. I'd seen her rehearsal this morning. They were in for a treat of a finale.

"The guy running the soundboard also worked at Bisa's parties yesterday," Manjeet said.

"How do you know?" I said.

"He's a smoker," Regina said. "He asked me for a cig. Manjeet did the rest."

"Let's just say, we hit it off," he said, looking very pleased with himself, and, I will say, dapper, in spite of the overabundance of merch draped all over him.

The shrieks and shouts and clapping continued until Bisa walked back onstage. Our conversation stopped immediately. It was impossible not to feel the energy. Boats in the harbor honked their horns and Bisa waved to her seafaring audience.

"What a gorgeous summer day. Are you having fun?" she said to her fans. They screamed yes in response. "Did you like the ferry?" More hollers, some laughter. "I love you. I love New York. And I love America."

She looked up at Lady Liberty.

"This country is my home," she said. "And I believe in giving back. You know I built a new music school for New York for hosting me this week. We need to work to make sure every child has the opportunity to find their talents and make them shine."

She raised her hands in the air to make her point and then began her last songs.

"I have to leave as soon as this song is over," I said. "Did you ask the tech guy about yesterday?"

"I love this song," Manjeet said. Regina had left us and, with hands also in the air, was dancing with abandon to the music.

"Focus, please," I said.

"OK," he said. "The guy went off to the side of the house, far enough away that no one would hassle him about smoking. He said from where he was standing, he saw Anna run out of the house and jump on a bike. She sped away very quickly, while two other people left the house, also at top speed. One was a guy with some kind of tattoo. I feel like he said it was on his head but that sounds weird. Anyway, that guy jumped into a boat moored in the opposite direction from where he was to the house. The techie, Levi's his name, thought it was cool that someone had arrived on their own boat. And then another person whipped down a path near him on a motorbike."

"Who?" I said, my heart racing as fast as the music. My photo had not lied. The blurry image on the bridge was the killer. I was so close.

"He didn't know. And he was distracted, because Bisa's manager and a gorgeous woman with a jewel on her eye popped out from a little cove on the side of the house where they keep the gardening stuff."

I'd been rooting for Ben to be the killer, but he was officially off my list. His story matched with the gardener's and gave him an alibi. It was a bit crushing.

"Then he saw another woman leave the house," Manjeet said. "She hopped down the path, and jumped on another bike to follow the others. That caught his eye because her hair blew up like a balloon after two seconds. Presumably, that was you?"

"It was," I said. "And thanks. Go, enjoy the end of the show."

"Be careful," he said.

Manjeet joined Regina. His dance moves were more angular, with side-to-side hip action, while Regina continued to swirl with her empty cocktail container raised to the skies. In minutes, our group would be reboarding the helicopter for Bisa's next concert. I saw Kayla already waiting by the stairs on my side of the stage, so I joined her. Our departure came quickly. In fact, when Bisa left the stage, Freesia was waiting with a towel and an atomizer, and the entourage left immediately, as the crowd still applauded. Bisa stripped off her Liberty Island red-white-and-blue costume to bike shorts and a crop top, while the tech team teased the audience with a light show before starting the end-of-show exit music. The extra time gave Bisa and our group a head start to the helicopter. Some fans, of course, were outside already. Alfonz and two other guards flanked us. I lowered my head and involuntarily tensed my body, shocked at how physical and overexcited the fans were. Bisa smiled at them, but her stride never slowed. She was ready for the next concert.

When we arrived at the helipad, the chopper's blades were already spinning and the engine roared. The blades churned against the hot air. Dev cut me off and joined Bisa and the medicine man, who had remained in the aircraft, waiting for her. They took off. Ben, Freesia, Kayla and I were left behind. I wasn't surprised that Ben looked unhappy to ride with me, but he had no choice. He'd ditched his family, who were probably crammed on a ferry, so I didn't feel bad for him. I imagine he wanted to sit up front by the pilot, but because of weight distribution, he had to sit behind me. While he was settling in, he knocked the back of my seat with his foot. He might not be a murderer, but Ben was such an irritating guy.

This chopper had a different pilot. Unlike our first, we buckled our seat belts without instructions. He didn't give us a heads-up on the wind factors, either. As the helicopter rose, I clutched my armrest with white knuckles, but to my surprise, we rose gently and followed behind Bisa's copter. I bit my lower lip, trying to be cool, but the idea that this wasn't unusual for Bisa made me realize how pedestrian, literally, my life was. I looked over to the pilot and smiled, but he focused on out flight path up the entire island of Manhattan.

Our next stop was Bill Rainey Park in the South Bronx, a spot nestled among many respected wall murals in the City. As far as I knew, the area sat in a fairly residential and commercial area, but the 6 train landed right by the famous Big Pun Mural and led right to the field. Since Big Pun was a Puerto Rican rapper, Bisa probably wanted to use the City to highlight her heritage, as well as her movie. It was an interesting choice given how mainstream her three songs and movie were. I respected the choice. She was keeping everyone on their toes, remaining an enigma.

When I spied the George Washington Bridge ahead of us, the pilot took a right and we crossed over the City. The helicopter then began to descend, which made me nervous. At Liberty Island, we had the whole back half of the island to land. It's not like we needed it, but I was comforted we had a lot of space. At this next concert, we approached Bill Rainey Park directly. The fans had already filled the park. Barriers were erected around the park, and guards dotted the perimeter so that only ticket holders could enter, but I saw people on rooftops and hanging out of windows and plainly sitting on beach chairs around the area. If they couldn't see Bisa, they could at least hear her. And given the JumboTron, I supposed some people might have a free view of the show as well.

My hands once again found the armrests and squeezed. Our

landing pad was a baseball diamond that jutted out, away from the stage and crowd. I noticed Bisa's helicopter hovered far above ours. Bisa kept her audience waiting and, as expected, the crowd went wild, exactly as it had at Liberty Island. When my helicopter lowered, the pilot directed us to get out. Again, he did not turn the propeller off. Our drop-off was in and out. I followed Freesia and Ben to stairs leading to a now-familiar offstage setup.

The new group of backup performers was already offstage, bursting to start the show. Bisa joined us shortly after. Freesia retouched her makeup and hair. A costume designer ran up to her and wordlessly fitted her with a tight gold jacket before wrapping her in jewels and a boa. Then both assistants stepped back to let Bisa take her pre-performance breaths. I held my camera up and took the shot. If Shawn had a problem with any of my photos, he could bring it up with Bisa. My shot would be a prized look at Bisa behind the scenes. The media and its audience would love it.

The green room was more crowded here than at Liberty Island, possibly because the location was easier to get to. The noise outside grew as the music shifted to the opening compilation. Shawn was seated in a lounge area with two friends and the studio executive. They high-fived each other as Bisa took the stage.

"I know I'm limited in the photos I can take during the concert, but can I get one of you guys?" I said to Shawn.

He smiled at me. Today he tore a white T-shirt that showed off his chain.

"You got it," he said, and turned to the group. "Bros, let's give the lady a smile for Bisa."

The group obliged. I took some photos and then looked at my viewfinder.

"These are good," I said, and showed Shawn the best of the lot.

"Nice," he said.

"Is Anna OK? I asked. "I was hoping to get a photo of you with Bisa and her, but she took off so quickly."

"Yeah," he said, leaning back. "I don't think she's coming back."

He seemed so sure of himself. I sat down right beside him.

"Kayla said you were the one who informed her that Anna had left," I said. "How'd you know that?"

"That's none of your business," he said. His warmth began to recede.

"It's just, I got her room," I said. "I'd like to make sure she's not coming back. What did Anna say exactly when she left?"

"She didn't tell me," he said. "But don't worry about it. I checked in on her room and it was in one of those Anna-fit conditions."

"You had a key to her room?" I said, tilting my head in a way I hoped was nonthreatening given how direct it was.

"Nah," he said. "She always—"

Shawn stopped talking.

"Oh," I said, another piece in the puzzle falling into place. "Right. You two are together."

"We're not," he said. He started to bounce a knee.

"Yeah, you are," I said as I started to understand a few things. "She told me."

Anna had done no such thing, but the dollar amount on her phone next to Shawn's name, plus the somewhat bitter expression on his face right now, said it all. He muttered a curse under his breath.

"A'right, but Bisa doesn't know." He did not make eye contact with me. "That woman's crazy. If Bisa finds out, she's gonna kill both of us. I told Anna that. Listen, I was in it for real, but Anna got tired of me, the way she gets tired of everything. And then, she tells me I have to invest in her company. If

I thought it was an investment, I'd have been happy about it, but I knew she couldn't make that business happen. Listen, those two women are family to me. I would never mess with either one of them. My thing with Anna was real, but Anna said she doubted Bisa would believe it. And Bisa is the type who will go berserk about things like the two of us."

"The investment was blackmail so she wouldn't tell Bisa?"

He nodded and looked around the room furtively to make sure no one had heard, although he seemed happy to have someone to talk to.

"Yesterday, I was supposed to meet her in her room. She left the key sticking out from under the door for me. I wanted to talk some sense into her about that toast she made," he said. "The room was trashed. She was gone. She came to get money from Bisa and took off."

I remembered Shawn telling me that money ruined Anna. I understood why he thought so. Like Ben, Anna had threatened Shawn's future with Bisa. I guessed money had gotten to him, too.

"Anna hid a lot from Bisa," Shawn said in a defensive tone. "I could have blackmailed her right back. Like, she was working in an old factory in Queens the entire time Bisa was shooting *All About Love*, but she told Bisa she was in California."

"Why would she do that?"

Shawn shook his head slowly. "That girl always wants to show her older sister that she can make it as big as Bisa has," he said. "Frankly, I was surprised she asked Bisa for the money. She only did that once before, back when she had a sort of drug problem, you know? But then she swore she'd never ask again. She was so embarrassed."

"Can I ask you something?"

"We should probably get going," he said, and stood.

"I noticed you weren't at the breakfast party when Anna left," I said.

"How do you know that?" He looked irritated rather than flattered that I'd noticed.

"It's my job to keep track of where people are at parties. You know, the comings and goings. I have to make sure I get the right shots of everyone in various groupings. I was going to suggest you, Anna, Bisa, and Dev pose for me, but you were gone."

"I don't remember," he said. "Maybe I was in the bathroom?"

"I'm sorry I didn't get the shot," I said to him.

Outside, the volume of the crowd's cheers increased.

"Sounds like it's time to go," he said.

"You don't need to worry about me telling Bisa about you two," I said, the two of us standing as we concluded out exchange. "I have no interest in upsetting her. I like my job. And also, that's not my style."

Shawn smiled.

"Maybe you'll keep working for her down the road."

"I don't think so," I said. "I'm not a roadie type. I have a small photography studio."

Shawn didn't stick around to hear my pitch about Liv Spyers Photography, or my motto: *I'm ready to capture YOUR story!*

Shawn was having an affair with Anna and was worried about what Bisa would do if she found out. I remembered his comment to me that he'd known Bisa and Anna since childhood. The sisters were more than his livelihood—they were family.

I wondered if he had it all wrong, though. Bisa might have been more worried about him than Anna, who ran hot and cold. In the short time I knew her, Anna had displayed her tendencies to me—giving me shoes one minute and closing the door on me the next. Even the shoes came with strings. Even so, something about Anna resonated with me, down to the fact that she lived in the studio where she made her shoes.

With Shawn and his gang gone to watch the show, I looked at Felix Montgomery, who stood by the craft table and poured himself a glass of champagne. He downed it quickly and then had another equally strong one, as if he needed to brace himself before going out to watch the end of the show. If he was ever going to talk to a stranger about Bisa, it was now, while he was a fish out of water.

"Mr. Montgomery?" I said.

He looked at me with an all-star smile that hid the solo-drinking guy I'd watched.

"I'm Liv Spyers, Bisa's photographer," I said. "She asked me to take photos during these next couple of days of the people who mean the most. You are at the top of that list."

Felix's smile began to look more genuine.

"May I?" I raised my camera.

"Of course!" Felix raised another glass of champagne and let me go to work.

"Thanks," I said. "I joined the double-decker bus tour last night and there were great stories about the two of you, things that happened during the shoot."

"We had a ball," he said.

"There was one about Bisa's allergy attack during friends-and-family day," I said. "Thank goodness for your aunt Trudy."

"They told *that* story?" he said. Both hands grasped each side of his champagne glass and I wondered if he was disturbed by my comment.

"Your aunt Trudy had Sudafed, right?" I said.

"Yeah," he said, "but Bisa didn't have an allergy attack. Something upset her that morning and I suggested she sneeze a bit so we could take an extended break. Don't tell!"

He smiled a charming smile and I wished I was having a regular conversation instead of interrogating him. Although, if I were not charged with my duty to find Anna's murderer, I probably would never have had the courage to even make eye contact with him.

"I wonder what upset her," I said.

"I know," he said. I could see he was happy to spill and me being no more than a non-threatening photographer, he felt free to loosen up. "Dev wanted to put an end to Anna's business aspirations. He thinks Bisa should focus on a jewelry brand and he gave her an ultimatum, which she rejected. She was very strong with him that day. Ultimately, he backed down, and somehow got back into her good graces."

"I think Bisa's about to sing the new song," I said. "I should get to work."

I wasn't supposed to take photos up front, but I could tell Felix was done talking to me, and between Freesia and Felix, I'd learned a couple more things about Dev. Felix followed to the stage as well, where Bisa now raised her hands. The crowd quieted as much as it could. From experience, I knew half the house thought she was looking straight at them.

"I grew up in Puerto Rico and then Ohio, but my sister and I used to come to Nueva York when we were kids to visit my old auntie. She died a long time ago now, but she would've been very excited to see me back here today."

Bisa held the mic gingerly as the crowd paid tribute to her aunt with their cheers.

"Anna, my little sister with big talent, I love you," she said, tears in her eyes as she looked up. "This song is one of my favorites in *All About Love*, which is coming out tomorrow."

Cheers continued, not for the movie.

"Today I'm going to sing it for my little sister."

The music started, but the opening was slightly different

from the opening I'd heard last night. It sounded like a clip from a radio interview. One guy said he only wished the other could have sung with B.I.G. The other said one day he would have the chance, at the pearly gates.

I raised my camera for a photo, but I didn't have the heart to take it. Tears streamed down Bisa's face. The music continued to a joyful beat and was probably going to be the anthem for every couple this summer, but I could see that Bisa knew her sister was gone.

Dev appeared and walked by me with long strides.

"This was not in the program," he said to no one in particular.

The concert would end in minutes and we'd be off to the last one. Bisa's decision to let me sleuth, while she performed, was paying off. I'd confirmed Ben's alibi, learned about Shawn's affair, and had a new lead about Anna's studio, which I decided I wanted to visit. I also didn't like what I was seeing and hearing about Dev. The more I understood about Bisa's fiancé, the more I thought Russell was right. Dev put Bisa on a pedestal, but he also thought he knew what was best for her. Neither of those things was good for anyone.

Dev motioned to Kayla, who approached and stood behind him. He whispered something into her ear. She checked her iPad and then scanned backstage.

"We're running a few minutes behind schedule," she said to me. "I'm going to put you and Shawn and Ben on the first chopper out of here. I'd like you all to board and then we can get you in the air the moment she finishes."

I followed her instructions as Bisa began her finale, along with my flight companions. As I walked to the chopper, I watched Felix get into a black car outside the park. Alfonz, Dev, Freesia, and Kayla remained behind. Our pilot was the same guy who'd flown us over. He was in the cockpit, but did not expect our arrival until the last song. As a result, he'd taken his hat and earphones off. When I climbed into the co-pilot seat, I saw he had a star tattooed onto the top of his head.

I counted my blessings that his seat was too high for Ben or Kayla to see. The last thing I needed was for one of them to make the friendly overture that I'd been asking about him.

CHAPTER 15

I held my camera tightly to my chest, similar to how Anna had gripped her phone at Todo Amor after she'd received her text that said, **Time's up.** Part of me was ready to use my small Leica as a weapon. I imagined heaving it against the pilot's skull and making a run for it, but my arms had lost their strength. The heat of the day wrapped around my throat and made my breathing choke.

"You OK, ma'am?" the pilot asked me. "You need to put your headset on. And seat belt. We'll be taking off shortly."

I nodded and put my seat belt on, but not my headset.

"I saw you the other day," I said. "I mean yesterday. At the party at Todo Amor."

The pilot looked ahead as if I hadn't spoken. His eyes were fixated on the building across the street, where two kids were waving a Puerto Rican flag out their window.

"Are you friends with Bisa? Or Dev? Why were you there?"

"I was working security," he said. "I'm a pilot but I moonlight sometimes. As long as I was flying today, they let me work the party, too."

"Who did?" I said. "Alfonz?"

"Who?" he said, and looked at me. "I don't know what your

problem is, lady, but we have to go, so put your headset on so we're ready."

"Everything OK up there?" Freesia said from behind. "I think my friend here is trying to be friendly."

"I'm being friendly," the guy snapped back.

"I'm Liv," I said.

"Yeah. I'm Freesia," my back seat companion said. "Thanks for the ride. What's your name?"

"Louis," he said.

"That's a cool tattoo you have on your head, Louis," I said. "Unusual place to put ink."

Louis adjusted his headphones so that we could no longer speak. I copied him. I wasn't sure what I should be asking him, but the earphones bought me time to think. I saw him speak into his microphone to someone on the ground. I tried to read his lips, but the mouthpiece covered my view. Once again, I clutched the armrests. I was climbing into the air in a tiny machine with a man who, I knew for a fact, was directly connected to Anna's death. This was the closest I had gotten to Anna's assailants and it was terrifying. If Louis was still around, that meant whatever Anna had of value, it had not been my shoes.

When we were a couple hundred feet in the air, my anxiety lessened. Louis, if that was his name, was stuck with me. If anything, he should be more uncomfortable than I was. I'd found the man with the star tattoo. I could track his name and contact information from the helicopter company and contact the police. I'd be much happier when my life wasn't in his hands, but the trip back to Roosevelt Island, where an audience waited for Bisa's last concert to begin, was only minutes away.

We flew south over the East River and my breathing steadied when I saw the island and then the red landing circle on the roof of Todo Amor. Ahead, I saw the Four Freedoms State Park at the southernmost tip of the island. The only structure between the park and Todo Amor was the haunted old small-pox hospital I'd learned about during my bus tour. The Jum-boTrons played the trailer for *All About Love*, and at this point, I'd seen the clip enough times that I didn't have to read lips to know what Felix and Bisa were saying.

As the helicopter descended to the roof, two ground crew members waved us down. Another man stood by the door that opened into the house. My heart skipped a beat, because I thought Harry might have made it to the island for the last show. As we drew closer to the ground, however, I saw his combed hair in perfect, straight lines. The Cardinal looked up at me and waved.

"Crap," I said, but couldn't hear myself over the chopper.

I hadn't spoken to Harry yet about what to do. He'd told me the Cardinal wouldn't show up at one of the concerts, but here he was at the house. I felt my phone buzz as well. I lifted it and saw Harry's name. Quickly, I clicked on it.

On my way to Todo Amor.

Oh, Harry. He was so close to recapturing his thief. I needed to buy time for him to get here.

I replied: **Meet me in my room. He's here.**

The chopper blades continued to spin as a ground flight at-tendant opened the hatch. He reached out his hand and helped me to the ground. Ducking under the whirling blades, I had no choice but to run toward the Cardinal. There was no escaping him.

I pointed to the roof door for him to follow me. We walked without speaking. At the second floor, I opened the exit door. Shawn and Ben were behind us, but I knew they would con-tinue downstairs and into cars that would drive them to the last performance. When I stepped onto the second-floor hallway, I was immediately aware of how different the house was without Bisa in it. The party team was at work preparing for a post-concert bash that would rival last night's party, but without Bisa here the house was quieter. My bag with the pepper spray was in my room, and for the second time, I thought I might use it. Without looking over my shoulder or speaking, I walked to my door and let us in.

"How were the shows?" the Cardinal asked when the door shut behind us.

"Why are you here?"

"I want my answer." He took up his perch on my chair. I put my camera on the table, picked up my bag, and sat across from him with it on my lap.

"I have a concert to photograph," I said.

"Yes? Or . . . no?"

"Yes," I said. "And . . . no."

The Cardinal crossed his arms, but he didn't look mad.

"Yes, we have a deal if you promise to keep my identity a secret," I said. "But not without promises."

I was really winging it to buy time until Harry arrived.

"I'm listening," he said.

What promises did I need? I looked at my phone. Only ten minutes had passed since I'd texted him. Harry would not be here for at least another ten or twenty.

"In return for letting you go, I would like your promise that you will disappear forever, so that the headache of following you around the globe will go away."

"I hear you but I'll be honest, or as honest as I get. I'm not sure I can hold up my end of the bargain," he said. "I can't help myself. It's who I am. I see a painting or a jewel or a sculpture and I can't sleep until I've figured out how to get it. It's like a drug."

"Perhaps I can entice you," I said.

"How?"

"I'll let you have one more heist. On me," I said. "And it will be so good that you'll never need that high again. Every time you look at your loot, the memory alone of stealing it will be enough."

"It would have to be something very unique for me to give up my livelihood."

"Like what?" I said. Oh, where was I going with this? "The *Mona Lisa*?"

If Harry didn't arrive soon, I'd be promising the Cardinal the Eiffel Tower.

"Vincent Peruggia already beat me to the *Mona Lisa* in 1911. It was recovered, obviously, but I'd never choose as my last heist something that's already been stolen. I need my own legacy."

"You drive a hard bargain," I said. "But I'm sure I can think of something."

"I'm not sure the prize itself would be enough. Your little comment yesterday about my lukewarm performance at the Neue got me thinking. I can't go away for good with that reputation. If you want me to disappear forever, I'd need to make one last splash."

I laughed at his audacity.

"You would want me to let you not only have at it with a priceless work of art, but also let you make a big splash while stealing it?"

"You ask me what I wanted. That's the truth. It would have to top my heist at the Neue. I was very proud of that one."

"You want even more attention than that dumb Neue benefit?" I said.

"The Neue's painting is one of the most expensive in the world," he said, looking as offended as I hoped he would. "You know it."

The Cardinal looked out my window, where we could now hear Bisa's last concert begin.

Outside my door, we heard a hand grip my doorknob. I held my breath. Harry was here at last. Unfortunately, the Cardinal heard the noise, too.

"Do we have a deal?" I said to get his attention.

"If you can find something too good to pass up, yes," he said.

"I can do that."

The thief smiled.

"You should answer your door."

I didn't move.

The Cardinal laughed.

"You'd better make good on your promise," he said, "because what you're doing is amateur hour. One more attempted sting like this and the deal is off."

Still, I waited for the door to burst open, but it didn't. Worse, the doorknob turned, ever so slowly.

"I'll get it," he said, and leapt across the room. Turning the handle, he opened the door and yelled, "*Boo!*"

Louis, not Harry, was in the hallway. In a split second, the thief jumped up, grabbed the top of the door frame, and swung himself past the thug. Shocked, Louis turned to watch the man escape. I used the brief moment to slam my door shut and stick a chair under the doorknob so that he couldn't come in. I ran into the bathroom next and locked that door, too. Only then did I realize my phone was on my table, along with my pepper spray. By the time I heard Harry at my bathroom door, I was seated in my bathtub and covered in towels.

"Are you OK?" he said, knocking at the door.

I uncovered myself and shook my head at the absurdity of the situation as I went to the door.

"He got away," I said when I saw his concerned face.

"I guess I didn't do too well being the cavalry coming to save you," he said. "What happened here?"

"The Cardinal paid me a visit. And funny enough, he inadvertently protected me from an intruder," I said. "The chopper pilot was the man with the star tattoo. He came to my room after we landed."

"Did he threaten you? Did you get his name?"

"Louis," I said.

Harry hit his screen and handed me the phone. Bernie answered. In a calm and grandmotherly way, she asked for Louis's description and jotted down everything I could remember. She promised to look into him and assured me not to worry about a thing. Meanwhile, Harry poured us each a Coke from the mini fridge and sat down at the table. His choice of seating was not the coziest, so I knew he was worried. Outside, I heard Bisa finishing her last song in the distance. She and the others would soon be returning to rest before a post-concert celebration tonight.

"One more thing, Bernie," I said. "Anna Reyes was living and working on her shoe production in a warehouse. Is there any way you could get her address?"

"Of course," she said. "I'm off."

And she was. I joined Harry at the table and traded his phone for an icy soda, which reminded me how hot the day was.

"Harry, I'm not sure Louis realized I was in my room when he came to the door," I said. "I was supposed to be at the last concert. I think he's still looking for something. Were you able to lift any prints from the jumpsuit or the fingernail?"

"We did," he said, "but it wasn't particularly fruitful. There were prints, but we couldn't make a match."

"What does that mean?"

"It means whoever ripped Anna's jumpsuit and manhandled her doesn't have a criminal record."

I took my mugshots from my camera bag and laid them on the table.

"It tells us one thing," I said. "But I already knew it. Ben Goldfarb didn't kill Anna. He has a record, but the sound-and-light guy from yesterday's party already confirmed he saw Ben with a woman. Ben was evasive about where he was because he's married."

Harry mirrored me by also leaning his head on his hand.

"From where I'm sitting, being a photographer is harder than catching thieves for a living," he said.

He reached his hand across the table and I welcomed his warm touch.

"Actually," he said. "You can rule out Alfonz, too. I found a record for him. Nothing serious. Disorderly conduct mostly. He hung out with a rough crowd in his youth."

"I thought Alfonz might have been the person on the motorbike, but OK," I said. "We have two off the list. And what do you want to do about the Cardinal?"

"Don't worry about the Cardinal. We've officially decided if we caught him once, we can catch him again. He'll figure out soon enough that you aren't with the ACU. In fact, he sounds desperate to have taken the risk to come back today when he'd already escaped. He must know his days of freedom are numbered."

"The thing is, I was trying to buy time until you got here, but I think I made a deal with him instead."

"A deal." Harry held his glass in both hands and bit his lip.

"Sorry," I said.

I recapped my tête-à-tête with his thief. About halfway through, Harry began to pace the room. I couldn't tell if he was mad or furious. When I finished, he was looking out the window with his hands on his hips. I suspected we were heading into our second fight in two days.

"You're a genius," he finally said.

His comment was a huge surprise.

"I know," I said. "But why?"

He pulled his chair so that the table wasn't between us and I liked where he was going.

"You said you'd give him a chance to steal something remarkable."

"And in a splashy, unforgettable way, so he could reclaim his reputation. Technically, I said in front of way more eyes than the dumb Neue benefit."

"That painting is one of the most expensive works of art in the world," he said. I decided not to let it concern me that the Cardinal and my boyfriend had similar sensitivities when talking about art. "Either way, he agreed?"

"Yes but we were interrupted by Louis," I said. "I told him I'd set something up and he'd know."

"How?"

"We didn't get that far."

We both let that sink in for a bit.

"I have an idea," I finally said. "He found me through Instagram. I've had a bunch of new followers these last few days. One of them is bound to be him. Why don't I use the platform to send him the message about where and when. You can be there to catch him in the act and I can take the fall for it."

Harry nodded his head.

"I like it," he said. "I'll set up an easy heist, you post the news. I'll catch him in the act. You know he would never stop."

"Never," I said. "I could see it in his eyes. He sort of has the same creative passion as Bisa. What if the heist isn't big enough to sate his appetite? I got the feeling he was looking for something as big as Bisa Mania."

There was another knock on my door. I didn't even ask who it was. At this point, I was prepared for anything.

Bisa was outside my door. Behind me, I heard Harry spill his drink. It was the comedy moment I needed. The guy could talk about murderers and thieves without flinching, but get him drunk with a pop star and he'll never stop cringing about it.

This is why I was, deep down, thinking about the *L* word, as Maria had said. Bisa saw the smile I was trying to repress by biting my lips, but she didn't join in my good humor. Instead, she walked straight into my room and flopped on my bed.

"Congratulations," I said. "The shows were amazing."

"We've already had one million downloads for each of the songs," she said. She put her hands on her forehead. "But more importantly, what did you learn about Anna?"

"Do you mean you've had three million downloads?" I asked.

"In five hours," she said.

"That's a good day's work," Harry said as he came out of the bathroom with a B-emblazoned blue facecloth to dab up his spill. "Would you like a Diet Coke?"

"No, I don't want a Diet Coke," she snapped, and then looked to the ceiling. "I'm sorry. This has been the hardest day. Did you learn anything? It was all I could think about during every performance. I'll have a Diet Coke."

Bisa's phone rang.

"Hi, honey bun. I'll be down in a few. I just needed a moment to compose myself," she said. She was quiet for a moment and then sat up. "Well, is he OK?" she asked. "Who was flying the copter all day if it wasn't him?"

She put her hand over her mouth.

"Dev," she said. "You're going to have to make excuses for me. I can't do this party . . . No, I can't . . . I need to be alone. Please don't bother me tonight."

She put the phone down and stared at me, and then at Harry.

"One of the helicopter pilots was found with a concussion," she said. "He's been out all day, they're saying. Someone else was flying us around today and we don't know who."

"I met him. He was at your party yesterday morning, too. He says his name is Louis," I said. "And he has a tattoo of a star on top of his head. He's the guy I saw in the boat with Anna."

Bisa began to fiddle with her sister's rings on her pinky.

"I have to get out of here," she said. "I don't feel safe."

"Were you serious when you said you weren't going to go to your after-party?" I said. "Can you do that?"

Bisa stopped fiddling and stared at me hard.

"Girl, I just sold three million songs in the last few hours," she said. "If I wanna miss a party, I'm gonna miss a party. You got that?"

I nodded. "It's only, I have a place for you to stay if you want to disappear. And the food is good."

"What are we waiting for?" she answered. "I'm not even going to change. Just put me in a car and take me away. I thought I'd invited my family to celebrate with me, and now I don't know who to trust. And you have a bed and good food? I'm in."

"There's one thing, though," I said. "If I don't tell my best friend to meet us, she will disown me."

"Do you trust this friend? More importantly, can *I* trust this friend?"

"Yes," I said confidently.

"As I said, what are we waiting for? No, wait! I need my disguise hair—then we'll go."

She left the room.

I looked at Harry, who still had the facecloth. Before either of us said a word, there was another knock at the door.

"Hello?" I whispered into the wood.

"Open up," Bisa said.

I opened the door.

"We're not leaving yet," she said. "This is my house. I built it. And I have one more thing I want to do before we go. I'm going to have Alfonz show us the security footage of the last couple of days. Decide what you want to look at and meet me downstairs in five."

"Bisa," I said, "maybe at this point we should rely on the police for help? Now that the pilot was found attacked, I'm sure an investigation will begin."

"Liv," she said, and pointed a finger at me. "You have to learn this early. If you want to get anything done right, you have to do it yourself. I'm not sitting around like some damsel in distress, while the police dicker around trying to decide if my sister is dead or not. No way. See you in my office in ten. Make that five."

She walked down the hall and I closed the door.

"You definitely have the harder job of the two of us," Harry said.

CHAPTER 16

I called Granny. I called Maria next, only to say she needed to stop by. After that, Harry and I headed downstairs and waited in front of Bisa's office door. I had my tote bag and camera, ready to go once she was. Harry stuck his hands in his pocket. He rubbed his hair a few times in the way he does when he's thinking. I tried to flatten it, but seconds later, it was sticking up again.

Around us, the party staff was at it again. Tonight, the décor's theme was centered around *All About Love*. The music had now hit the market, so it was time to focus on the movie. And next week, Bisa's attention would be on her tour.

"I have an idea for tomorrow night," Harry said. "With the Cardinal."

"Excellent," I said. "Tell me it's in Paris and not Radio City Music Hall. I've always wanted to go to Paris."

Alfonz joined us, looking like a kid who'd been sent to the principal's office.

"Bisa said she wanted me to meet with her and you guys," he said. His arms were squeezed against him as if he was trying to make himself look smaller.

"Any news about the poor pilot?" I asked.

He shook his head. "We've been able to keep it out of the press for now."

"But who hit him?" Harry asked.

"Beats me." Alfonz's eyeballs were wet. "I should've noticed something. I don't understand how this could have happened."

Bisa walked down the stairs, with Dev behind her. She carried a medium-sized bag that was bursting with personal items, and in her other hand, she carried a short black wig and glasses. Dev also looked like he was heading to the principal's office, but, where Alfonz looked like the kid who knew he'd done something wrong, Dev looked like the kid who was going to have his parents complain to the school. He was both nervous and contemptuous.

"Bee, you need to come and get dressed," he said. "You are being unreasonable. The police will figure out the pilot situation. If we can, we'll get some good PR for you. But you have a party to host. If you don't show up, the film execs will be livid. Cyril already thought he should have been invited to fly with us today."

Bisa stopped at the bottom of the stairs and looked firmly at her fiancé, as if she was really seeing him for the first time.

"It's very important that, tonight, you appreciate me as a woman, as a regular person," she said.

"But you're not a regular person," he said. "That's one of the things I love most about you."

She sighed and walked to us, pressing the code for the doors to open. Alfonz, Harry, and I walked in. Dev began to follow us, too, but Bisa pressed a button to shut the door on him.

"Al, can you pull up the house security footage on my computer?" she asked.

"Sure," he said. "But we didn't put cameras on the roof. There won't be anything to show the attack."

"I'm not interested in the attacker," she said. "Liv already identified him for me. A guy named Louis with a tattoo of a star on his head."

"Freesia talked to him, too," I said.

"Tell the police to call Freesia about it, would you?" she said to Alfonz.

"Sure thing, Bisa." Alfonz pressed his lips together and absently rubbed his forefingers over his thumbs. He walked to the desk where Bisa had logged in to her computer. A screen hanging from a wall behind them flickered on so we could all easily see what was on her laptop.

"We want to see footage from yesterday morning's party," I said.

The screen already showed that Alfonz was logging in to footage from security, but he stopped and looked at me when I gave him my instructions.

"Why?" he said.

"Don't ask her why, Al," Bisa said. "We don't have time. Just pull it up."

Alfonz returned to his system. He opened and closed a couple of files. As he did, his brow moistened. He pulled at the neck of his shirt.

"It's not here," he finally said. His voice broke and I thought he might cry.

"Where is it?" Bisa said.

Alfonz looked at her helplessly.

"I don't know," he said. "Either someone turned off the system or erased it. Nothing's here. There's nothing. Bisa, I'm so sorry. I'll resign. I don't understand what's going on."

"That's enough, Alfonz," she said.

Looking inconsolable, Alfonz left the room. While the doors were open, I noticed that Dev was gone. When the doors closed, Bisa flipped on her wig and put on her glasses. Then she opened the back door.

"Do you have a car, Harry?"

"I have a driver waiting," he said.

"Even better."

"Do you have Find My Phone?" Harry said as we headed across the back grounds outside. "Turn off anything that can track your phone."

"You think this is the first time I've needed to go MIA for a night?" Bisa said, already ahead of him.

The car pulled around and we left. Harry sat in the front; Bisa and I were in the back. The driver didn't get a glimpse of Bisa in her disguise and we made sure not to speak until we arrived home, especially since Bisa's voice was so recognizable. I mostly prayed during the ride that my family wasn't organizing a parade to welcome her. I'd said Bisa needed a night away from fans and attention after her big day. Under no circumstances were they allowed to tell anyone. Not even my parents. I hoped that was enough.

Fortunately, when we pulled up to my tree-lined street at about seven o'clock, the Carrera residence was quiet. Even the neon KEYS sign in my grandparents' store was off. I breathed a sigh of relief as our small group wearily climbed the stairs. When we walked through the door and I smelled Poppy's famous stew, all of my stress melted. I wanted a warm piece of garlic bread, dripping with butter.

"*Carina,*" Granny said to me with a big hug when she heard the door open. "And Harry! Welcome dear boy. We've missed you. And Ms. Bisa, we're honored to have you here. We're proud of Liv and now she brings home celebrities. Two years ago, she was a college dropout working at Starbucks, and now look at her!"

I looked at the ceiling, wishing her bio of me would soon be over.

"I never graduated, either," Bisa said. "When life calls, you go running. I got a record deal and I couldn't pass it up."

"Come to the kitchen," Granny said, leading the way.

It's not unusual to head right to the table in my family. Food is the ice breaker for everything.

"We have stew with meat and potatoes and carrots. I know it's not very summery, but after the big day you all had, you need some iron. And we have a salad with garbanzo beans I made yesterday. And the bread will be out in a minute. Bisa, if you don't like stew, we also have fettuccine Alfredo. It only takes a minute to make. And for dessert, I made my famous pineapple upside-down cake."

"Mrs. Carrera, this is all so kind of you, but I am on a paleo keto diet," Bisa said as Poppy greeted her with a large glass of wine. "And I don't drink, either. Do you have Diet Coke?"

"I'm sorry," Poppy said. "We don't believe in diet sodas. Have the wine. It's much better for your blood."

"I'm sure there's something keto and paleo in the stew. And there's cheese in the Alfredo sauce. Can you eat bread? You have to try this garlic bread. It's Liv's favorite."

Before Bisa could answer, Granny stuck a piece of bread in her mouth.

"Oh my God," she said. "I forgot how good bread is."

"She can't remember the last time she ate bread?" Granny whispered to Harry, who was setting six plates around the table.

"I wouldn't refuse the food," Harry said to Bisa. "They might send you back home."

I began to put the food platters on the table and Bisa didn't fight it. She went to the kitchen drawers and opened a couple until she found the serving forks and spoons. We were about to sit down when there was a knock on the front door. Bisa looked so relaxed since the first time I'd met her, but she stiffened at the sound.

"Don't worry," I said. "It's Maria."

"Maybe worry," Poppy said. "She's a huge fan."

"Do you know Mateo DeLuca?" Granny asked as I went to the front door to let in my best friend.

"What's so important?" Maria asked.

"Follow me," I said.

"How were the concerts? I was really dreaming you'd get tickets," she said as we walked to the kitchen. "I know it was an impossible ask, but it was like when the Taylor Swift tickets sold out and the system broke and I spent a day convinced they'd feel bad and call me with tickets. A girl can dream."

Maria stopped at the door to the kitchen. Bisa was scooping a hearty serving of stew onto her plate as if she'd never heard the words *keto* or *paleo*.

"Hi, I'm Bisa," she said to Maria. "Liv told me I can trust you to keep my visit here a secret."

"I'm going to need a very large glass of wine," Maria said.

Bisa held hers to my friend.

"She only drinks diet drinks," Poppy said, shaking his head sadly.

"Can I do one thing before we eat?" Maria said. "One thing, and then it's like you're a working stiff like the rest of us."

She pulled out her phone and Bisa stood up for her usual selfie with a fan, but Maria pressed her screen. The *All About Love* theme song began to play.

"I've already learned the words," Maria said.

"The food is going to get cold," Granny said.

I sat on Harry's lap while we watched Bisa and Maria sing *All About Love*. Granny and Poppy boogied in a corner and I rested my head on my boyfriend's shoulder in the first normal moment I'd had in days. The celebrity world was exhausting.

"OK, *mangia*," Poppy said when the music ended.

Over dinner, Bisa joined my grandparents in a lively discussion about music from the old days. I was surprised she cared about tunes I thought only they liked, but music was her passion and she was like an encyclopedia. Her phone rang a couple of times, but she ignored calls from Dev and Kayla. Texts besieged her phone as well. It was only at dessert that she answered a call.

"Hey, Russ," she said. "Everything's fine. I'm here with the Carerras . . . the photographer's family . . . Don't tell anyone."

She was quiet as she listened to Russell. I couldn't hear what he was saying, but the softness that had returned to Bisa's face began to recede and the woman who managed an empire returned.

"OK," she finally said. "I'll call her."

She looked at our table of expectant faces.

"I have to call Kayla," she said. "She called Russell and said it's urgent. She wouldn't go behind Dev's back to call Russell if it wasn't really important."

Our party had become subdued. Except for Poppy, who enjoyed his cake. When Bisa left, he nudged me. "Who's the lady?"

I took his hand in mine, realizing he'd forgotten who our guest was.

"She's a friend of mine," I said.

"Big eater," he said with a giggle.

Bisa came back to the kitchen moments later. We looked at her expectantly, but I could see she didn't want to talk.

"We've all had a big day today," I said. "And tomorrow's a big deal, too. Maybe we should settle in for the night. Granny, can I sleep on the sofa? I'll give Bisa my room."

"Not at all," Bisa said, and brought her dish to the sink. "I've already put everyone out enough lately. I'm tired of it, too. Granny, Poppy, if you have an extra pillow and blanket, I'd be very grateful if you could lend me your sofa for a night. And maybe a little Tylenol. My body took a beating today."

"You should have had the wine," Poppy said. He hadn't forgotten everything.

"You can sleep wherever you want, Bisa," Granny said.

"But in the morning, I'll be downstairs to watch NY1 on my little set in the kitchen."

"Don't you love Pat Kiernan?" my pop star guest asked. It was maybe my favorite moment of all time.

"Night," Maria said.

"Wait, I have a question. Let me walk you to the door," I said.

As we walked down the hall to the front door, I could tell Maria thought I wanted to download, but I was still on the clock.

"In your law studies, what have you studied about wills and estates?" I said.

"Wills and estates? We just had dinner with Bisa!"

"Sorry. I know," I said. "It's just a quick question."

"I mean, my boss deals in real estate mostly, but he's done some wills," she said as we reached my grandparents' front door. "Why do you ask?"

"How do prenups work?"

"I don't have to be a lawyer to tell you that," she said. "My friend, Betty, from college had to sign one. When a couple gets engaged and one party has more money than the other, people negotiate a prenup so that if things don't work out, the person with no money can't take the other one to the cleaners."

"Sounds very unromantic," I said. "Is the amount based on percentage of the rich person's estate or a pre-negotiated amount?"

"Could be either," she said.

I hadn't stopped thinking about Dev. There was no way Bisa would get married without a pre-nup, no matter how persuasive Dev was. If the deal was based on a percentage of Bisa's estate, however, Dev stood to gain with Anna out of the way. The idea made me shudder.

"Oh. My. God," Maria said. "Are you and Harry? And is he asking you to sign one?"

"No!" I said. "We've been dating for less than a year. Do you not know me? I was thinking about Bisa and Dev. She should make him sign one. *Puh-leez.*"

"Night, I love you," Maria said, making the letter *L* with her fingers followed by little heart signs.

Making my way to the living room, I found the world's two newest besties, Granny and Bisa, in the living room, making up the sofa. It was only about nine o'clock but Bisa looked like she could sleep for a week.

"Antony and Harry, turn off the radio!" Granny yelled up the stairs. "Bisa doesn't want to listen to the Yankees game. She needs her beauty sleep."

Poppy grumbled, but did as he was told.

"Good night, sweetheart," Granny said. "I'll leave you two girls alone."

We returned her good night in unison. When Granny was gone, I turned to Bisa to hear what Dev had said during her call to him.

"Alfonz has gone missing," Bisa said. "I hope I wasn't too hard on him."

I was thinking she might not have been hard enough on him.

"I'm sure he'll turn up tomorrow," I said. "Hang in there. I'm just downstairs. If you need anything send me a text."

"Thanks," she said. "Man, we've just met and you've done more for me than the people who I've thought of as family."

"Oh, please," I said. "I have much crazier relatives than some of your gang."

"It's true," Harry said poking his head into the living room.

Bisa laughed and let us make our exit. Harry sat on the stoop and I joined him.

"Do you remember when you said the Cardinal would only be happy with something as big as Bisa Mania?" Harry said.

"Yup." I leaned my head against his arm.

"I can only think of one venue that would make that big of a splash."

"Where?"

"The heart of Bisa Mania. Tomorrow night," he said.

I lifted my head.

"You want me to invite a thief to my client's movie premiere?"

"Actually, I want you to invite a thief to steal something at your client's movie opening. From your client. Hear me out," he said. "The ACU has a good relationship with the British government. No matter what the price of a royal jewel, it has a mystique and priceless value to it in the eyes of the world."

"Where are you going with this?"

"The UK has given us permission to borrow the Cartier Halo Tiara. It's worth almost two million dollars."

I punched Harry in the shoulder and went into my apartment. Harry followed.

"What are you thinking? Bisa can't wear some Cartier tiara tomorrow," I said.

"It's covered in diamonds," he said. "It would be a win-win for everyone."

"With all she's been through, I don't want us to be responsible for even more turmoil."

"We'll get him before she even knows he's there," he said. "I promise. All you have to do is post about it after the UK Trust of Royal Jewels calls and she says yes to wearing it. She'll never know a thing."

"It doesn't matter. If you want her to help you, you'll need to tell her," I said.

"Bernie would never green light that."

"Then I can't help you."

I knew it was a brilliant idea. The Cardinal wouldn't be able to resist the opportunity to steal the tiara at Bisa's big premiere. But Bisa was a human being.

Harry's phone rang.

"Answer," I said. I went to my room to make sense of Alfonz's disappearance. It wasn't looking good for him. He'd brushed me off the day I'd seen Anna's body; he'd clearly erased the security footage from the day she'd died, while doing an impressive act of remorse tonight; and he denied knowing about the pilot when it was his job to make sure people were who they said they were and doing what they were supposed to do. Hell, the day I arrived, the guy had practically thrown me off campus because he didn't like how I looked. The first thing he ever said to me was that he'd been doing his job a long time and knew a fraud when he saw one. Shawn, Ben, and even Dev had much bigger problems with Anna, but for some reason, Alfonz seemed to have brutally ended her life, along with Louis. I wondered why.

My phone buzzed. A photo appeared on my screen from an unfamiliar number I knew to be a temporary one from Bernie. It was a picture of the Cartier Halo Tiara. I Googled it. Not only was it worth a fortune, but it had been popular in the royal family since it had been made for the Queen Mum in the 1930s, including, drum roll, Kate Middleton who wore it in her wedding.

I walked into my studio, still resolved that Harry had to be truthful with Bisa.

"I told Bernie I need to sleep on our plan," he said.

I lit a candle on my kitchen counter and opened a bottle of water.

"She also had some news about the helicopter pilot," Harry said.

"The real one? Is he OK?"

"I'm talking about Louis. The police found him. In a burned-up car. He's dead."

"Like murdered."

"Wow!" I sat on my kitchen stool and Harry joined me. "Alfonz killed them both."

"We could decide that's what happened," he said. "But Bernie also got the address to Anna's warehouse. Call me old-fashioned, but I'd like to know why he did it."

"Me too. Where are we going tomorrow morning?" I asked.

"Brooklyn," he said. "Industry City."

"You know you need to tell Bisa," I said. "If you really want to make this thing with the Cardinal happen."

Harry nodded, but he was miles away.

CHAPTER 17

My alarm rang the next morning at six. Harry had left even earlier to change and meet me at Anna's studio. We'd picked the early hour in order to be in and out before Bisa awoke but she wasn't as tired as I expected. After a light rap on the door a few minutes later, I found her at my stoop.

"I have a car waiting for me," she said. "Harry spoke to me this morning."

"He did?"

"Girl, he can trust me," she said. "You've got my back. I've got yours."

"Wow," I said. "That was a big deal. He's never told anyone outside of the ACU other than me. His boss is going to kill him."

"His boss doesn't know," she said. "And I understand why. I won't tell my people the real reason this wonderful offer came in either. I don't trust any of them. We're all good. Meanwhile, I got a call from the UK Trust of Royal Jewels. The Cartier Halo Tiara is being flown here as we speak. I'm going back to Todo Amor now."

"Are you really going to wear it?" I asked.

"Who am I to turn down so many diamonds? And anyway, do you think Dev would let me pass up an opportunity like that?"

"You're a queen," I said.

"I'm tired of being a queen," she said.

"Still, be careful tonight. If you can't find Alfonz, get some-one by your side you can trust. There are a lot of crazy people out there."

Bisa laughed.

"If that freaky little thief attacks me, let him," she said. "All the more publicity for me and all about diamonds. Anyway, I'd rather a good story about losing a tiara than losing my sister."

"About Anna," I said. "She had a warehouse in New York."

"He told me about that too and I can't talk about it," she said. "I'm too sad about her to now be mad at her too. You do what you need to do and let me know. I don't mean to drop the ball."

"No," I said. "It's too much. We'll let you know what we find."

"You are good friends."

I hugged her tight.

"I'll see you tonight," she said and ran up my stairs to her waiting car.

I was worried about Bisa, but proud of Harry to have made such a tough call to get the job done right. I turned on my espresso machine and let the aroma of a couple of shots fill my studio. My small room was filled with a reddish hue from the light shining against my red silk privacy curtain. I put on Bisa's new songs. The music was great. I hoped the movie would be, too. I sat on my desk chair and posted my photo of the tiara with the teaser: **Guess where this will be tonight? #RadioCity-MusicHall**

As if Bisa didn't already have enough, the wheels were now in motion for yet more trouble. I checked the news to find, al-ready, a splashy announcement that Bisa would be wearing a fancy royal diamond tiara to the movie opening. Ben worked fast. There was a lengthy description of the tiara's royal heritage and rarity. If all went according to plan, the Cardinal would understand my message and be there to steal it. I realized how odd my idea of good fortune was, but all bets were off for the time being.

"*It's all about love, sugar,*" I sang to myself.

I dressed in shorts and a T-shirt with sneakers instead of my boots. At seven, as planned, I was on the subway heading to Thirty-sixth and Fourth in the Sunset Park section of Brooklyn. Anna's workspace was not located in a beaten-up old warehouse, like I'd imagined. Industry City was a hip center of sixteen buildings on acres and acres of old industrial land. Small studio spaces housed engineering, design, manufacturing, and production, while the property hosted art exhibits, sold great food, and had tons of events. If Anna's business had taken off, Industry City would have been a perfect place to design and make her chic yet artsy shoes. For me, there's no better place to be than at my studio in the busy neighborhood of the West Village, but Industry City was so cool, I couldn't help fantasizing about being connected to the talent that filled the workspaces. Even if Harry and I hadn't had a specific mission for visiting, I'd have happily spent the day there.

Instead, I found my guy at Building No. 2, in front of the Brooklyn Roasting Company, where he offered me an iced latte, for what would be my third coffee of the morning. He was dressed in shorts and sneakers as well, with a lime-green T-shirt that looked gorgeous against his summer tan. I gave him a nice, long kiss.

"Was Bisa up when you left?" Harry asked.

"She told me everything," I said. "I've never liked you more."

"I'm glad you like me," he said with a seventh-grade style shove to my arm that made me blush.

"I wonder what we're going to find upstairs? Anna wasn't killed for nothing."

"I've been wondering the same," he said.

The morning was so pretty it felt unnatural to be scoping out motives for murder, but we headed to the building Bernie had given us and took a large, industrial-sized elevator up to the fourth floor. After a couple of lefts and rights, we arrived at studio 3. A small sign was tacked to the door: A.R. SHOES in a block font, blue letters on a silver background. The design perfectly complemented the shoes Anna had given me only two days ago.

"Did Bernie get you a key?" I said, noticing the lock.

"Nope," Harry said. "I thought you were the key genius of the two of us."

"And you were right," I said, and pulled out from my tote a key ring, which carried the master keys of many brands. I wanted all of them in case I ran into trouble, but I went directly to a key with a black rubber cover on the top. I pushed it into the lock and easily opened it.

"How did you do that so easily?" Harry said.

"I did a little research this morning," I said. "I googled the office and found a photo of it when someone else was using it. Up close, I recognized the lock. Before I came here, I took my grandparents' master keys. I took them all, in case Anna had changed the lock, but we're in luck."

I opened the door and we stepped inside.

"Huh," I said.

Anna's studio was surprisingly neat. On one side of the room, she had set up a drafting table with a small desk beside it. Birch-white floating shelves hung from an exposed brick wall and were filled with eye-catching clear-plastic boxes. One entire shelf, the largest of the lot, was filled with boxes containing sequins and crystals in all shapes and sizes. They were the kind of display you wanted to dig your hands into. I imagined Anna poring over her bits and bobs as she designed each new shoe.

Across the room, empty white shoe boxes in a pyramid shape filled up the entire wall. Wide, open shelves stocked with the pale silver tissue paper that wrapped her shoes stood next to them. There was a label maker, and blocks of drafting paper and wood. There were plastic molds for the heels in different sizes. The pièce de résistance, however, were the bolts and bolts of satin and silk fabrics, lying in rows beside a large table with a ruler and cutter. The setup was inspiring. Everyone said that Anna could never turn her dreams into reality, but this small studio challenged the general theory.

Between two large windows, there was a dresser. I opened the drawers.

"Shawn was right about one thing," I said. "She was living here."

I poked my head into the small bathroom. It was filled with bath and beauty supplies. It took me a moment to figure out where she slept, until I found a rolled-up sleeping bag in the shower stall. I suddenly wasn't feeling any FOMO for life at Industry City. I'd take my iron window bars and homemade muffins any day over this arrangement.

"It makes no sense," I said. "Why did Anna stop production of her shoes? Where did the money go? Her sister was a ready and willing client, as far as she knew. And Shawn and Ben were feeding her healthy sums each month."

Harry sat at Anna's desk and opened the drawers. I went to the bathroom and poked around for something unusual. I opened the studio's one closet and reached up to the shelves in order to see if my hand hit something unusual. I flipped through Anna's sketch pad on the drafting table.

"Look at this," we both said in unison.

I brought the pad over to the fabric table. Harry carried a couple of manila envelopes and a folder. He opened one and dumped a pile of receipts onto the table.

"She was good at keeping track of her bills," he said. He opened the folder.

"Budgets," I said, looking at spreadsheets similar to those I make for my own business. "When I looked at Anna's phone, all I found was an empty page with the heading *Debt*. The fact that it was blank had misled me to believe that Anna couldn't manage money, like I'd been told by everyone."

"Look at the balance sheet," he said, lifting another page from the pile. "This first line indicates she had two deposits of one hundred thousand dollars in cash one year ago. And shortly after the second deposit, she took the entire amount out again."

"Bisa gave her that amount at about that time. But what about the other deposit? That's a lot more than she was getting from Shawn and Ben, especially all at once," I said. "Does she list a source of where the money came from?"

"I don't think it was from a bank," Harry said. "There's no documentation."

"What if she's paperless?"

"Given these spreadsheets and how detailed she was with keeping receipts from everything else, I don't think so," he said. "What did you find?"

I shook the sketch pad to make sure every piece of unbound paper fell to the table. A few of the pages were sketches of shoes. Some were scribbled out, as if she'd decided she didn't like the direction of her work. I put those aside until what remained behind were printouts from news stories.

"Look at these," I said, reading the headlines.

"They're all about drugs," Harry said.

We each picked up a few pages and read them.

"Not just any drugs," I said. "These are about something called MX322. It's known on the street as S'nuff. Have you heard of it?"

Harry laughed. "Buying S'nuff off the street isn't my thing," he said. "But look at this. Does the description of the drug's effects remind you of anyone?" He handed the page to me.

"*An endless supply of energy, creative inspiration, sugar cravings,*" I said. "Harry, this sounds like Bisa."

"That's what I was thinking," he said.

"If Bisa found out that Anna was on to her," I said, "she might see it as a huge threat. Especially if she was on drugs. Bisa's brand is built on the goddess thing, not drug addiction."

I dropped the paper on the table as this new possibility gathered steam.

"Bisa showed us the ring she'd found in my suite. Do you think she really found it? Or was the whole thing a ruse? Oh my God," I said. "I had her over for dinner with my grandparents."

"I still don't understand," Harry said. "Why did Anna stop production?"

"Maybe she was afraid that Bisa, her only client, at least out of the gate, was falling apart," I said.

Harry put his finger over his lips in a sign to keep quiet. I raised my hands and mouthed *why?* He pointed at the door. Someone was outside and turning the handle. Two days ago, I might have been scared, but now I was mostly fed up. I marched to the door and opened it, half hoping to see Bisa, but quite surprised to see who our visitor was.

"Alfonz?" I said.

Bisa's hulking head of security took a step back and seemed to want to bolt.

"Excuse me, Liv," Harry said.

I stepped aside to let Harry into the hallway, where he grabbed the huge man's thick arm and, before my very eyes, flipped him onto the ground.

"That was very impressive," I said.

"I aim to please," Harry said, and dragged a groggy Alfonz into the studio.

I shut the door on all of us, but not before I glanced in both directions in the hallway, to make sure no one had seen us.

Alfonz sat up and rubbed his head. "What the hell, man?"

"Why did you go missing last night?" Harry said.

Alfonz looked at him with sheer disgust. "What are you talking about? I came to the City from Todo Amor and got hammered. And I passed out on a park bench."

Alfonz was wearing the same clothes he'd had on yesterday, except that now they were massively wrinkled. He did look like someone who slept on a park bench. And now that he'd pointed it out, he did smell a bit like a brewery.

"And you woke up and thought, *Hey, I'll go over to Anna's warehouse?*" I asked. "How'd you even know about it?"

"Shawn," Alfonz said. "I followed him here once, while Bisa was shooting the film. I heard him on the phone with Anna and I wanted to make sure I was hearing things right. I knew Bisa would be furious if Shawn was fooling around with her little sister. Shawn doesn't have a good track record with women. He's already had two wives. I was going to confront him, but he assured me it was over and not because of him. I thought, *OK, Anna can take care of herself.* I didn't tell Bisa about this place, though. It would have really upset her to think that Anna was in town and avoiding her. Once upon a time, those two were inseparable."

"And what about now? Why are you here?" Harry asked. "You didn't answer Liv's question."

Alfonz cursed for a few seconds while he tried to compose himself. When he was done, Harry offered him a chair.

"Here's the thing," Alfonz said. "You should stay away from this place and anything to do with Anna. Frankly, I could be asking you two the same thing. What are you doing here? At least I knew Anna. Who are you two?"

"You still didn't answer the question," Harry said.

"Because I don't give a flying fig about your questions."

Alfonz stood up. The guy was big.

"I don't know what you two are up to," he said. "But you don't know what you're playing with here."

"What did Anna have that everyone wanted?" I asked.

"Who's everyone?" Alfonz said.

I shrugged.

"Her room was ransacked at Todo Amor, for one," I said. "Or did you do that, too?"

Alfonz sat back down again and looked genuinely confused.

"Or what about the text Anna got before she fled Todo Amor? *Time's up.* Did you send it to her from a burner phone?"

"No," he said. "But I'm pretty sure I know who sent it."

Harry and I looked at him expectantly.

"She borrowed money from some unsavory characters," he said. "I assume that's also why she showed up to Todo Amor. She wanted Bisa to bail her out, no doubt. There. That's what I know."

Harry, who had been quiet, sat down next to him.

"How do you know she borrowed money?" he asked the guard.

"She told me."

He was lying. I knew it. Anna would never tell Alfonz anything personal. She'd told me herself that she loved making his and Kayla's life miserable whenever she was around them.

"And you're not going to tell us why you're here?" Harry said.

Alfonz crossed his arms and looked as if he was contemplating some form of violence against us.

"No, I'm not. And I don't have all day," Alfonz said. "It's time for you to leave. And if you don't, I'll call the police."

Harry scratched his head.

"You'll do what?" I said.

"You heard me. I'll call the police."

I looked at Harry, absolutely baffled.

"Al," Harry said slowly. "Do you know who Louis is?"

I casually walked over to the fabric table, where I'd left my tote bag and its contents of one can of pepper spray which I was becoming eager to use.

"Who's Louis?" Alfonz said.

"He's the guy who impersonated the pilot yesterday," Harry said.

"What about him?" Alfonz said. "I don't know anything about that guy."

"He's dead," Harry said.

Alfonz stood and took a step away from Harry. He looked at both of us in disbelief. "What are you talking about?"

"Louis, the fake pilot, is dead," Harry repeated.

"I didn't kill him," Alfonz said.

Harry and I didn't move, but Alfonz continued to step backward, his eyes on us, as he inched to the door.

"How did he die?"

"You don't know?" I said.

"I don't know anything," he said. "I have nothing to do with this. I've just been doing my job."

He reached the door and turned the doorknob. "Don't be idiots," he said. "Get out of here."

Alfonz opened the door and ran. I started after him, but Harry beat me to the door. He stood in front of it and caught me midleap.

"Whoa," he said. "What are you going to do when you find him?"

"Go get him," I said. "He's getting away."

"This is quickly turning into a double homicide case,"

Harry said. "And as Alfonz said, we don't know who we're up against. You need to stick to your own MO."

"Follow the photos and put the story together," I said.

"Exactly," Harry said.

I looked out Anna's window. Alfonz was nowhere. My camera was on Anna's worktable. I pulled a metal stool out from under it and sat down to work. Specifically, I flipped through my saved photographs until I came to the ones I took of Anna's ransacked room.

"What did Anna have?" I said, searching the photos. "It must be staring right at us."

"I don't see it, either," Harry said.

Underneath my camera, the articles about S'nuff and its effects lay on top of Anna's spreadsheets. The drugs were smooth, ovoid in shape, and, of all things, sparkly.

"Wait a minute," I said.

Across the room, Anna's container of gems sparkled as the sun hit them. I approached the decorations meant to adorn shoes, and lifted one jar at random.

"When I spoke to the Cardinal, he said it would be hard to find *snuff* in a place like Todo Amor," I said. "I thought he was using some old-fashioned term for a drug. He's a weird guy."

I dumped the baubles in the jar onto the table. "Maybe he meant that in a place drowning in crystals, S'nuff could be anywhere."

"Oh, boy," Harry said.

Harry approached the pyramid of shoe boxes and opened the one at the top. He retrieved a pair of new shoes and brought them to me.

"I think we know what Alfonz was looking for," I said. "I'm starting to see why someone threw Anna's shoes all over her room. And why they broke into my studio and took mine."

"Do you think Anna disguised S'nuff as gems and glued them to her shoes?" Harry asked.

"At least someone thought she did," I said. "But they don't seem to have had luck finding them."

I sat on Anna's desk chair, and sighed.

"Was she a user? If so, what a weird way to stash your drugs. And she didn't look like a user. The people pictured in these articles look really strung out. Anna looked healthy. Her behavior was a little out there, but she didn't seem manic or anything."

"Maybe she was a dealer," Harry said. "That would explain her cash influx."

"But how'd she get the drugs, to begin with? The Shawn and Ben money train didn't start until later," I said.

Harry blew a frustrated breath and shook his head. "She could have been an intermediary."

"Through bedazzled shoes she wasn't selling? I think I'm more confused than ever," I said.

Outside the building, we heard a police siren. The sounds of ambulances and fire trucks and police cars are like ambient noise when you live in a big city, but when you've broken into the studio of a murdered woman, the alarm and spinning red light signal that it's time to leave. Without skipping a beat, I gathered up my belongings. We quickly shoved the papers we'd found into a desk drawer and then hightailed it to the elevator. The entire ride down, I don't think I breathed once.

When we exited the building, I realized the police hadn't come for us at all. A yellow tape was set up around a dumpster behind the building across the street. Police guarded the area and we heard the sound of an ambulance approaching. I looked at the ground behind a young officer, who looked as if he might have just thrown up. A body lay behind him with a blanket covering most of it, but not all of it. Both hands, those of a young woman, had fallen from the confines of her makeshift shroud. Her left sleeve covered her wrist. It was part of a sparkling silver jumpsuit.

"Let's go," Harry said.

I lifted my camera and took a photograph of Anna Reyes before following Harry out of Industry City. Harry and I ran to the subway. I leaned against the wall by the entrance as people went in and out of the station. I'd seen Anna fall from the bridge, and I'd known since the moment Alfonz and Kayla dismissed my concerns that something was very wrong at Todo Amor. However, now that I saw the blue-gray hands of the once-vivacious woman, I struggled to accept what I'd seen.

"Why was she dumped there?" I said, outraged.

Harry leaned his forehead against the top of my head and held me. "It's a good question," he said. "Why throw a person off of a bridge, retrieve her body, and then dump it later in a very public place?"

I looked up at Harry.

"That's what the Cardinal said too. Except for the part about today."

"Maybe I've been spending too much time trying to think like my thief," he said.

"Catch him tonight and put an end to that." I winced.

My phone buzzed. Bisa's name filled my screen, but I couldn't answer. Surely, Anna's body had not been identified yet, but the news would be coming soon. Gently, Harry took my phone from me.

"Hi, Bisa," he said.

He was silent. I could hear muffled sounds from the other side of the line, enough to know that Bisa was upset. I buried my head in my hands, sure she had heard the news.

"We'll head there now," Harry said. "Meet you there."

Harry handed my phone back to me.

"She knows?" I said.

He shook his head. "Not yet. She's back at Todo Amor. She says Kayla's losing it with Alfonz gone and Louis dead," he said. "And she's threatening to skip the movie opening tonight."

"Maybe you shouldn't have invited the Cardinal there after all," I said.

"Which train will get us back to Todo Amor?" Harry asked.

CHAPTER 18

When we walked through the sweeping doors of Todo Amor, I was happy for Bisa that the parties and concerts were over. She would soon need the solitude. The party team was packing the lighting and music equipment, furniture, and plants into trucks. The set was coming down and soon only the inner circle would be left. Since I'd arrived two days ago, the group was smaller, but I knew its leader would stay strong. Bisa was a survivor and there were people in that house who loved her in their own ways.

Kayla's voice echoed to us from upstairs.

"I'm not going to be next," she said.

A door slammed shut. Kayla appeared at the top of the stairs. Her hair was disheveled, her clothes a wrinkled mess, and her cheeks were smeared with black mascara. She looked like a heartbroken woman as much as a frightened one and I wondered if there'd been something between her and Alfonz. I hadn't noticed any chemistry between them, but I hadn't been looking, either. They didn't jump out as the couple type. Alfonz was a massive guy who dressed in black, while Kayla was a rigid woman whose iPad had been an appendage.

"What are you doing here?" she said, pointing to me as she stomped down the stairs. "And you, Harry? Get out!"

Harry turned and left immediately. I held my ground.

"Liv, your job is done," she said. "Your check will be in the mail. Time to go."

Kayla had definitely forgotten our friendly banter from yesterday's concerts and her promise to keep me on speed dial.

"Is everything OK, Kayla?" I said. "It's been a hard couple of days."

Kayla squinted at me. "What do you want?"

"To get some fresh air," I said. "This place is a madhouse."

"It is," she said, and looked back upstairs. "I spent last night worrying that Bisa and Alfonz were both dead. I dealt with Dev all night, throwing a fit that she was missing. Without Alfonz to help, he was going to call the police, but we were afraid of the story going public. And Ben, Shawn, and even Cyril were furious with me for losing Bisa. How was it my job?"

"It's like, when you work here, you're expected to do everything," I said. "Meanwhile, it's a gorgeous July day."

"And what about that pilot?" she said.

"It's all crazy," I agreed. "I need the sun and some vitamin D."

"That sounds nice," she said.

I wasn't sure what she'd say next, so I took her hand and walked us through the kitchen and to the back lawn. A couple of chairs were still out from yesterday, so I guided us in their direction and took a seat, in hopes that she might calm down outside of Todo Amor's grip.

"I don't have sunscreen on," she said. "I'm very pale."

"Two minutes will be good for us both," I said.

Rather than join me on the chair, Kayla lay on the ground.

"You're right," she said. "I was going to be a vet. On days like this, I wonder why I didn't pursue that dream. Bisa has a way of making you feel special, though."

"And her energy is unmatched," I said. "Who was that guy in the helicopters yesterday? He was giving Bisa meds."

"Dr. Michael?" she said, raising her hands and looking at

them in the sun. "He is Bisa's homeopathic doctor. He gives her vitamin drips and other nutritional supplements to keep her going."

"Is that all? Nothing stronger?"

Kayla laughed. "Are you kidding? A Diet Coke is a big deal for Bisa. She's into nothing stronger than a ginger turmeric gummy and an IV of vitamin whatever."

I looked up at the tree above us and watched the leaves rustle in a breeze. We sat in silence for a moment, which seemed like an improvement for Kayla. I was enjoying the quiet, too, but we both had things to do.

"Have you ever heard of a drug called S'nuff?" I asked.

Kayla dropped her arms and turned her head toward me. "How do you know about S'nuff?"

Her expression was different from any version of the Kayla I'd met so far. She wasn't sad or worried or even pompous about her seniority over me. Her eyes looked vacant and her cheeks sank.

"I was thinking about Anna Reyes and her former drug addiction," I said.

Kayla propped herself on her elbows. "How did you find out?"

"She offered me some when I went to her room," I lied. "But how did you find out?"

"She offered drugs to you?"

Kayla studied my face with wide eyes. I started to understand her interest in my line of questions. Anna wasn't the one using S'nuff. Kayla was. It made perfect sense, now that I thought about it. Who could keep up with the demands of Bisa without some help? It was different for Dev and Shawn and Ben. They were Bisa's partners. Kayla, however, was her assistant. She needed to anticipate Bisa's needs, be available to her at any time, day or night, and keep the show going for someone whose idea of a day at the office was three concerts in one day.

"She never offered it to you?" I said.

"No," Kayla said. "She knows I don't do drugs. I only know because she told me she was struggling with her addictions again."

Alfonz had made the mistake of telling me that Anna confided in him, and now Kayla had, too. The trees rustled above me again and I studied them, feeling that I was getting closer to putting the pieces together of this intricate puzzle.

I'd met Anna Reyes only shortly, but we'd bonded over our shared entrepreneurial spirit and our love for her shoes. She'd shared with me her disdain for Kayla and Alfonz. She'd publicly embarrassed her brother-in-law-to-be immediately after his proposal to her sister. And she'd talked Bisa into giving her a hefty check Bisa had not been able to afford. Shortly thereafter, I saw her fall from a bridge and then watched as Louis retrieved her body, which had landed on the piling below. Since then, I'd learned she was blackmailing Ben and Shawn and had taken out a six-figure loan from someone who was not happy she hadn't paid it back. Her **Time's up** text indicated that any good graces she had with her debtor had ended. Her room had been searched and then cleaned up, as if no one had ever been there. And my studio was searched after I'd inherited Anna's suite. After this morning, I now knew that the drug S'nuff had played some role in these horrors of Anna's death. I had no answer to the Cardinal's question of why anyone would want to recover Anna's body from the river, but I did know Anna had something that someone wanted. Drugs.

I closed my eyes and ran through the pictures I'd taken, the important ones that were imprinted in my memory. The wide-lens shot of the party before Anna fled where all of the key players were missing. The image of blood below the bridge. The items strewn around her room at Todo Amor. I discarded others I'd thought had been important, but now knew weren't, such as the photo of Shawn leaning into Anna and the tension across Bisa's face when Dev proposed. There were stories there, for sure, but in the end, they didn't reveal what had happened to Anna.

I opened my eyes with a start. Kayla seemed to have fallen asleep and I did momentarily worry that she was too pale for the sun, but rather than wake her, I took out my camera. From the depths of my soul, I did not want to see Anna's lifeless body again, but I had to, at least this one time. I zoomed in on the hands that had fallen from the covering.

"Holy mother," I said.

Kayla stirred.

"Is it time to go back inside?" she asked.

Anna's hands lay open from both sides of the small blanket the policeman had used to cover her. I studied them now and realized that all of her beautiful blue fingernails were gone. I knew them intimately, since she had both booped me with one and then I'd found one on the bridge. Harry hadn't found any fingerprints on the nail, but perhaps it was because it had fallen off quickly.

I opened my bag and searched for the fingernail Harry had given back to me after the lab results had come back. It was blue and crystal studded. I held it close to my face. All of the jewels sparkled brightly in the sun, but some were brighter than others. The lab technicians had searched for fingerprints, but we should have asked for more tests.

"Where did you get that?" Kayla asked.

From her reclined position, she was now on hands and knees. She lunged at me and grabbed the baggie with the nail inside. Once in her hands, she looked at it greedily.

"Give that back, Kayla," I said. "It's part of a murder investigation."

"You think I'm an idiot?" she said.

Suddenly, with the speed and strength of a wild animal, Kayla flew down the greens behind Todo Amor and along a path to the south of the island, where Bisa performed her last concert. I took off after her. As I did, I heard a window open and Harry's voice call after me.

"Call the police," I yelled, not stopping and finally certain that it was time to make the call.

Once again, the heat melted my makeup and my hair grew three times its weight, but I persevered until I rounded a corner at the old smallpox hospital. There, I let myself scream in frustration for a second. Kayla was climbing over the chain-link fence, which protected the public from its crumbling walls. I took a deep breath and followed.

Kayla was already over the fence and climbing into the ruins when I arrived. She laughed and skipped now, presumably thinking she had escaped from me with Anna's drug-covered fingernail. Before my very eyes, she popped the evidence off the nail and ate it. Then she sat down on the grass, waiting for its effects to kick in.

And, so, this is how I found myself climbing a chain-link fence into one of the allegedly most haunted grounds in America on a Friday morning in July. I was keenly aware of the sign that warned me to stay away and cautioned that my life was at risk from falling rock. I cursed as I scurried down the other side of the fence and skinned my shin in the process. I had planned to wear a mini-dress to the premiere but now that wasn't going to happen.

Kayla heard my thud when I landed. She stood up—no, jumped up like a science fiction creature—and ran to a scaffolding that led up to a hollow space in a decaying wall that once was a window. Before I knew it, she was lost inside the ruins.

"Kayla!" I said. "This is not safe."

I hoped she would come back out after these cautionary words, but I knew I was kidding myself. I felt my pockets for my phone, but it was gone. Looking back through the fence, I saw it had fallen from my shorts while I'd climbed over. From inside the ruins, I heard a crash and then a scream.

"Kayla?"

There was no answer. Truly, I wanted to head back to safety, but I couldn't leave Kayla if she'd run into harm's way. I studied the building and found a hole in the various gates and chains, which were meant to keep people out. After walking around the corner of the building, I spied an opening large enough for my body and ducked inside.

Suddenly, it was as if I was in a jungle. Fully grown trees flourished in the middle of the old building. Birds flew from limb to limb and the floor of one corner of the building extended for a few feet and ended with a door still shut from whatever room used to be there. I took a few steps forward and my foot hit a beer bottle. I guess Kayla wasn't the only one to break into the space. At night, when the building was lit and the moon was full, it must be a wild place to visit.

"Kayla," I said again.

From somewhere ahead of me, I heard a moan.

"I'm coming," I said.

Kayla's curses and moans led me to her prone body, which was trapped under a large tree limb. I kneeled beside her and tried to lift the limb. When I had a good angle and grip, I decided to take advantage of my upper hand.

"Admit it," I said. "You threw Anna over the bridge. And then you had the guy with the star tattoo on his head pick up her body so you could collect the fingernails with the drugs on them."

Kayla burst out laughing. "You think I did that? You think I organized a boat to pick up a woman I'd thrown off a bridge so I could collect her fingernails? Are you crazy?"

When she put it that way, yes, I did feel crazy.

"Get this tree off me, you witch," she said.

"First, tell me what happened."

"I don't know what you're talking about," she said.

"I don't believe you," I said. "And you know what? My job with Bisa is over. I was only hired to take photos of the parties and the concerts. Which means I have nothing to do today until I go as a guest to the movie tonight. I have all day to wait you out."

Kayla tried to lift the tree off of herself, but even the manic effect of S'nuff didn't give her enough strength. After a few attempts, she dropped her head to the ground, breathing heavily.

"How long does this stuff last?" I said.

"Fine!" she yelled at me. "Anna was trying to blackmail me."

Now that made sense.

"Why?"

"She saw me when we were filming *All About Love*. I was out one night at a club, one rare night off, and she was there, too. I was partying a lot that night and she saw me take the drug. She followed me into the bathroom and told me if I didn't pay her, she would tell Bisa. My boss has no patience for drug users, especially after Anna's battle a couple of years ago. But she didn't use heavy stuff. Anna just partied too much. If Bisa knew what I'd gotten into, I'd be fired. And for what? All I was doing was trying to keep up with her. S'nuff helped me get through endlessly long days and weeks. And with the tour ahead, I wasn't going to stop."

"And you didn't tell Bisa you saw Anna?"

"Are you kidding? Invite Anna over to tell Bisa about me?"

"Did you pay her?"

Tears started to stream down Kayla's cheeks. They weren't from the pain of the tree on her legs. I had a pretty good feeling she couldn't feel the pain. The tears were remorse.

"I met Anna on the bridge," she said. "We arranged to meet there and I would pay her. When I got there, I didn't find her. And I haven't seen her since."

"Did you search her room for drugs?"

"No," she cried.

I heard footsteps in the ruins.

"Liv? Are you OK?" Harry asked.

"Over here," I called out to him.

Harry's head popped up over a branch. "I found your phone on the street. Are you OK? What's with her?"

"S'nuff. She's an addict," I said. "Anna glued the drugs to her fake fingernails, and when Anna saw I had one, she took it and went crazy."

"Anna glued the drugs to her nails?"

I nodded.

"Why? I mean, the shoes I sort of understood. She could sell them and no one would know a transaction had occurred. But her nails? Someone could have ripped them off her."

"Someone did," I said. "When Anna was at the party, she had blue fingernails. I found one on the bridge. When I saw her cadaver today, her nails were gone."

"Who are you working with?" Harry asked Kayla.

"You guys are crazy," Kayla said. "Get me out of here. I told Liv, Anna tried to blackmail me because she saw I was using. She wanted to meet me on the bridge to collect or she'd tell Bisa."

"No," Harry said. "There were a million places she could have met you. The bridge is too far-fetched. Come on, Liv, let's go."

"Don't leave me," Anna said. "OK, OK. You're right. I saw Anna leave. I saw she was in a panic. I didn't know why, but I knew I didn't want to be beholden to her anymore. When she jumped on the bike, I knew she was trying to leave the island. We have a couple of motorbikes, so I took one. I planned to cut her off on the bridge and tell her to leave me alone. I reached her about halfway across the bridge, where we got into a fight. I'd taken some S'nuff in the morning. Not a lot. Enough to get me through the day without anyone noticing.

But when Anna started pushing back, I lost it. S'nuff can do that to you. Before I knew it, I'd put my hands around her neck and I choked her. I didn't mean it. She collapsed and I knew she was dead, but I didn't mean it."

"So, you threw her body into the river," I said.

She nodded, now sobbing. "And I threw her bike onto the other side of the median," she said. "I tried to throw it in the water, but the handlebar kept getting stuck. Then I got back on my bike and rode to Queens. There, I took the turn and returned to Todo Amor from the other side. I even saw you on the bridge."

"What about Bisa's loan to Anna? The one that went through during the engagement photos," I said.

"Once, when Anna was in rehab, I had to deposit a check for her," she said. "I had the password and ID. I'd never used it again, but Anna dropped the check during our fight. I thought Bisa would get suspicious if it wasn't cashed, so I went into her account and deposited it. I didn't know they had a deal to hold it for a few days. I was in shock. I wanted to save Bisa from heartache for as long as I could."

"Anything else we should ask her," Harry said to me.

I shook my head.

Harry lifted the branches with one hand and grabbed Kayla into an arm hold before she could get away.

"Honestly, I didn't notice the drugs glued onto the fingernail until today," she said. "And I never searched Anna's room. I stayed as far away from anything to do with her as I could. I love Bisa more than anything. I didn't mean to hurt her."

I looked at Harry. "It would have been hard for her to break into my studio while she was running the parties the other night," I said to him.

Harry nodded in agreement. "Who was Louis?" he asked her.

She shrugged, limping to the edge of the building, while leaning on him for support. "I think he was an associate of Alfonz's," she said. "I don't do checks on everyone he hires. I trust he knows his people."

I thought of the petrified look on Alfonz's face when we'd told him that Louis was dead. It was not the look of someone who was calling the shots.

"I think Alfonz was working for someone other than Bisa," I said. "Also, Kayla, you were right about the sun and your skin. It's a little blotchy."

Two police cars waited for us at the gates of the ruins. A caretaker of the island unlocked one of the gate's padlocks and we handed Kayla over to them.

"We'll take it from here," an officer told us. "And we identi-fied the body of Anna Reyes. The police are at the house now."

"Thank you, Officer," Harry said.

We walked together toward Todo Amor. It wasn't the time for either of us to intrude on Bisa's devastating news. She knew her sister was dead, but to hear it confirmed was unimaginably sad. Bisa had trusted Kayla with every aspect of her life. She had lost two members of her family.

To my surprise, an armored truck pulled up to the house. The driver got out, looking confused by the commotion, but Dev ran down the path to greet him.

"Is she really going to the opening tonight?" I said to him.

I didn't expect Dev to answer me. He'd never paid attention to the help. Now, however, he looked me in the eyes. I didn't know if Bisa had told him we'd been helping her, or if Dev needed to talk to someone, anyone, but he nodded in answer to my question.

"She's a really strong woman," Dev said.

"Kayla confessed to the killing," I said. "Perhaps that will give Bisa some peace."

"I don't think anything will ever fill the hole Anna left be-hind," he said.

I was surprised to see tears in Dev's eyes.

"I still don't understand who put Anna in the dumpster," he said.

It was a good question. Kayla was worried about blackmail. Someone else was looking for Anna's drugs. I suspected Alfonz had the answer. There were still many unanswered questions surrounding Anna's death, but at least her killer had been found.

Dev turned back to the truck driver to sign for the Cartier Halo Tiara. ACU agents were hiding around the island to protect it, but we knew the Cardinal would not strike until tonight.

CHAPTER 19

"Antony," Granny said early that evening. "I laid out your blue tie. Take that one off, it has a stain. Come on. Let me help you."

"I've got it, Granny," Maria said. "You finish putting on your lipstick. You look beautiful."

"Livia, those nails," Granny said. "Since when are you dressing like a pop star?"

She was referring to the two-inch-long blue nails that were covered in sparkling jewels.

"Since Bisa," I said, and gave both of my grandparents a hug.

The scene in my house by early evening was as wonderfully chaotic as Bisa's opening night was probably, originally, meant to be. As the arrival of the armored truck had predicted, Bisa lived by the rule that the show must go on. Harry said that when he told her the story behind the UK Trust of Royal Jewels's sudden generosity, she hugged him and promised never to breathe a word to anyone. She was mad at first, but then decided that catching the Cardinal would have given her sister a kick. Perhaps the idea of balancing some justice in the world motivated her as well. Whatever her motives for wearing the tiara, she was a brave woman. But I already knew that.

Ben and Shawn stepped up to take over Kayla's responsibilities, and by midafternoon, Granny received a call that she, Poppy, and *the friend*, aka Maria, were invited by Bisa to attend the premiere. The news of Anna's death was being held from the media for a day so that Bisa had time to mourn privately, and my family had no idea what had happened. To them, the lady who had needed a break from fame by having a sleepover last night had reciprocated the favor with movie tickets. I liked their version of the story better and felt no need to give them the details. If I had, they would never have let me work for Regina again. Once I felt that the gang was ready to go, I slipped out to meet Harry, who was waiting for all of us in a fancy stretch limousine.

"Are you sure you're up for this?" he asked me for about the tenth time.

I nodded as my family and Maria joined us, and stepped inside the car for the ride uptown.

Radio City Music Hall is familiar to many as the home of *The Christmas Spectacular*, but tonight, it was the home of Bisa's *All About Love*. I realized the red carpet, the paparazzi, and the fans at Todo Amor were nothing compared to the fanfare that greeted us outside the theater. Bisa had found relative privacy in Roosevelt Island compared to the night's fans who lined up five rows deep across the avenue for a glimpse of the stars arriving for the movie. News vans with cranes to lift the cameramen up for aerial views were parked in specially allotted spaces. The paparazzi lined the red carpet. As each celebrity arrived, they had an opportunity to pose at a step-and-repeat with the logo for *All About Love* splashed all over it.

As planned, Harry and I ducked out of our car a block earlier and now stood among the paparazzi and wearing press passes. I raised my camera to fit in, but rather than look for the next celebrity, I kept my eyes open for the Cardinal. My only moment of distraction was when I saw my grandparents crash the step-and-repeat with Maria in order to get a shot of their own. I had a strong feeling that there would be a new framed photo on their mantel in the coming days.

The screening was scheduled to begin at seven, but at five minutes before, neither Felix nor Bisa had arrived. The theater held over six thousand people who were now inside and waiting for the show to begin. My grandparents had probably been to the bathroom twice.

"Are you sure this is going to work?" I said to Harry.

"Be patient," he said. "This is New York. Seven o'clock can mean eight. You never know."

"What about the other thing?" I said, flashing my nails.

Click. Flash. Snap. Zoom.

Suddenly, the media came to life and the action really began. Bisa's stretch white limousine pulled up in front of the theater. A doorman rushed forward to open the door. To my surprise, Felix, not Dev, emerged. He waved to the crowd across the street, who went wild, and then nodded a charming hello to the media. Then, he turned back to the car as a silk blue glove reached out to him, followed by a beautifully shod foot in blue silk, with a solid but chiseled heel, covered in jewels and made by none other than Anna Reyes.

Bisa stepped out of the car. No one would ever guess that the death of her sister had been confirmed only hours earlier. She was perhaps more serene than usual, but she smiled radiantly at her fans and the press. As she waved, I sensed her mood lighten, as if the love she felt from her fans and followers gave her a small reprieve from her grief.

The crowd gasped not only at their idol, but also at the tiara she wore atop her gorgeously plaited head. Freesia had outdone herself with Bisa's hair and makeup while showing off the royal jewels. The actress-singer looked a true princess, even though I knew, deep down, she'd decided she didn't want to be one.

"No sign of Dev?" I said, happy to see Bisa had come around to see that Anna had been right about her fiancé all along.

"This is certainly Felix's big night out," Harry said with a laugh.

Felix looked like the guy who was bringing the prettiest girl at school to the prom. His own celebrity status paled in comparison to Bisa and he actually didn't seem to mind. As planned, Felix led Bisa to the step-and-repeat, where Harry and I were now stationed. We were not in prime position to photograph their arrival, but Harry needed to keep his eyes on the prize. In hopes that the Cardinal would find the area below the cantilevered marquee that was open enough for one of the Cardinal's infamous flights, the expectation was that this moment would serve as the perfect time for the thief to strike.

"You promise you'll get the Cardinal before he gets to her."

"That's the plan," he said, still focused on every aspect of the orchestrated moment.

Bisa and Felix posed. I could feel Harry hold his breath. The movie stars stood one way, then another, but the tiara stayed firmly on Bisa's head. There was still no sign of the Cardinal. The stars of *All About Love* waved once more to the crowd and headed inside.

"What now?"

"I guess we're going to the movie," Harry said.

I was thrown by his calm, but I followed him inside. We made our way to seats that gave Harry a clear view of Bisa. When the lights went out, every set of eyes focused on the screen but ours. We spent ninety minutes staring at the top of Bisa's head. The diamonds on her head shimmered in the light reflected from the screen but there was still no sign of the Cardinal. I feared Harry would be searching for the thief for months to come.

Toward the end of the movie, I indulged myself. I pried my eyes away from Bisa to watch the last kiss in what was an adorable rom-com. The characters Bisa and Felix played were poised on the waterfront of Roosevelt Island, with the bridge behind them. I knew Granny was loving it and would be sending a handwritten note of congratulations before the end of the night. I glanced across the audience to see if I could spy my family. Instead, my eye caught the silhouette of an usher by one of the exit doors. I knew that figure anywhere by now. It was Alfonz. I nudged Harry and nodded in his direction. Alfonz seemed to be staring right at me.

"Come on," I said. "It's time to make some noise."

When we stood up, we blocked a few people's view. They let us know with grumbles and complaints to sit down.

"I'm going," I whispered loudly back at them.

This was followed by a few shushes, but I'd succeeded in drawing attention to myself, which was my plan. Rather than walk to the exit at the end of the theater, we headed to stage left, as I'd been informed it was called, where an usher guarded a door. We flashed our passes and he opened it for us. We had not exited the theater, but, instead, had entered through an offstage door.

Backstage at Radio City Music Hall was almost as remarkable as the public spaces. The facility was bigger than anything one could imagine. We entered at a space under the stage, where lights and scenery and other theatrical treats were stored. Above us, I could hear the movie playing. We followed the path to another door, which led us upstairs to stage level.

"Who are you?" a stagehand asked us.

We flashed our passes again and waited in the wings for the movie to end. As the credits began to roll, the applause rose to a deafening cheer, and in less than a minute, both Felix and Bisa walked through the door with the stagehand. The curtains closed over the screen and six thousand cheers of *bravo* and *speech*, minus maybe one cynical film critic among them, began to fill the theater.

"Is everything OK?" Bisa asked.

"All good," Harry said. "Don't worry about a thing."

The curtains opened again. The stagehand gave Bisa a bouquet of about fifty roses and signaled for the stars to take the stage for a bow, standing center stage on red *X*s marked for them. Harry stepped into the shadows. He had his work to do. I had mine.

"OK, Liv, let's go," a voice said behind me.

It was Alfonz.

"What's up?" I said without turning.

"You have the drugs," he said. "I saw the nails. I know you found them today at Anna's studio. Let's get this over with."

"I had a feeling you were behind this," I said to Alfonz. "Bisa isn't your only boss, is she? Anna was going to repay a loan she took out with the mob, and you were there to make sure it went smoothly. You followed Anna when she fled, didn't you? And when she got to the bridge, you saw Kayla intercept her and throw her over the bridge."

"Louis was supposed to take the money, not me," he said. "He was supposed to meet her after the party, take the money, and leave on a boat he had. But he crashed the party, and didn't see her leave early. I followed Anna and called Louis to tell him to follow by boat. Lucky for him, Anna landed on the concrete instead of the water."

"If this was all about the loan, how do the drugs fit in?"

"Louis's boss is the biggest mob dealer in S'nuff," he said. "Anna got a loan from him last year for her business, and she saw the drugs during their meeting. Dumb woman, she stole from him and then afterward she panicked. It didn't take long to connect the dots between the day their drugs went missing and Anna's visit. They roughed her up, but couldn't prove anything. She didn't use them or sell them. They couldn't find them. She stopped working. I think she even started blackmailing Ben and Shawn, hoping to raise enough money to appease the mob if she was caught."

"Why'd you get the idea that they were at Todo Amor?" I asked.

"This woman Ben was hitting on, a blonde with a jewel attached below her eye like a beauty mark," he said. "She came in all shy and demure. Next thing you know, after an hour, she's a crazy person and acting like she's on the drug. One of the tablets fell off of Anna's fingernail and she took it."

"And you thought she hid the drugs on her shoes. You went looking for them in her room," I said. "You thought they might be on her shoes, so you fished her out of the river."

He nodded.

"And you searched my studio?"

He shook his head. "That was Louis," he said. "But then we learned Anna had been hiding her stash in plain sight. The fake fingernails had been discovered with the drugs and one was missing."

"It was the safest way for her to keep an eye on them," I said.

"That one nail you have, Liv, is worth one hundred fifty thousand dollars on the street. I only went to Anna's studio to see if she'd stashed any more. Bisa was going to fire me. I needed extra money.'"

"And that's what everyone has been looking for?"

Alfonz nodded. "Just so we're clear, I worked for Bisa and no one else. Kayla must have erased the security footage because it honestly wasn't me. And I was doing Louis a favor regarding Anna. I couldn't have cared less about Anna, but it's always good in my line of business to have a good connection with people like him."

"And so, you let him fly the helicopter so he could keep an eye on everyone who might have the nail or the drugs."

"Let's put this behind us," he said. "You're a photographer, not a drug lord. Let's let everyone do the job they were meant for."

I buried my hand into my purse as if I was playing with my nails and grabbed the little can of pepper spray.

"OK," I said, and turned around. "Did you guys get that?"

"We sure did," a policeman said. "Stand away from the lady, sir."

Knowing the case was tied with a bow, I turned to Alfonz. "Boop," I said, and sprayed him in the face, knowing Anna would appreciate it.

While Alfonz yelped, I breathed a sigh of relief that the security I'd been promised had come through.

Alfonz, however, had his own idea of how the night would end. Before the handcuffs had been placed around his wrists or the first words of his Miranda rights had been recited for abetting a murder, working for a drug lord, and contributing to unimaginable trouble at my best job ever, he dashed blindly toward the stage to escape.

The night's arrests had started slowly, but now they came fast and furiously. From high in the rafters, opposite to us and above Bisa and Felix, I suddenly saw the Cardinal as well. He held a cord tied to the rafters so that he could sweep down below and swipe the crown from Bisa's position on the red X, in front of six thousand eyes, before disappearing in the mysterious ways only he knew how.

If I'd learned anything, you had to capture the Cardinal in the act of his heist—otherwise, he'd be gone before you could say *tweet*. The Cardinal jumped, or flew as legend had it, at a perfect angle toward his prize. I took a step forward in hopes that I could somehow stop him, but I found help in the most unlikely form.

Alfonz.

As Bisa took a step forward to take a bow, Alfonz blindly pushed her off her mark and Felix rescued her from falling. With the stars off to the side, both Alfonz and the Cardinal crashed into each other. The Cardinal hung limply from his rope. The police jumped on Alfonz before he could run again. The curtains closed quickly.

"That wasn't part of the plan," I said to the Cardinal as he walked by me in cuffs moments later.

"Everyone here," the Cardinal said, looking at our assembled group, "do you see this woman? She's an agent with the ACU." He glared at me. "I told you I'd ruin you if you messed with me," he said. "And you can bank on the fact that I will escape again."

"What's the ACU?" Felix asked.

Bisa watched Alfonz being taken away. He would never have been able to save Anna, but he could have done so many other things to protect her. He could have told Bisa she was in New York while they were filming *All About Love*. He could have turned in Kayla after the murder and saved everyone extended fear and heartache. He could even have comforted Anna after Louis sent his text warning of **Time's up**, which had scared her so badly. Instead, he helped the mob recover her body and their drugs. And when everything had fallen apart with his job for Bisa, he'd offered his allegiance to the mob by seeking me out tonight for the drugs.

The stage door banged open behind us, and both Regina and Manjeet rushed toward me.

"Are you OK?" Manjeet said, hugging me. "We saw you

leave and then we saw the two guys and we decided to help stop them."

I laughed.

"We're good," I said. "They've been caught, but I appreciate the sentiment."

"Whatever we can do, luv," Regina said.

"How about a bonus for this job?" I said.

CHAPTER 20

One week later, I handed my credit card to the waiter at Ai Fiori.

"You don't have to do this," Harry said.

"Even without being able to sell her engagement photos, Bisa made a fortune, and I got my bonus," I said. "And Regina let me keep the Leica camera. I think it's fair to celebrate. And since you had to stand by me after this week's paparazzi leak, I feel I owe you."

Harry gave me a cheeky smile.

To explain, the morning after Bisa arrived to her premiere with Felix instead of Dev, word spread that her engagement had been called off. Instead of rumors about Felix and Bisa, however, a photo of me in my closet at Todo Amor hit the tabloid market. Rumors began to spread that Dev had been hiding a paramour at the mansion and Bisa had returned her ring. Turns out, Miles, the waiter I'd seen everywhere, was not a waiter after all. Part of the paparazzi, he had found a way in and had made some cash on my closet dwelling. Even building a fortress on Roosevelt Island had not been enough to protect Bisa's privacy.

"Fair enough," he said, his hands raised in surrender.

The restaurant was designed for slow dining, which was perfect. While I waited for my card to return, with a huge dent in my credit line, I enjoyed a little canoodling in our corner table.

"Any word from the Cardinal these days?" I asked.

Harry laughed. "I hear he's plotting his escape, but I don't think that's going to happen again."

"I'm going to hold you to that," I said.

"Madam," the waiter said, handing my card back to me, "there was a call from a Ms. Reyes. She said she has a car waiting outside for you."

I looked at Harry. "Do you know anything about this?"

He shook his head and looked as intrigued and surprised as I did. We left the restaurant to find Bisa's white limousine waiting for us. A driver opened the door.

"Where to?" I asked him.

"Ms. Reyes said you'll be pleasantly surprised," he said.

A week ago, I wouldn't have expected to hear anything so uplifting related to Bisa. The news following the opening of *All About Love* was heartbreaking. The movie and Bisa's new songs received rave reviews, but the tragedy of Anna's death loomed large. I didn't hear from Bisa, but I watched the news as she buried her sister in a private ceremony back in Puerto Rico. I hadn't heard from the superstar, although Granny had received a note from her, thanking us all for our hospitality.

When the car reached SoHo, it stopped in front of an art gallery. Russell Bays's name was printed across the window. Front and center was a portrait of Bisa. As a lover of portraits, painted or photographed, I was immediately enchanted by the swirling blues and silver shades that reflected the energy Bisa exuded in life.

We entered the gallery.

"Am I seeing what I think I'm seeing?" I said.

"It's like opposite day," Harry said.

Bisa waved to us from across the gallery. She wore jeans, a

T-shirt, and no makeup. I hardly recognized her except for her sparkling blue shoes. Russell, who stood by her side, gave her a kiss on the cheek and she outright blushed. From the corner of my eye, a familiar figure appeared.

"Oh, good, you're here," Granny said. "We wondered what was taking so long, right, Antony?"

"She's got me wearing my blue tie again," Poppy said. "Apparently, Mateo DeLuca might be coming by later and she wants to show me off to him."

I tried to keep a straight face, but Harry burst out laughing.

"Here we have the heart of New York," Bisa said, coming to our small circle.

"I'm actually a Jersey girl, but that's sort of every Jersey girl's dream to hear, so thank you," I said. "It's nice to see you here with Russell."

"I learned that Dev and Ben were planning every detail of my wedding," she said. "I'm sorry, but no one plans Bisa's wedding."

I nodded in agreement, remembering the huddled conversations I'd witnessed between the two men. I'd never have guessed they were picking flowers and color schemes.

"Anyway, I'm much more interested in carrying on my sister's legacy than selling diamonds," she said. "Anna left behind a lot of drawings. I'd like to turn them into something the world can enjoy."

"I will be your first customer," I said. "Those shoes are the best. Manolos can eat it."

"I'm glad to be off the pedestal," she said. "I'm working on a new album and a Bisa 2.0. I hope my fans will accept it."

"I'm pretty sure they'll embrace anything you do," I said.

She squeezed my hand.

"Hey, guys," Russell said, joining us.

"Your work is amazing," Harry said, shaking his hand. "Thanks for having us."

"Actually, I was hoping you'd make it," Russell said. "I haven't seen you since our morning together and Bisa told me how much you did. I wanted to thank you."

"No need to thank me," I said. "I'm not the kind of person who sits back when I see bad stuff go down. Bisa had a lot on her shoulders. I just wish I'd known to trust you so I could have helped more."

"What is she talking about, Antony?" Granny said to my grandfather, who shrugged and took a slider from a passing waiter.

Russell walked to the back of the gallery and returned with a small package wrapped in brown paper.

"For you," he said, handing it to me.

I opened the package to find an oil painting. With a white background in the same wild strokes I'd seen in Bisa's painting, the subject was simple. The letter *L*.

Granny smiled impishly. "Oh, look," Harry said, admiring the canvas over my shoulder. "An *L*, for *Liv*."

"It's not for *L*—" Granny began, but I put my hand over her mouth and my lips on Harry's.

Sometimes I can play hard to get.

Acknowledgments

Click

Many thanks to the team, including, but not limited to....! My agent, Christina Hogrebe at Jane Rotrosen Agency; my editor, Norma Perez-Hernandez, along with Larissa Ackerman, Kait Johnson and the design team at Kensington Books. I couldn't be luckier to work with such a talented group of people. Thank you so much for your support in getting this book to the finish line, and making it sparkle. And also, for getting me on BookTok.

Flash

To my friends who shine so brightly… especially Gretchen Eaton, Peggy Boulos Smith, Jill Furman, Valerie Steiker, Meredith Lipsher, Jennifer Sheehan, Elizabeth Kennedy, Alicia Cleary, Alysia Macaulay, my old neighbors at 1133, the LOR, and the gals of Hot Flash Yoga.

Snap

To my readers whose reviews and comments and emails make writing a pleasure.

Zoom

Tommy, Carly. Mom, Dad. Mark, Jen & Cate. You are everything to me!

Visit our website at
KensingtonBooks.com
to sign up for our newsletters, read
more from your favorite authors, see
books by series, view reading group
guides, and more!

Become a Part of Our
Between the Chapters Book Club
Community and Join the Conversation

Betweenthechapters.net

Submit your book review for a chance to win exclusive
Between the Chapters swag you can't get anywhere else!
https://www.kensingtonbooks.com/pages/review/